Tango

Susan K. Kehoe

 FriesenPress

One Printers Way
Altona, MB R0G 0B0
Canada

www.friesenpress.com

ISBN
978-1-03-913837-7 (Hardcover)
978-1-03-913836-0 (Paperback)
978-1-03-913838-4 (eBook)

1. Fiction, Romance, Suspense

Distributed to the trade by The Ingram Book Company

ACKNOWLEDGMENTS

For Mel and Allison

Chapter 1

LATER, JESSICA COXWELL WOULD THINK BACK ON THE O'Connell's gala as the end of her life as she knew it. It had been a catered affair at the exquisite estate of Thoroughbred racing's current elites, Ryan and Laura O'Connell. She recalled every detail of the evening, as she positioned herself inside the front door of the marble-floored foyer where twin staircases spiraled upward to the second floor. Playing hostess at these rare events were so different from her day job as feed manager at their stables.

She accepted the embossed invitation from Mr. and Mrs. Brompton and welcomed them to the gala. "It's good to see you both," she said.

The gray-haired woman dripping in diamonds, nudged her husband and commented on the chandelier. "That's new since we were here last," the woman said staring up and admiring the five-foot long cascade of lights and Waterford crystals suspended above them.

"Lovely, isn't it?" Jess said, directing them to the lounge. *It's a good thing I was born and raised, here in Lexington. I know most of these people from working on their horse farms. I need to keep an eye on the two foreign visitors too*, she thought.

Senator Smith-Hyde and his wife came in next. "Hello, Jessica. The O'Connells did well at the sales. Selling five yearlings with She's A Charmer getting highest bid is quite the feat," he said. "Is Neil here?"

"Yes, he flew in this morning," she replied. Neil, Ryan's older brother, had arrived from Ireland. He owned the filly's sire, Arctic Cat, a highly valued breeding stallion.

The party had progressed well. So far, no one had spilled their drink or complained about the food. When all the guests had arrived, Jessica circulated around the room, keeping a sharp watch for anything that could disrupt the evening. She heard her name called. It was Grace Hailstone, one of the elderly high-society matrons.

"Jessica, where are you keeping the gluten-free foods? I must be so careful," the very large lady said.

"Mrs. Hailstone, all the specialty foods are on a separate table. Come with me," she said and led her to the buffet with its tables draped in white linen, adorned with silver utensils, candelabras, and flowers. Hors d'oeuvres were well-marked with small hand-made cards labeled "gluten-free," "vegetarian," "seafood" and "contains nuts."

A separate area held the regular delicacies, which were equally well-labeled. Waiters were already refilling glasses of bourbon and wine. The French doors were open to the garden and the late September air was warm enough for the distinguished couples in tuxedos and evening dresses to stroll outside. Jess knew the incognito security staff, including Neil's elusive body guard, were stationed somewhere on the premises. The nondescript man who always accompanied Neil, was reputedly ex-SAS, if she took the gossip as gospel.

Jess watched Ryan zeroing in on any girl he could. Laura usually kept a pretty tight rein on him, but it was too busy tonight. She watched as he steered a shapely blond out to the garden. The girl looked familiar. Jess remembered seeing her in the office earlier in the week, applying for a job. Cynical, it occurred to Jess that the girl was probably starting her orientation that very moment.

Looking around the room, she saw many of the wealthy horse owners her father had once worked for. In his youth, Joe Hartford had cleaned stables, groomed and exercised the horses for Garnet Hamilton, now the white-haired and overweight patriarch filling his plate at the buffet. Later, her father was barn manager for the elderly Wilsons presently holding court by the fireplace. His last job was feed manager for the O'Connells. That career ended abruptly with his untimely death in a car accident two years prior. Jessica had gotten her love of horses from him. She was the feed manager and the odd job person now, doing staff scheduling, and payroll as well as making transport and veterinary arrangements for the horses. Knowing all the local breeders and every horse and pedigree on the place was a real asset at events such as the gala. She always thought of her father when she attended one.

Jessica mixed and mingled, overhearing snippets of conversations varying from the local scuttlebutt on births, weddings, affairs, and pending divorces, to discussions of bloodlines and racing results. She kept an eye on potential troublemakers who imbibed more than their fair share but needed to be handled with kid gloves because of their status in the community. The displays of haute couture and gemstones on the wives would probably pay off her mortgage.

She checked in with the two foreign visitors, Monsieur Marchand from France, and Señor Diaz from Argentina.

"Señor Diaz, is there anything you need?" she asked.

The short, stocky raven-haired man smiled. "I'm fine, Señora. Accommodation is good. I'm delighted with She's A Charmer and Full Moon. They'll do well in my stable. I'll be looking at other horses tomorrow."

Jess introduced him to other breeders in the room who immediately congratulated him on his successful bids. Monsieur Marchand was on the other side of the room deep in conversation with the Smith-Hydes.

Ryan's brother Neil made eye contact. He was in his early forties, not particularly handsome but ruggedly attractive. In his dark-gray silk suit and open-necked shirt, he had more impact than any of the other men in their tuxedos. He was also one of the few men who looked good with designer stubble whether he wore jeans or a suit. He had the uncanny ability to make Jess feel uncomfortable, even from twenty feet away; it was the way his gray eyes looked at her from head to toe, mentally undressing her. Despite his reputation with the ladies, Neil had never propositioned her. It was more of a game as he knew she wouldn't take the bait.

The stable staff suspected his successful European importing business had shady dealings, but it was his breeding stable outside Dublin that was his claim to fame. Arctic Cat was his main breeding stallion. Neil was also an equal partner in Ryan's stable. Ryan was definitely a paler imitation of his brother, lacking the substance and aura of his older sibling.

Jess avoided situations where she might be cornered by either man. At least Neil was more of a gentleman than

Ryan, who routinely invaded her personal space. Female staff called him "the handyman" behind his back. He was well known for his groping, partying, and gambling.

Around ten o'clock, Ryan commanded everyone's attention, calling for silence. Neil and Laura stood beside him. Gradually, the guests gathered around and the chatter died down. Ryan had a huge smile on his face, basking in the attention.

"Tonight is a celebration of our success at the yearling sales. However, I have a much more important announcement to make, which will put this stable on the map. My brother Neil has brought Arctic Cat from Ireland to stand at stud here in Lexington for this season. The horse is presently in quarantine in New York. We expect him to arrive within the week once he's cleared by the vets."

At first there was dead silence, which escalated to a hum of murmurs, then an outburst of clapping and cheers. The crowd engulfed the O'Connells in a wave of congratulations.

Jess had heard stories of the twelve-year old horse. His offspring were starting to make a name for themselves in winners circles across Europe, but the stallion himself had a nasty reputation. She'd heard that he was unpredictable to handle, biting and kicking, and had injured several handlers. However, no one could argue with his performance on the track or in the breeding shed.

By midnight, guests began to head home. Jess assisted the inebriated Mr. Brompton and his wife into their limousine, thanking the gods most guests had chauffeurs or had shared a ride with someone else. Jess had ordered limos for the foreign visitors.

Despite the lateness of the hour, Laura O'Connell still looked beautiful in her designer gown, ever the southern belle. She came over to talk. "Thanks, Jess. The evening went really well, for once; not a hitch."

"I'll be glad to get home. I'm tired," admitted Jess; she'd been up since five and had spent all day organizing feed for the twenty-five hungry horses on the property before going home to get ready for the party. She watched as the caterers started packing up.

"It's too bad your husband couldn't come tonight," Laura replied.

Andy had warranted an invitation, being a professor of agricultural economics at the college and knowing many of the land owners in the elite crowd, but he'd turned it down due to his schedule.

"He's got a mile-high stack of papers to be marked for Monday morning. He's been so busy lately with some new program at the college; he never seems to have time anymore," she said, rolling her eyes. "See you later, Laura."

With home only a few exits away down the I-75 and with little traffic, Jess was only twenty minutes from home. The subdivision was in slumber with draped windows, only the street lights illuminating the way. As she pulled into the driveway, she noticed all the house lights were dimmed, except for the front hall. Andy had probably gone to bed already, so she quietly unlocked the door. She undressed in the bathroom, thankful to remove her high heels and little black dress. Parties really weren't her thing. However, it was nice to see the big-name breeders, keep up-to-date with the industry, plus a little overtime money always came in handy. Generally, she was a jeans and T-shirt kind of girl.

Andy was snoring soundly so she slipped into bed, trying not to wake him. When she placed her head on the pillow, Jess noticed a very faint floral scent. She dismissed it as fabric softener and instantly fell asleep.

*　　　　*　　　　*

BOTH OF THEM WERE EARLY RISERS AND WERE UP AT SIX o'clock.

"How'd it go last night?" Andy said, getting orange juice from the fridge.

"Exciting news—Neil brought Arctic Cat from Ireland for this breeding season. That was the biggest surprise. Other than that, nobody got too drunk. The O'Connells aced it at the sales, so everyone's happy. There was a breeder from France and another one from Argentina. I'll ask Carla if she knows him," she said, thinking of her Argentinian friend who was taking an eight-month apprentice stable management course at another stable in town. The two women had bonded instantly when they'd met.

"The marking's going slower than I'd like," said Andy. "I think I'll go for a run before I tackle the rest," he added, putting on his Nikes.

"I'm going to clean this house today. I never got around to it last weekend," Jess said, eyeing Andy's trim, athletic body. She admired his dedication to his fitness regimen. He was thirty-four and in excellent shape. He waved goodbye and was out the door. Through the living room window, she watched his dark head bobbing as he hit full stride, quickly disappearing out of sight.

Jess sat quietly, enjoying her morning coffee and her favorite treat—a bagel and cream cheese. Looking at her to-do list, she decided that the upstairs needed cleaning the most. The bathroom came first, then the bedroom. After changing the bed linens, she hauled the vacuum with her, accidentally knocking over the waste basket, scattering debris. Muttering at her own carelessness, she turned off the vacuum and started picking up the litter: tissues, Post-it notes, and a condom wrapper.

She stood there speechless, staring at it. Andy never used them; she was on the pill. She checked the rest of the litter but no condom. Next, she searched the garbage she had emptied from the bathroom, but didn't find anything. He must have flushed it. Frantic now, she did the unthinkable and searched his dresser, finding a box of condoms in his sock drawer; four of the six were missing. She rummaged through his jacket pockets, but nothing. Running back to the laundry hamper, she found her pillowcase. Smelling it, there was that scent; the fragrance wasn't fabric softener but perfume. Her logical mind searched for reasons. The only possible conclusion was that Andy had brought another woman into their home and made love to her in their bed. Her brain went numb.

Jess put the vacuum away and sat in the living room remembering how she and Andy had met. He had accompanied one of her classmates to her graduation ceremony for the Equine Management Program at the university. He taught agricultural economics at the college. She had been instantly charmed and they'd married within the year.

I thought my marriage was good. We don't argue. We're both professionals. We've got a lot in common and an active group of friends. I love him. I thought he loved me, she thought.

Jess stared at her reflection in the hall mirror and saw a twenty-six-year old with ash-blond hair in a pony tail, all five-feet-six of her looking slim and neat in her snug jeans. She was constantly on the move at the stables and rarely had time to sit at her desk. Her belly was flat. Her skin was blemish free with no makeup. The overall picture was one of a wholesome, happy woman; until now.

Who was the mystery woman, this rival? Fighting a growing anger and knowing he'd be home shortly, Jess grabbed her car keys and headed to the mall. She sent a text to Carla.

"Emergency. I'm at the coffee shop if you're free."

Jess sat in a booth sipping her coffee, oblivious to the shoppers passing by. She didn't even see Carla approach until the mocha-skinned, curvaceous brunette sat down across from her.

"Jess, what's wrong?" Carla asked, staring intently at her.

"Andy's having an affair," Jess said.

"What! You can't be serious. Tell me," said Carla, her dark brown eyes full of concern.

So, Jess did. "I've got to find out what's going on. I'm angry, Carla. The thought of him touching me now, when he's been with somebody else, makes me feel dirty. How could he use our bed?" Her eyes started to fill with tears. She blew her nose. "I've got to have more proof than the wrapper before I confront him with it."

"Slow down, Jess; slow down. For the sake of argument, if you find out he's had an affair, what then?" said Carla.

"That's a no-brainer. I trusted him. If he's broken that trust, then I can't—I won't— tolerate it. I'd divorce him."

"Whoa! Divorce isn't an option for me; I'm Catholic. If I was in your shoes, I'd scream and beat his chest, try to claw his eyes out or call him every foul name I could think of, or burn his underwear! Lord, I hope this never happens to me. How are you going to find out who she is?" she said.

"I've been thinking about that. Laura O'Connell uses a security company. Surely, one of the officers must know a private investigator. I don't intend to go creeping around in the bushes with a camera and binoculars. I don't want to go on Facebook either. I'll phone Laura when I get back home - wait a minute, she's away today, I'll have to call her later."

Carla clasped her hands across the table and looked Jess straight in the eyes.

"Whatever happens Jess, you are strong. You're working and quite capable of being independent if that's the route you choose. You don't know the situation yet. I've never seen or heard anything bad about Andy. He's always seemed a good guy. What you've found is highly suspicious, but there might be a perfectly logical explanation. Knowing you, you're going to tear yourself apart worrying about it."

"Thanks Carla. You're thinking more clearly than I am. Enough about me. How are things going for you?" she asked

"Just four weeks left in my internship at Fitzgerald's stable, then I'll be going home. Dad's booked my flight for Buenos Aires on November 5th. My wedding's in January."

"Do you have your wedding dress yet?" Jess asked.

"Mum has a seamstress lined up to make it as soon as I get home. I'm so looking forward to seeing Mateo. It's been hard to be away from him, but I think the course will be invaluable to me for not only running his stable but others too. Polo's a real big deal in Argentina, and he's good at it."

"I know it's been difficult for you, being away from your family," Jess said, thinking of all the times they'd laughed and cried about Carla's life in Buenos Aires.

"I want to get home and see my parents again but I'm going to miss you. You should take some vacation and come to see me."

They talked a while longer and finished another coffee.

"You know Jess, I wasn't kidding about the vacation. I'll get my uncle to teach you the tango; he's a famous dance instructor," Carla said. They both laughed.

"Right. I haven't danced since I was in high school. As a kid, I did tap and ballet. I could waltz, but Mum and Dad wouldn't let me do the Latin dances; they were "too sexy." Andy sort of putters around, doing the university shuffle," said Jess with a grin on her face that quickly faded. "This is a mess."

"Hang in there. Look, I've got to go. I promised Barb I'd help her with the yearlings this afternoon. I need the over-time money. Take care of yourself, and don't do anything stupid. Give the vacation some serious thought—lots of sun and fun. You'll have snow here."

"I will, Carla but right now, I'm trying to figure out how I'm going to go home and behave like nothing's happened," said Jess.

"Pretend you're an actor in a play or something. Good luck. Call me if you need anything," said Carla, giving her a hug before she headed out the door.

Carla was right. The best thing she could do was pretend she didn't know, but it wasn't going to be easy.

Chapter 2

ANDY WAS WORKING IN HIS OFFICE WHEN SHE GOT HOME. "Hi Jess, where'd you get to?" he asked.

"I met Carla for a quick coffee," she said avoiding his gaze. She quickly began to clean and dust the downstairs, trying to distract herself from her thoughts. She gathered up the local newspapers, which she set to one side to re-read in case there was any pertinent gossip she might have missed. It felt awful to be thinking like that. She figured she'd deserve an Oscar if she could pull off the charade, pretending she was ignorant of the situation.

He emerged from the office around one o'clock. "There. I'm finally done," he said. "What's for lunch?"

"How about a ham sandwich and some soup?" Jess said, checking the contents of the fridge.

"Sounds good to me," he said, putting his hands around her waist.

She almost froze, but took a deep breath, slowly exhaling.

"Are you okay?" he asked with a frown on his face.

His look of concern nearly broke her heart. "I'm not feeling a hundred percent today. Maybe just tired," she said, grabbing the ham, bread, lettuce, mustard, and the jar of homemade soup.

She put the soup in a pot on the stove to heat and quickly made his sandwich. She felt him watching her. He'd picked up right away that something wasn't right and that surprised her. He usually wasn't observant. She set the steaming bowl of soup and sandwich on the table.

"Aren't you having any?" he asked.

"Not right now. Do you want me to thaw some steaks? We could barbecue tonight."

"That would be great. I'm going to be busy this week. I'm setting up the student job fair on Wednesday. Admin's got over twenty companies booked so far, including that new agribusiness company from Chicago. Last year at least thirty of the kids were hired for either summer jobs or full-time ones because of the contacts they made. A couple of them are doing a research study on renewable energy projects on farms," he said, looking out the window. "I think I need to cut the grass; it's looking ragged. What's on your agenda for the afternoon?"

"I've got pedigrees to prepare for the two fillies Señor Diaz bought and I should give Mum a call," she said, heading upstairs. The guest bedroom had been turned into her office space; they'd replaced the double bed with a Murphy bed in case they had company.

She sat at the computer, filling in the generational chart but found it hard to concentrate on bloodlines. She double-checked every entry, knowing accuracy was critical. She printed off a couple of copies, and given her state of mind, she decided she'd better check them again later. There was the steady buzz of the lawn mower and the sweet smell of freshly mowed grass. It was probably going to be the last cut now fall had arrived.

The mower went silent and she heard the door close downstairs as Andy came back in. He sprinted up the stairs and looked in on her. "Are you done with the paperwork?"

"Yes, I just finished."

"I'm going to have a beer. Do you want one?" he said, his six-foot frame bent over her as she sat at the desk. Normally, that proximity would have been inviting, but not today.

"Sure, sounds good to me," she said and they went downstairs. Sitting out on the patio with a beer in her hand, she remembered she needed to call California and talk to her mother. She pulled out her cellphone and punched in the numbers. As mother and daughter, they weren't close. Her parents had divorced when she was sixteen and her mum had quickly remarried a Thoroughbred trainer in California. At the time, Jess opted to stay with her father in Kentucky, since she intended to enroll at the university for the horse program and could live at home. The call went through and her mum picked up.

"Hi, Mum. It's Jess. How are you?"

"I'm fine," Margaret replied and went into a long, detailed spiel about the clothes she had bought for some event out there and how well her husband, John Newell was doing with his horses. Personally, Jess didn't like the man. Her mum continued, telling her all about Marty, Jess's brother, who had been hired by one of the Silicon Valley companies as an analyst.

Jess told her about the O'Connell's party, the yearling sales, Andy's job fair, and the pending arrival of Arctic Cat. Finally, the call was over and Jess figured she'd killed another twenty-five minutes of the afternoon. Looking at Andy, she said, "I need another beer; can I get you one?"

He took the beer and they sat together until it was time for the televised Sunday football game, which Andy always watched. Jess was quite content to sit and say nothing while he cheered on his team and ranted at the referees. Supper time rolled around and Andy barbecued the steaks with his usual flair, applying the spicy sauce and flipping them until the aroma permeated the whole house and garden. It seemed like all the neighbors were doing the same thing, as the last days of summer slipped into the glorious, blazing colors of fall.

Trying to make things look normal, she made his favorite potato salad and put some garlic bread under the broiler. They ate on the patio. Jess picked at her food.

"Jess, you've been really quiet today. What's wrong?"

Quickly making up an excuse, she said, "I've just been thinking about Dad. There's Mum out on the coast having the time of her life and he's dead. Doesn't seem fair somehow. The police never did find out why he swerved into that culvert. He'd driven that road for years," she said, the memory just as sharp as it had been the day it happened.

"Could've been a deer or anything," he said.

"I suppose so," she shrugged.

Later that night when they were in bed, even when she turned away from him, he put his arm around her. *Please, no sex tonight*, she silently prayed. She felt his warmth, but he didn't pursue it and just held her. She was thankful then started to feel guilty for doubting him, wondering if there was any other possible explanation.

*   *   *

EARLY MORNING AT THE STABLES FOUND JESS CLEANING buckets from the morning round of grain feeding and setting them up for the evening shift. The attendants were leading the horses out to pastures, separate ones for mares, fillies, and colts. Today she was rotating the horses to different paddocks as part of her pasture rotation protocol. Every animal looked glossy and full of vitality. She watched the colts nipping each other and galloping around, blowing off steam. On the recommendation of their Wainright feed expert, she checked every horse for its monthly body score assessment. Too fat, too thin—a body score of six out of ten was perfect. Some horses didn't need much grain; others needed more.

The stallions had their own yards and attendants. She walked over to the stallion barn and inspected the renovations to the stall for Arctic Cat. It was the standard twenty foot by twenty foot but had a new door with close-fitting bars and a warning sign on the wall outside telling people not to put their hands in. All the paddocks were double-fenced for safety reasons. With Arctic Cat's reputation, the O'Connells weren't taking any chances on visitors getting bitten. The daily routine continued; stalls were being cleaned and fresh shavings put down. The blacksmith was trimming a mare's feet. Jess was expecting a shipment of baled hay to be delivered.

She noticed a taxi arrive as Neil said his goodbyes to Laura and Ryan. Neil's bodyguard stashed the suitcases in the trunk. Although he'd accompanied Neil many times, she'd never really gotten a good look at him. He was in his mid-thirties, probably about five ten, wearing a suit that couldn't hide the broad set of his shoulders and tapered waist. His ash-blond brush cut gave him a bullet-shaped head, an ominous look. She'd caught glimpses of him some mornings, running the paths in his gray track suit, but never the same routine two days in a row. Occasionally, she'd seen him doing one-handed pushups. He was more like a gray ghost; there one moment and gone the next. His eyes were always vigilant, and she'd never seen him smile; not a man to mess with. The taxi pulled away, heading for the airport. Jess wondered why Neil needed a bodyguard. Were the rumors of illicit business dealings true?

On her break, Jess called Laura O'Connell. When Laura picked up, she said "It's Jess. I've got a favor to ask you. Do you know a local private investigator?"

Without hesitation, Laura gave her the number for a Brad Hollingsworth. Jess thanked her and hung up. The name was familiar. He'd been a local cop, but she hadn't seen him for a long time. Taking a deep breath, she phoned him. He answered his phone promptly.

Jess identified herself and told him she had a marital problem that needed investigating. He agreed to meet her later that afternoon in the mall parking lot. He'd said he'd be driving a black SUV. She gave him her cell number. That arrangement was fine she thought as she hung up. The woman in Andy's life was a faceless adversary she needed to identify and Hollingsworth could be the right man for the job.

In the afternoon, a big transport truck arrived carrying nine hundred small, square bales of prime quality alfalfa mix hay. She checked a few bales for mold then had staff bring the front-end loader to stack them in the Poly tarp storage barn. Jess looked at the remaining space available in the barn and estimated she'd need another couple of loads to fill it, enough to get them through the winter. She'd ordered more grains and supplements, that were scheduled to arrive the following week. According to the vet, fetuses grew the most in those last two to three months and the mares would need extra feed. She increased the grain rations accordingly. Foals were due in January or February at the latest.

After work, she met Hollingsworth downtown as planned. She immediately recognized him. He'd often been the cop on duty for the high school dances. There was nothing subtle about him. He was a big, hefty man in his sixties, dressed in casual clothes. Time had thinned his hair and widened his girth, but it was still the same broad, friendly face. "You must be Jessica. I'm Brad. What can I do for you?"

"I think my husband Andy's having an affair. I want to know who she is and how long it's been going on."

"First of all, I charge two-hundred dollars a day and need a retainer."

"No problem. I can write you a check right now," she said, removing her checkbook out of her purse and writing it, right there and then.

He nodded. "Tell me about your husband. Where does he work? What does he look like? Have you got a picture?"

She showed him a recent photo of Andy on her phone. "He's a professor at the Agricultural College. There's a job fair Wednesday in the big hall and he'll be there wining and dining the reps. I'm guessing he'll hook up with the woman," she said, writing out a check. "You can call or leave a text on my cell."

"I'm sure I've seen him before, at the summer fairs. I'll be in touch as soon as I have something," he said, shaking her hand. They parted company.

She knew Andy wouldn't be home until late, so she picked up a takeout pizza from Mario's. As soon as she got in, she saw the blinking light on her message machine and checked her calls. A group of her friends were going out Friday to celebrate a birthday. She decided to skip it, preferring to see Carla. Only four weeks, then she'd be gone. She really enjoyed the girl's company and would miss her effervescent yet practical personality.

She ate her pizza, finished reading the pile of newspapers that held nothing of interest, and decided to go to bed early.

*   *   *

JESS HAD NO IDEA WHAT TIME ANDY GOT IN, BUT HE WAS UP bright and early Wednesday morning, looking none the worse for wear. "I must have been really tired. I didn't even hear you come in," Jess said. "Are you all set up for the job fair?"

"Yeah, pretty much. Don't bother waiting up tonight, Jess. With all the reps in town, we'll be going out for supper." He gave her a quick kiss on the cheek.

"That's okay, Andy. I'll pick something up for myself, on the way home," she said, heading to her car.

Just before she pulled onto the roadway, her phone rang. It was Carla. "I've just got a minute. Did you find a P.I.?"

"Yes, I did. Laura O'Connell knew somebody. He's on the job, so hopefully I'll find out what's going on."

"Keep me posted. I've got to go," said Carla, disconnecting.

Jess headed to the stables, very thankful that she was going to have her usual busy day and wouldn't have time to dwell on Andy. After the morning feed, she stopped in the office to check some files and found the new girl sitting at the spare desk. It was the same one who had been at the gala. She surmised the girl was replacing Beth, who was on maternity leave. She couldn't imagine Laura being too pleased to see the buxom blond as staff when she'd only been a guest at the gala.

"I'm Jessica."

"I'm Becky."

"If you need help with anything, let us know. Annie's our accountant, she takes care of all the paperwork and accounts. She's been here forever, even worked for the previous owners before Ryan bought the place. I'm in charge of horse feed, vets, blacksmiths, staff schedules, and payroll sheets. What duties has Ryan assigned you?"

"Answering the phone, advertising, correspondence, that sort of stuff," she said.

Annie smiled at Jess and rolled her eyes in the direction of the newcomer. They'd seen a steady stream of girls come and go over the past five years.

Jess double-checked the pedigrees she'd done and found them accurate. She placed them in an envelope and headed over to the main house. Ryan's car was gone so she gave the envelope to Mrs. Porter, the housekeeper, to put in his office. Laura didn't seem to be around either. The two children were at school.

She went back to the yard with her list of horses and continued doing her body scores, talking to the individual attendants who were assigned to each animal. One old brood mare was having tooth issues and Jess notified the vet to float her teeth the following week. The day passed very quickly and it was two o'clock before she knew it. Tomorrow she'd do payroll and the new schedule.

On the way home, she picked up takeout from the Chinese restaurant, ordering beef and broccoli, plain rice, chicken, mushrooms, and an egg roll, as well as some salmon from the sushi bar. Jess relaxed in front of the TV and enjoyed her meal. Her fortune cookie read: *You are going on a journey. Your lucky numbers are: 3 19 24 37 45.* Right, like she was going anywhere!

Since she had the whole evening to herself, Jess threw in a load of laundry, checking the pockets in Andy's pants. She had no idea what she was looking for and decided it was pure paranoia. Later, when she was putting the clothes away, she checked in Andy's drawer for the box of condoms. It was gone. Hell.

She lay in bed for a long time, her thoughts ricocheting in her head. She was driving herself crazy. Maybe Brad would find some evidence. Tonight was the perfect night for Andy to meet the woman. After all, he had a valid excuse for not coming home until later.

Chapter 3

JESS KEPT HERSELF BUSY ALL MORNING. SEÑOR DIAZ WAS visiting the yard, accompanied by Ryan. The Argentinian was examining the chestnut filly, She's A Charmer, taking photos with his phone. The horse was a beauty with a sweet disposition and good conformation. Señor Diaz laughed when the horse stuck her nose in his pocket, looking for alfalfa treats. He rubbed her forehead and ears, then carried on his examination, running his hands over her legs, and picking up her feet. Jess watched him. He was very thorough and kind. He was used to horses; she could tell from the horse's relaxed response. He asked Ryan about the filly's X-rays as the two men walked away.

Just after lunch, her phone rang. It was Brad Hollingsworth.

"Jess, can you meet me after work at the mall? I've got something for you," Brad said.

"Already?"

"I'm afraid so," he said, not elaborating.

"I'll be there," Jess said, feeling a heavy weight settle on her.

*   *   *

BRAD WAS SITTING IN HIS CAR WAITING FOR HER. HE ROLLED down the passenger window. "Get in, Jess."

She slipped sideways onto the leather passenger seat, took one look at his face, and knew it was bad news.

"There are some days I hate my job. This is one of them," he said, handing her an envelope. "You were right. He has been seeing someone. I got photos last night and I checked around. Her name's Angel Mercer and she took one of his summer courses. Here's her phone number, car plate, make and model and her email, and Facebook information. I suggest you don't open this until you get home. I'm sorry, Jess."

"How much do I owe you Brad?" she said quietly, her eyes brimming with tears.

"Another two hundred dollars will cover it."

"I should say thanks, but somehow that's not the right word." After paying him, she slowly walked to her car. The fact Andy was dating a student was insane. He was completely out of his mind! If the college ever found out he'd been intimate with a student, he could kiss his job goodbye. So much for ethics. Gathering her scattered thoughts, she started the car and headed home, concentrating on the road and traffic.

Thankfully, Andy's car wasn't in the driveway. She ran up to her office, and phoned the stables, taking the next day off with the excuse that she had a medical appointment. At that moment, all she felt was a gut-wrenching wave of anger and she hadn't even seen the photos yet.

Bracing herself, she slit the envelope open. The photos were clear and precise. The curtains hadn't been pulled and the lamp light was very revealing. The girl looked no more than eighteen, lying naked on a couch with Andy equally naked, kneeling over her. Behind the girl's head was a young man, kneeling on the floor his arms stretched out over the girl's shoulders, his hands on her breasts. Jess didn't recognize him, but he looked young enough to be a student too.

Photo number two showed a tangle of bodies and limbs, various body parts in every orifice.

There were also several pictures of Andy and the girl fully dressed engaged in an intimate conversation in the hall just outside the college library.

Jess was so appalled that she ran to the bathroom and threw up. The photos made her decision very easy. There was only one option here: get out of the situation and remove herself totally. Infidelity was one thing: sex with another man was totally unexpected. Was this the reason he'd never wanted children? Had he always had these tendencies? She couldn't think of any indications. Feeling numb, she made copies of the photos and put the originals back in the envelope. Right then she started making a list of everything she needed to do. She had to keep busy, keep the anger at bay, and keep herself organized.

> Bank: get a safety deposit box and put the originals there for safe keeping; open up new bank accounts that Andy couldn't access. Give her brother Marty power of attorney for the finances.

> Insurance policy: change beneficiary to Marty.

Make a doctor's appointment and get blood work
and swabs done to make sure she hadn't caught
some awful disease from dear sweet Angel and
whoever else.

See her lawyer to get a divorce.

In all of their time together, Andy had never given her
the impression he was interested in men. Had she failed to
see it, or was he really very good at hiding it? She wasn't
against people of other sexual persuasions; it just wasn't part
of the package she wanted. She couldn't stay in the house
that night. She didn't want to see him until she'd got some
defenses in place. Disbelief mingled with a boiling anger
she'd never felt before. It was overwhelming.

She left a note for Andy stating she'd see him tomorrow evening, with no further explanation. She threw a few
things in her duffel bag, grabbed her toiletries, and headed
to her car. She drove to the other side of town and checked
into the Days Inn, parking around the back, out of sight.
As soon as she got to her room, the tears started. Her phone
buzzed a few times, but she ignored it. Sleep that night
was elusive.

Friday morning, she arrived at the bank promptly at nine
and opened a new checking account. Never again would she
use the joint account. She signed up for a safety deposit box
and placed the sex photos in it.

She called the doctor's office and got an appointment for
the following week. The lawyer's office was just down the
street, so she stopped in there. Scott Ames had been her
father's lawyer.

"Hi, Mrs. Johnson," she said to his longtime secretary. "I need to see Mr. Ames as soon as possible. Is there any chance he could see me now for a few minutes? It's really important," she said.

An hour later Mrs. Johnson ushered her into the office. Mr. Ames was in his sixties, with a straightforward conservative attitude. He never seemed to age and always looked the same in his crisp gray suit with the blue shirt and tie. His office was old-fashioned with ceiling-to-floor bookcases of leather-bound law books, but there was a computer on his desk.

"Jessica Coxwell, I haven't seen you for a long time. What can I do for you?" he asked.

"Mr. Ames, I found out yesterday that my husband Andy's been having an affair. She is one of his students. I hired a private detective, Brad Hollingsworth, to check it out, and he managed to take some very explicit photos of Andy not only with her but also with a young man," she said, handing him the envelope.

"I have the originals in a safety deposit box and my own copies, so these are for you. First of all, I want to remove Andy from my will. I'll make my brother Martin my power of attorney for personal care and property as well as executor and beneficiary of my will. Secondly, I want to initiate divorce proceedings. As you know, both my name and Andy's are on the deed and mortgage on the house. I don't care if it's sold or if Andy buys me out. I just can't live there, nor can I afford it."

Ames opened the envelope and both eyebrows went up when he saw the pictures. There was total silence for a few moments and he put them down on his desk. "This must be a horrible shock to you. Kentucky is a no-fault divorce state. You don't need to produce these to get a divorce. We can start the paperwork now. What you need to do, is to try to amicably settle the issue of the house. If he's willing to pay you out or sell it, the divorce could go through quite quickly as an uncontested one. If he challenges it, then it would have to go to court. That will cost time and money.

He'd be a complete fool to contest it quite frankly, with the evidence you have. He's absolutely at the tender mercies of yourself and these young people. His reputation is completely on the line." He phoned his secretary to prepare the documents.

By the time they had discussed the situation in detail, Mrs. Johnson had the divorce application ready. Jess read it over and signed.

"Mr. Ames, do I have to stay in the house while all this is happening?" Jess asked.

"I would recommend that you stay if you can. Keep your temper, even if he provokes you. Pay your share of the expenses as you normally would until we have something definite on paper. I'd advise you to get all of your valuables to a safe place. Has he ever been violent or abusive?"

"No, never. I couldn't imagine him getting violent, but obviously there's a whole other side of him. Marty and I split Dad's estate, the sale of his house, and Dad's life insurance policy. Do I have to share any of that with Andy?"

"No. Inheritances are specific to the beneficiary. The courts will decide on the settlement of assets and debts. I'm assuming that he makes more money than you do."

"Oh yes. Andy's making over a hundred thousand a year. I make less than half that."

"The courts could be more lenient since you're at a monetary disadvantage."

"I'm not asking for any support or anything like that. I just want the money out of the house. We both contributed to the down payment. Dad gave me some money towards that."

"My secretary will call you when the new will's ready to sign. Jess, you need to stay calm over the next few months. I will need a list of your assets, bank accounts, stocks, 40lKs, pension plans, etc. It won't be easy and call me if you need anything," he said gently steering her out of his office.

Jess stopped at her insurance broker's office and changed the beneficiary on her policy to Marty, then drove back to the hotel. She couldn't tolerate the idea of seeing Andy yet, so she took the room for another night. Andy had sent her a text. "Where are you? Call me." There was also one from Carla. "Jess, are you alright? You didn't answer your phone and I'm worried."

Jess sent a text to Andy. "The situation has changed. Can't come home until tomorrow. See you then." She didn't even feel like speaking with Carla, so she sent her a text. "I have the evidence. Unbelievably graphic. Overwhelming. I'm okay. I'm spending the night at a hotel. I just need time to get my head together. Jess"

JESS SAT LOOKING OUT THE WINDOW, THINKING ABOUT THE next step. There was a stack of boxes of her father's belongings in the man cave at the house, where they'd been sitting for two years. She'd been putting off opening them. *I'll need to rent a storage unit and at least start to move things out plus start looking for an apartment*, she thought. Obviously, her standard of living was going to take a big hit.

She turned on the television more for background noise than anything else, but it was six o'clock and the local station announced the arrival of Arctic Cat at the O'Connell stables. The camera angle showed the ornate wrought-iron gates of the estate standing wide open as the horse trailer pulled into the circular driveway in front of the columned entrance to the house. Laura, Ryan, and most of the stable staff were waiting on the lawn. Arctic Cat backed off the trailer, on a lead line controlled by his Irish handler. The twelve-year-old animal was magnificent. Close to seventeen hands, his glossy bay coat, black mane, and tail gleamed in the sunshine. He looked around his domain as though he owned it, then pranced and snorted for the cameras. Ryan stood there with his chest puffed out and a grin on his face, a successful entrepreneur. The camera cut to local news. Jess turned down the sound but left the television on. She made a mental note to check with Arctic Cat's handler on Monday morning for the horse's feed requirements.

Sitting on the bed, with the pillows tucked behind her, her growling stomach reminded her she hadn't eaten all day. Jess picked up the room service menu, selecting a hot roast beef sandwich with coleslaw and fries, a coffee, and a newspaper. Twenty minutes later there was a knock at the door and the food arrived. She tipped the girl and locked the door. Dutifully, she ate her supper, barely tasting it.

The whole thing didn't seem real. One blessing was that she wouldn't have to pretend any more. She had never been a convincing liar. Andy had stepped over a line, leaving her no option but to leave. If his situation went public, it would not be because of her.

Jess read the paper and scanned the want ads, looking at the prices of apartment rentals. Prices were high. None of them appealed to her or the neighborhoods weren't right. She'd have to take a closer look over her budget and decide how much she could afford for rent.

Next, she decided it was time to call Marty. With the west coast time difference, he'd be home from work by now. He'd only moved to California eighteen months before. There were times she really missed her big brother. He'd always been someone she could talk to and he had the knack of making practical suggestions. She dialed the number and Marty's wife, Sarah, answered the phone. "Hi, Jess. Yes he's here. Just a minute."

She could hear Sarah yelling down the hall over the noise of the kids, "Marty—phone."

Picking up, he asked, "Hi, Jess, how are you?"

"Marty, can you talk to me for a few minutes? I've run into a big problem. I need your help," Jess said.

"Sure, let me go to the bedroom; it's quieter there. Okay, that's better. What's up?"

"I'm divorcing Andy. It's a nasty situation. I've taken the liberty of giving your name as my power of attorney, and making you beneficiary and executor of my estate. I have also given your name to the bank as next of kin. You're beneficiary on my insurance policy too. I hope you're okay with that," she said. "He's been unfaithful, but it's much more complicated than just an affair and I only found out about it a couple of days ago, so I'm not dealing with it very well yet." The tears welled up.

"Jess, what the Hell happened? All of us got along so well. I don't remember him even looking at another woman," Marty exclaimed.

"Well, he's been seeing one since the summer and there's more to it that but I don't want to talk about it right now," Jess said.

"Listen kiddo, I'm here for you. Do you want me to come back to Kentucky?" he asked.

"No, Marty. I don't know all the legal stuff yet. I'll send you copies of the paperwork when I get it all together."

"Have you told Mum?"

"No, I've been putting it off. She thinks Andy's Mr. Wonderful. Hell, I thought he was Mr. Wonderful until I discovered this. I don't want Mum pestering me every day. You know how she is—drama queen." She paused "Let's change the subject. How are things with you?"

"They're good, Jess. The research component makes the job interesting and I've got the skill set for it. The money's great. It's over an hour's commute on a good day. We're all adjusting to the west coast life style. House prices in the city are astronomical," he paused. "Are you sure you're okay?"

"Marty, I'll be working my way through it one step at a time. Thanks for being there for me.

"Take care of yourself kid, and keep me up to date on what you're doing."

"I will. Bye."

Chapter 4

SATURDAY MORNING, JESS SAT IN THE HOTEL ROOM PREPAR-
ing herself for going home. She decided the best strategy
was to put on a calm, totally in control façade no matter
what happened, no matter what she felt. She wasn't going
to provoke Andy or react to what he might say. She realized
it would be a tall order, but it was in her best interest to
stay neutral and settle the legal stuff quickly. She couldn't
change who he'd become, even if she still loved him, and
she couldn't condone his betrayal. If he didn't want her, he
could have said so. *I wish it didn't hurt so much*, she thought.

Jess checked out of the hotel and started the drive home.
Remembering there was a storage place just off Man O' War
Boulevard, she made a quick left at the lights. A small storage
unit was all she was going to need. The attendant showed
her the eight-by-fifteen unit that was sixty dollars a month.
She paid for the month on her credit card and pocketed the
key. She couldn't predict how long she'd need it.

She pulled into the driveway and walked up the path.
Andy opened the door before she even got to it. He went to
put his arms around her but she backed off. "Don't. Touch.
Me," she said very quietly, walking around him into the

house. She dropped her duffel bag on the chair and went to the kitchen, turning on the coffee maker.

"Jess, what the hell is going on? Where have you been?" He stood with his hands on his hips, looking both worried and angry.

"I'll explain in a minute, so park yourself," she replied, turning her back on him, getting the coffee. Her mind was shouting, "Keep in control!" He sat down. She sat opposite him, the coffee table between them and took a deep breath to calm herself, sipping her brew.

"I know you're having an affair-"

Andy interrupted her. "It was just a one-time thing. She doesn't mean anything to me. You know how I feel about you."

"That's a lie, Andy. You've been going out with Angel Mercer since July when she took your summer course," Jess replied in an even, unemotional voice, keeping her eyes firmly fixed on him. "Item number two: Who's the guy? How does he fit in with you and Angel? You claim you love me, but under the circumstances that's highly unlikely."

Andy just looked at her.

She reached into her duffel bag, pulled out the copies of the photos, and handed them to him.

Moments passed as Andy sat in silence flipping through each page then looking back to her. For one fleeting second, he looked like a trapped animal. It was like seeing a total stranger. His eyes were blank, there was no expression. She'd obviously caught him off guard. He put the pages on the coffee table and ran his fingers through his hair.

"Jess, these photos could destroy my career. Where are they? Who's got access to them?"

"They're in my safety deposit box, so you don't have to be concerned on my account. I have no intention of using them in a public way. You've jeopardized your own career and ethics. I'd rather not have it public either. I'd look like a complete idiot. I've started divorce proceedings."

A look of surprise came on his face. "But Jess—"

"Come on, Andy. At some point, you had to know I'd find out."

"I never thought it would be anything more than a fling," he said, avoiding her eyes.

"Since when is having a fling okay?"

There was silence. Somehow, he'd shrunk.

"Do as you please, Andy. I'm not going to yell and carry on. You have an ongoing relationship with two people and had the nerve to bring her here. It doesn't matter now. You decide about the house; either buy me out or put it on the market. I can't afford it so either way is fine by me; just let me know, so I can inform my lawyer. An uncontested divorce is a lot cheaper than a court battle."

"Jess, let me explain."

"Don't bother. I can't trust you to tell the truth. You've chosen to go that route," she said, pointing at the photos. "You haven't left me any leeway." Having said all she intended to, she put down her coffee cup, grabbed her duffel bag and went upstairs to her office.

She pulled down the Murphy bed and put the sheets on. About an hour later, she heard the front door slam and Andy's SUV start up. *I've done it. I've actually done it*, she said to herself and let out a big sigh. From now on, that was how she was going to treat him. She'd tell him what she wanted and not be so submissive.

Jess spent the next few hours moving her clothes from their bedroom to the office closet, examining every item. Anything she didn't want went into a bag for the thrift shop. She also made space for her dresser and moved it into her room.

She decided she'd better do a wash, so she gathered up her work clothes. The basket contained some of Andy's things too, but she set them aside. He could do his own laundry. The dining room table was covered with pieces of paper with Andy's scribbled writing, most of it figures. He'd been going over his finances. Could he afford to buy her out?

For the next half hour while the laundry was in, she rummaged around in the garage for cardboard boxes and started packing her photos and paintings from the living room and den. A lot of them had come from her father's house—pictures of him in his youth with family and friends, riding Thoroughbreds; the clothing and cars were vintage 1960s to 1970s. Fortunately, he had written the names of everyone on the back of each photo. None were familiar to her. She'd never met her grandparents. They were long gone.

Jess called Carla. "Hi, it's me."

"Thank God you're alright. I've been worried," said Carla.

"I'm home. I talked to Andy this morning. He's gone out. Can we get together? I'm going to need a place to live. What are the chances of me renting your place when you go? I can't afford most of the apartments in the paper."

"I don't know. I'll ask Mrs. Hibbard. You've been here before. It's just a small granny flat, but it's handy to everything and there's parking for your car. She's charging me seven hundred dollars a month. I don't think you could get a better place for that kind of rent. How about we go to The Keg and have some supper?"

"I've got some things to do first. How about five thirty?" Jess asked.

"It's good. See you there."

Jess went back upstairs and started figuring out her budget. She was really glad she'd paid off her car loan. It would be tight with the house expenses, storage unit, and rent on Carla's apartment. In the meantime, she decided she'd go through her father's things. There would be cutlery, china, linens, and pots in those boxes. Her mother hadn't taken much with her when she'd left for California. John had probably bought her brand-new things. That reminded her to call her mother.

Margaret answered her phone as soon as it rang. "Hi, Mum. It's me again. I thought I should let you know that I've got a serious problem."

"What is it, Jess?"

"Andy's having an affair."

"Oh my God. How could he do that to you? I'm speechless. Jess—are you alright?"

"I'm getting by. It's hit me hard. It's been going on since the summer. I've already seen Mr. Ames to start divorce proceedings."

"Jess, how are you going to manage?"

"I'm working. I'll be alright, Mum. I'm looking for an apartment. Andy can buy me out or sell the house."

"Are you sure that this is the way to go? No chance of reconciliation? Do you want me to come?" Margaret asked.

"No, Mum, that's not necessary. Would you just listen to me? My mind is firmly made up. It's over and yes, I've told

Marty. I've changed my will and accounts so he's my power of attorney now."

"Promise me you'll keep in touch," Margaret said.

"I will keep in touch and on a regular basis, I promise. Right now, I've got to go. There's so much to do," she said, hanging up. She was surprised her mother had been so concerned about her. There was such a disconnect between them.

About an hour later she heard the SUV pull in. Andy came in the door with the real estate agent Mark Gray on his heels. When the subdivision had opened, Mark had been the agent who'd sold them the house. Andy had obviously decided to sell.

"Hi Jess," Mark said. "Good to see you. Andy tells me you guys want to sell this place."

"Good to see you, Mark" she said. "Go ahead and have a look through it; see what you think," she said, thankful Andy wasn't wasting any time. They'd paid one seventy-five for the house six years ago with fifty-five thousand down: twenty-five thousand from her and the rest Andy's money. It had been a brand-new subdivision. Property values had gone up but she wasn't sure how much.

Fifteen minutes later, Andy called her down. "Mark says comps in the area are selling for upwards of two twenty-five, but this lot's bigger and has the double garage, so he figures we should ask two forty-five." He looked perfectly calm, normal in fact.

"Good," she said. "We can always drop the price if it isn't moving."

Andy added, "Mark, we want an early closing date too. Neither one of us can carry this place for long."

"You need to stage and clean the house as soon as possible. Nothing on the kitchen counters; it has to be spotless. Bathroom should have all the towels neatly displayed. Andy, that includes the garage and your man cave downstairs," Mark said as he pulled the paperwork out of his briefcase. They both read over the agreement and signed.

"I'm going to take measurements of all the rooms right now. I'll put up a "for sale" sign on lawn before I leave. I think that's it. We're on a roll," he said, pulling out his laser measuring gadget. "I will get a picture of the front of the house for an ad in this week's paper."

Once Mark left, Andy came up to see her. "Jess, listen to me for a few minutes. I didn't mean to deliberately hurt you. I've known for a long time that I was different, even as a teen. It's just been since the spring that I had to admit to myself that I was attracted to men as well as women."

"You may not have known before, but right now I'm collateral damage," she said, feeling the anger start to rise. "I'm going downstairs to sort through Dad's stuff, then I'm going to meet Carla."

"What about supper?" he said.

"What about it? I don't feel like cooking. I'm sure you can find something in the fridge," she said, heading to the basement.

The first box she opened had kitchen stuff: cutlery, spoons, steak knives, can openers which would be useful, so she refolded the lid and wrote "kitchen utensils" on the side in black marker.

The next box had the Mixmaster, toaster, and steam iron. The mixer and iron would never be used, so she set them aside. She looked at the box of her mother's fine porcelain tea cups. They could go to the women's auxiliary at the church. They were always putting on lunches. She worked steadily through half a dozen boxes, finding linens she'd keep.

A box of her father's clothes had her close to tears. The shirts and pants were good enough to give away, but she threw out the underwear and socks. Marty had helped her pack up Dad's things after he'd died. For the most part, they'd just thrown stuff in boxes. Such chaos. She remembered at the time thinking the office was a mess. So unlike him.

As a veteran, her dad was usually meticulously neat and orderly. His death had been so sudden, they'd been in shock. At the time, one of the policemen, who had been his friend for years, had commented about the condition of Dad's house and wondered about his state of mind. If it hadn't been for the brake marks on the road, they were at one point questioning suicide. The accident had happened in early evening, so it was unlikely he'd fallen asleep at the wheel.

Glancing at her watch, she saw it was five o'clock. Time to meet Carla. Jess went upstairs, grabbed her purse and car keys, and drove to the mall.

Carla was already at The Keg Bar & Grill, along with the rest of the girls. The knot of giggling women shuffled along the bench seats in the long, paneled lounge, making room for Jess. The first round of drinks was well under way. Aromatic smells emanated from the kitchen. The mirrors of the bar reflected the huddles of customers, bustling staff taking orders and carrying food trays, with the hum of conversations, and the clinking of glasses and plates. She needed this. Good friends and a little fun.

Spaghetti was the evening special so she ordered it. A glass of red wine went down nicely. The basket of garlic bread was quickly emptied—she was ravenous. They dissected their week, with humorous stories of work, husbands, and kids.

"I saw Mark Gray's car in your driveway. Are you selling?" Leah asked.

Jess took a deep breath. It hadn't taken long for the news to get out. "Andy and I are splitting, so we're selling the house."

There was dead silence as they all stared at her, mouths open and wine glasses poised in mid-air.

"I thought you two were the perfect couple," Karen said.

"So did I, but apparently he's got someone new. I only found out a couple of days ago, so I'm pretty shook up," she said, her fork now aimlessly moving the spaghetti on her plate. She found it hard to look at her friends.

She wondered if any of them would stick by her. Her social life would spiral downward. She'd seen it so many times before. Invitations from couples would stop. Many of her friends here were married to Andy's friends, and they would take his side. Her church-going friends wouldn't approve either. The older southern belles would put up with the humiliation of their husbands' behavior because they had never worked and couldn't support themselves or their lifestyles. Laura O'Connell came to mind. Jess felt she had just entered the world of the pariah, a social outcast.

"Jess, would you give Mrs. Hibbard a call?" Carla asked, gently touching her hand. "She's interested in renting the apartment."

"Thanks, Carla. I'll do that. Actually, can I go home with you and talk to her now?" Jess asked. "The sooner I know what I'm doing, the better. I haven't seen your place for a while. I need a better idea of how much space you have so I can downsize."

"Sure," said Carla.

"I want to dispose of my wedding dress. Does anyone want it?" she asked.

They all shook their heads.

"Never mind. I'll find a home for it," she said.

The mood of the evening changed and the meal ended sooner than usual. Her announcement had put a damper on things. Carla and Jess left together. She glanced back at the others who were gathered in a tight circle, looking at her and talking. Change had begun.

Chapter 5

CARLA'S APARTMENT WAS A CONVERTED DOUBLE GARAGE, just one big room. Jess looked at the layout and tried to imagine where her furniture would go. The place was bright and airy with two windows looking out on the street at the front and a large single window at the back overlooking the garden. There was a tiny kitchen with a refrigerator, a stove, and about six feet of counter top space including the sink on the right-hand wall. The postage-stamp-sized bathroom was located in the back corner complete with toilet, basin, and shower. There was a large closet by the door. The whole room wasn't much bigger than a stallion's box stall.

Dad's antique dining room set was just too big to fit. She loved that cherry table; the color and grain were awesome. She'd need some kind of storage for linens. There was enough room on the back wall under the window to set up her computer desk, filing cabinet, and bookshelves. Her Dad's big recliner would fit and so would her dresser. She'd have to negotiate with Andy for the smaller television. He could have the fifty-two-inch one. It didn't look like she'd have room for a single bed, but she could use the sofa bed and the dinette set already there. It would save her from having to buy her own. Money was definitely a consideration.

"I think this would work for you until you know what you're doing," Carla said.

"True enough. Let's see Mrs. Hibbard," she said.

Jess liked the look of her future landlady. Mrs. Hibbard was a short, stocky woman, probably in her mid-fifties and a widow. She welcomed them and they talked for a while. Jess explained her situation.

"Do you expect any trouble from him?" Mrs. Hibbard asked.

"Not at all. He's a professor at the university. He's found another woman and that's it. I'm expecting a quick divorce. Our house went up for sale today. I'd like to have the apartment as soon as Carla vacates, if you think I'd be a suitable tenant. I've got some of my own furniture, but I'd like to use the dinette and sofa bed, if that would be okay with you? If you need references, I work at the O'Connell's stables as their feed manager."

"I'm not concerned, Jess. Carla's told me a lot about you. I think this will work for both of us. Rent is seven hundred a month including heat but you pay your own electricity," Mrs. Hibbard said. "I'll remove any furniture you don't need."

Jess thanked her and left a deposit.

As they were leaving, Carla gave her a big hug. "Jess, don't forget what I said. I really would like you to come to Argentina for a holiday. You've got no supports here—no mother, no sisters, and I'm not sure the girls will step up to the plate. They're married to Andy's friends. From what you tell me, your Mum won't be much help. Get your passport and come any time. I mean it."

"I love the idea of a vacation. I've never been abroad," Jess replied. "But right now, I need to get all the legal stuff started and organize myself." As she hugged Carla, the tears flowed again.

By the time she got home, she was calm. Andy was sitting on the couch watching television. He acknowledged her and said, "Your mother called. She gave me an earful."

"I wasn't expecting her to do that. Next time, check call display and don't pick up. I don't need her interference." She went upstairs to shower.

Afterward, she continued sorting clothes and, with sadness, carefully folded her wedding dress in its plastic garment bag and placed it in the disposal bag. She felt like she was discarding a big piece of her life. Tomorrow was Sunday and she'd continue going through her father's things, which she could unload after work on Monday. Looking at her to-do list, she added "Passport and photos." Vacation—why not? The passport office was on Lansdowne Drive, not far away. She'd have to rummage through her paperwork to find her birth and marriage certificates. Maybe the passport office did photos too.

*   *   *

SUNDAY AFTERNOON, JESS CLEANED ALL THE KITCHEN CUP-boards, dusted, and washed the shelves and replaced all the contents neatly. Andy spent most of the day cleaning the garage. Out of habit, she prepared lunch for both of them, then headed downstairs to continue working on her father's stuff. There were two boxes of photos to sort through and some old photo albums but Jess decided she could do those at some other time. She sealed the cartons and added them to the pile ready for the storage unit.

She opened a box marked "books" and looked at them. She couldn't imagine why she'd kept them. There were vintage Philip Marlowe and Mike Hammer detective stories, from the fifties and sixties, a large number of Louis L'Amour westerns, and some leather-bound history books on World War II. She flipped through each one and most of them ended up in the thrift store boxes. There was one leather-bound one that looked like an encyclopedia, but when she opened it, it was a hollowed-out book with an envelope inside.

Jess had read about such things, in old detective stories but had never seen one. It was a safe place to hide something; it looked so real. She opened the envelope and there were two horse photos inside. The same horse appeared in both pictures, or did it? The one dated 2014, with Neil holding the lead line, had a circle drawn around the faint, three-inch scar on the right inner foreleg. The second dated 2015, was posed the same way but there was no scar. In her father's clear handwriting, he'd written *Arctic Cat* on the first and *Not Arctic Cat?* on the other.

She compared the two photos. The horses looked identical, except for the scar. The dates clicked. In 2014, he'd gone to Ireland on a holiday and stopped in at the stables to see Neil's horses. In 2015, an old friend had passed away and he had returned to attend the funeral, then taken a tour of the stables again. He hadn't been home more than a couple of weeks before he died.

The implications hit her! Had the horses been switched? Her father had hidden the photos. He had the proof. Somebody knew he had them. Was he killed because of them? Was the mess in the house proof someone had searched for them?

Stunned, she sat there for a long time, trying to make sense of it. If that was true, who was responsible? Was she in danger if it became known she had them? The only people threatened by the photos were the O'Connells, all three of them. Jess returned the photos to the envelope and decided to put them in her safety deposit box. She took all the boxes that were ready, plus the bags of things for the thrift shop, and loaded them into her car.

*   *   *

SHE WOKE UP AT FIVE O'CLOCK AND GOT READY FOR WORK. Andy was still sleeping, so she left early and headed for the stables. Even as Jess prepared the morning feed and carried the buckets to the stallion barn, the threat that the O'Connells were involved in her father's death loomed over her.

It felt like she'd been away forever, not just three days. She greeted all the handlers and then went over to Arctic Cat's stall. She recognized the short, compact red-haired man from the news program. He looked to be in his mid-thirties. He was also the handler in the 2015 photo of the phony Arctic Cat. The little voice in her head said, *Be careful.*

"Good morning, I'm Jess, the feed manager." Jess eyed the horse who was ignoring them, quietly eating his hay, but his ears were flicked back, listening. "He's magnificent."

"My name's Mick, Mick Barstow," he said. "Magnificent he is, but he's unpredictable, so always be wary. I've got the scars to prove it," he said, his rolling Irish brogue intriguing her.

"How long have you been his handler?" she asked.

"Over five years now," he said.

"That's good to know. What's his normal diet? He's a bit overweight, probably a body score of eight." If a switch had been made, this man could have been party to it.

"He was cooped up in quarantine for over a week. He's been active out in the yard all weekend." Then he proceeded to list the ingredients of the horse's feed.

Jess quickly wrote everything down. "This hay will be similar to what he was getting in Ireland I expect. He'll have to get used to winter weather here. It'll be a lot colder with snow by the end of November for sure. Does he have any health problems?"

"He's not had any in the five years I've handled him. His appetite's fine and his droppings are firm as you can see," he said nodding to the pile of manure in the corner. "No gut problems. Neil wants me to stay with him. It's a grand opportunity for me to come to the US." he said with a grin.

"I'll go and get his feed for you then," she said. The horse moved and she got a good look at him. No scar was visible on the right leg. Was her father right? If not Arctic Cat, then who?

After she prepared and dropped off Cat's feed for Mick, she went back to the office. Annie and Becky looked really busy, papers covering their desks.

"Glad you're back, Jess, we're up to our eyeballs in paperwork," said Annie.

"What's going on?"

"I'm getting the export papers ready for Señor Diaz. The fillies are being shipped to Buenos Aires on Thursday."

"That's great. I like him. He's good with horses. Did Monsieur Marchand buy any?"

"Not that I know of. He looked at the colts, but they didn't suit him, so he's checking out other stables here and in Louisville."

"So that leaves us with three colts. Ryan needs to get them sold." She wondered if Ryan had called any of the bloodstock agents to expedite sales. "We'll be short of stall space by January once the breeding season starts, now that we've got five stallions," she said, sitting at her desk. Opening up her computer, she started a page for Arctic Cat, filling in his feed chart and body score sheet. She made up a duplicate card for the feed room.

"How are you doing, Becky?" Jess asked when that job was done.

"Annie's been showing me the accounts, but the phone keeps interrupting. I'm learning," the blond replied.

"Jess," Annie interjected, "I forgot to tell you. The vet will be here today to do his post-quarantine assessment on Arctic Cat."

"Great. I'll take the camera with me. I'll need to start his profile. Pretty easy—bay, no markings." Jess rummaged through the bottom drawer for her camera. She put the profile page on a clipboard, ready for the vet, writing in Cat's tattoo and microchip information from the export–import form completed by his Irish vet. She wondered if the numbers would match the records.

Jess's phone rang. It was security telling her that the grain truck had arrived. "Send him to the silos. I'll be right there," she said.

After a quick conversation with the Wainright driver, she had him unload the corn. Enough spilled during delivery, to attract the ever-present local pigeons. Jess took the invoice to the office and gave it to Annie.

Right after lunch, the vet arrived. Jess gathered up the clipboard and camera. Mick had Cat ready with the lead line chain under the horse's upper lip. Ryan joined them. He positioned himself beside her, close enough to whisper in her ear, "Quite the horse, isn't he?"

"He sure is, Ryan. Impressive animal," replied Jess, side-stepping.

The vet took out his scanner and moved it over the left side of the horse's neck. He had no trouble finding the microchip and called the numbers out to Jess, who entered them on the form. They matched the export form. Mick tightened his hold on the lead shank while the vet checked the lip tattoo.

The stallion started tossing his head, becoming agitated. Jess wondered if Mick deliberately aggravated the horse by the way he was applying tension to the lead shank or if the horse was indeed resisting. Hard to tell.

The vet rolled up Cat's lip. "This tattoo is so faded I can't read it. How old is he?"

"Twelve," said Ryan.

"Jess, mark down it's illegible," the vet said, and stepped back.

Mick released the pressure on the chain and Cat's head came down. Hmm.

"I need to take five photos. Can you bring him outside? The light's better," Jess asked. She took photos from the front, the rear, and both sides, then a close-up forehead shot.

"When a horse has no markings, the Jockey Club wants a frontal head shot to pick out the whorl pattern on his forehead," she said to Mick, then felt silly because he probably knew that.

The vet gave the horse a quick once over, keeping a wary eye on him. Rectal temperature—normal. Cat stood. "That's it, Ryan. He looks good to me," the vet said, packing up his gear. "We're done. I'll sign him off."

Jess was a little surprised that he hadn't collected mane hairs to confirm the DNA, but noted the box had been checked off by the quarantine station on their paperwork.

Mick led Cat back to his paddock then released him. Cat whirled around and bucked, cavorting across his acre with exuberance, his nostrils flared, his tail kinked high. Jess smiled.

Ryan started to crowd her again, but Jess edged away and went back to the office. She downloaded the photos to her computer and printed a copy for the records. As afternoon approached, Jess sat at her desk with a multitude of ideas bouncing around in her mind.

Who was this horse? Was it possible to remove a microchip from one animal and put it in another? Could a tattoo be changed or removed? A substitute would have to be closely related to even come close to matching the DNA hair test. Had Neil somehow managed to do this? If so, then a whole lot of people were implicated—Neil, Ryan, Mick. Maybe the Irish vet. Did this have anything to do with her father's death? Who knew he had the photos?

She knew her speculations were wild. However, if they were true, then she had to be extremely careful or she could end up in the same boat. On the other hand, with all the turmoil in her life, there was a distinct possibility that she was just being paranoid. Unbelievable.

After work, Jess drove over to the storage unit and unloaded the boxes from the car, then dropped the bags, including her wedding dress, into the thrift shop drop box. She slipped over to the bank, put the photos in her safety deposit box, and picked up groceries. Andy wasn't home when she got there. The house looked well-staged, clean and bright, but somehow sterile. Jess fervently hoped that Mark would be showing the house soon and good offers would come in.

Andy didn't come home, so she made herself a grilled cheese sandwich and a bowl of soup. It felt very strange to be alone. She'd never lived alone in her entire life. As much as it hurt, she'd have to get used to it.

Jess sat at the computer and researched microchips. All the articles stated they were as hard to find as a grain of rice and could not be removed. All the tattooing articles suggested the removal process was painful, had to be done repeatedly over months, and needed a dry environment to prevent infection. A wet horse's mouth certainly didn't qualify. Even the laser treatments had to be done several times. None were practical for a horse unless it was sedated.

The alphanumeric registration number sequences made altering letters impossible. How then?

Thinking of the time frame, she looked up the sports pages of the Dublin newspapers: the *Times*, the *Star*, the *Examiner,* and the *Post.* Bingo! There had been a fire at one of Neil's stables a month before her father's visit in 2015. Neil had lost three horses in the fire. One of them was Wing Commander, a full brother to Arctic Cat.

Oh, my God. Neil probably got insurance money for those horses. But what if it was Arctic Cat who had died and Neil stood to lose all the breeding fees? Seventy thousand euros times fifty mares was three million, five hundred thousand. That would be a good reason to substitute Wing Commander. They were full brothers. They looked identical, even down to the direction of the forehead whorl. Wing Commander was two years older, so that would make him fourteen now. Maybe that was why the tattoo had faded. The horse in the stable had to be Wing Commander.

How could she uncover the truth? Mulling it over, Jess needed to explore the facts about her dad's accident, if it was an accident. Had he been forced off the road? Jess decided to start with the car. She picked up her phone and called Brad Hollingsworth.

"Hi, Jess. What can I do for you?"

"I've got a question, Brad. Were you on duty the night my father died?"

"No, Jess. I was working days. The accident happened in the evening."

"Did you ever see the car?"

"Yes. The front end was completely demolished. They had to use the jaws of life to cut the driver's door."

"Was there any damage to the back bumper?"

"I couldn't tell you, Jess. By the time I saw it the next day, it was in the impound yard. I never really examined it. Why are you asking? Is there a problem?"

On the spur of the moment, she invented a story. "Someone suggested that he'd been rammed from behind and I wondered if there was any evidence to support it, you know, photos and stuff. Also, how would I go about getting a copy of the coroner's report?"

"You'd have to go to the station and talk to Detective John Peterson. He was there that evening and he can find the file and open it. I think Irwin Carter was the coroner."

"Thanks for the info, Brad," she said and hung up. She looked up the website for the *Kentucky Herald*. Entering the date, she wasn't quite prepared for the front-page headline that glared at her: LOCAL MAN KILLED IN CRASH. The picture clearly showed the twisted metal of the SUV, nose down in the ravine beside the culvert, the hood wrapped around the large tree, accompanied by a portrait shot of her father. She looked at the shattered windows, the mangled driver's door, and the compacted interior and realized her father never had a chance. The engine was almost in the front seat. The angle of the photo showed the front of the car but not the back bumper.

Her phone rang. It was her mother. "Hi Mum."

"Oh Jess. I'm so glad you're home. How are you? I was worried," said Margaret.

"I'm okay. Things are going alright at this end. We're being civil to each other. The house is up for sale, so I've been cleaning. Andy said you told him off. I know you're trying to be helpful, but it just makes him mad, and I don't want to deal with that, alright?"

"My poor baby—"

"Mum, I'll manage. I've found a small apartment. Right now, I'm going through all the boxes of Dad's stuff that I've never got around to sorting. Most of it's going to the thrift shop. I'm glad I have a job. It keeps me busy and at least I can support myself. Look, I'm going to bed. I've got a busy day tomorrow. I'll call you on Sunday."

"You do that, baby," Margaret replied.

Chapter 6

THURSDAY WAS A BUSY DAY FOR JESS, PREPARING THE TWO fillies for shipment; their attendants blanketing them and wrapping their legs for the flight. The transport trailer was ready. All the export paper work was accounted for, including their X-ray reports and vet evaluations. Jess left a note for Laura, telling her she was going to work through lunch, so that she could leave half an hour early for her doctor's appointment. Also Mrs. Johnson had left a message that she needed to come in to sign her new will.

Ryan cornered her in the hall outside the office. Pressing her against the wall, he said, "I hear you're available now. That's nice," his body pushing against hers.

She removed his hand from her shoulder, slipped sideways away from him and glared at him. "You heard wrong, Ryan. Just because Andy and I are splitting, does not make me available, to you or anyone else for that matter," she said and stomped off to the office to join Becky and Annie.

She left at one thirty, thoroughly glad to be out of there. Sitting on the exam table, she explained everything to Dr. McMurray's nurse and was promptly given a gown and told to undress. Dr. McMurray had known her since she was a baby. When he finally came in, she explained the situation.

"Any symptoms or discharge at all?" he asked. He inserted the speculum and inspected her thoroughly. "Jess, it looks good to me. Labia are nice and clean," he said taking swabs. "I'll send these for all the usual diseases like gonorrhea, chlamydia and syphilis plus we'll get the lab tech to take some blood for HIV. Any itching or lesions like herpes?"

"None," said Jess.

"I don't see anything to worry about," he said.

"Do I continue to take the pill, even though we're not intimate?" Jess asked.

"Probably would be a good idea, until all the details are sorted out. An unwanted pregnancy would be a huge complication. Do you need your prescription refilled?"

"Can you renew it for at least six months? I'm seriously thinking about taking a long vacation this winter, just to get away from here for a while," she said.

"Good idea. We're supposed to have a harsh winter with lots of snow and wind. Where are you planning on going?" he asked.

"I was thinking of Argentina. My friend Carla lives there. I'm going to need a guarantor to get my passport. May I use your name?"

"Certainly. I've only known you for twenty some years," he joked. "I should have all the results back in a couple of weeks. The office will call you," he said as he was about to leave.

"I've been going through Dad's stuff. I never did get around to unpacking everything after he died. What was his state of mind at the time? Someone suggested he might have been depressed or suicidal."

"Joe? Good heavens, no. He was always the same—even-tempered, dry sense of humor. I never saw him depressed, even after your mother took off."

"Thanks, Dr. McMurray. I thought they were wrong too." She got dressed and then the lab tech came in and drew her blood. She was relieved to get another chore off her list.

As she got in her car, she glanced at her watch. It was five-fifteen. The scrap yard was open until six. She got there about ten to the hour. Old Mr. Miller was wiping grease from his hands with the tail of his flannel shirt, getting ready to close the chain-link gates.

"Hi, there, Mr. Miller," she said.

"Well, long time no see, Jessica. What can I do for you?"

"Do you remember the day Dad died?"

"I sure do. His car was a complete write-off."

"I know there was a lot of front-end damage, but was there any damage to the back?"

"It was dinged up pretty bad too: dents under the back window, damage to the side panels, and the back brake-light assembly was smashed on the driver's side."

"People have asked me over the years what might have caused the crash and I've never really had a good answer," she said.

"I don't know, Jess. He'd just had the car serviced 'cos I met him up at the dealership. I was delivering parts to them and he was in the lounge having a cup of coffee. He was telling me all about his trip to Ireland. Damn shame," he said, chaining the gates shut. As she walked out of the yard, he turned the big Doberman loose.

"Thanks, anyway," Jess said, climbing in her car. She stopped in at the police station on the off chance that Detective Peterson was working. The sergeant on duty told her the detective would be back Sunday afternoon. "I'll call him then," she said.

Andy's car was in the driveway when she got home. She could hear him running the vacuum cleaner upstairs. Andy stuck his head out his bedroom door.

"Hi, Jess. Mark's booked a showing here tomorrow afternoon around two."

"Okay, leave the vacuum up here. I need to do my room too. Just let me get changed. I want to ask you a couple of questions," she said.

He'd brought home a bucket of fried chicken and offered her some. That surprised her. There were a couple of beers in the fridge, so they took one each.

"I'm going to rent Carla's granny flat. There isn't much space; I'd like the small television."

"What other furniture do you want?" he asked.

"A sofa bed and dinette come with the place. I'll take my computer desk, the two bookcases, and my filing cabinet, plus Dad's recliner. I'm still going through his stuff downstairs, but it looks like there's cutlery, linens, pots and pans, and Mum's old set of dishes. That will be more than enough. I'm going to have to sell that cherry table and chairs. As much as I love them, they're just too big," she said. "You can do what you like with the rest of it."

It seemed odd to be casually discussing dismantling their lives.

"I'll probably get an apartment in town, but I haven't had time to start looking yet," he said. "I suppose Ryan's giving you a hard time."

"Yeah, but I can handle it, just like I always do. I might start looking around for a different job," she said.

"What have you got in mind?"

"Well, I don't know yet. Haven't had much time to think about it. Do you have any plans?"

"Not particularly. I'll stick with this position now and see how it goes," he said.

There was an element of caution in his voice, which made Jess wonder if he was worried about still having a job. Not that it really mattered to her now. She washed the dishes, then headed downstairs to the den to sort more boxes.

*   *   *

ON FRIDAY, ANOTHER LOAD OF HAY WAS DELIVERED AND later the grain truck arrived loaded with oats. Jess worked through her lunch hour again, giving her time to see Mrs. Johnson at the law office. Jess read the papers through and signed them. She asked for two copies, one of which she would send to Marty.

After that she went to the post office on Lansdowne, scribbled a quick note to Marty, saying the original would be kept at her lawyer's office, and sent it off. While she was there, she picked up the passport application and inquired about the photographs. Yes, they did do them. She decided to work on that over the weekend. She hadn't seen her marriage certificate in quite some time. It had to be in her legal file at home.

It was after six when she got home, but Andy wasn't there. She figured he would probably be out all weekend. She crossed her fingers that the house would sell soon and wondered how the showing had gone for Mark; his business card was on the kitchen counter.

She spent the evening watching television, feeling lonely. There was a difference between being alone knowing someone would be home later and being alone period. It still seemed really strange. She'd always lived with someone, whether it was her father or Andy. Part of her was angry with him for being unfaithful and part of her wondered what it would feel like to deal with the reality of his sexual orientation. Different?, Scary?

Jess sent a text to Carla saying she would be available for a coffee if Carla had time. She wanted to get more details from her about Argentina. It was sounding better all the time.

*   *   *

JESS HADN'T HEARD BACK FROM CARLA, SO SHE WENT FOR groceries. On the spur of the moment, she drove towards the stables. She had deliberately avoided the ravine road since the accident. Now she wanted to see exactly what her father had seen. Traffic was fairly steady and there was a pickup truck behind her that was just itching to pass. Every time she looked in her rearview mirror it seemed closer, until she couldn't even see the license plate, just the huge chrome grill. She slowed coming into the curve with the yellow and black warning arrows and for a moment saw the gap at the side of the guardrail as she drove past, her heart pounding and her hands clenched in a death grip on the steering wheel. She stayed on the road and pulled over at the first turn-in she came to, allowing the guy in the truck to go by with his screaming turbo-charged engine and throaty roar of the dual exhausts. She was trembling.

Jess got out of her car and when there was a break in the traffic, made her way across the bridge to the open end of the guardrail, where her dad's car had left the road. The half culvert, channeling any rain water run-off, lined the gully from the road down to the water's edge. She followed it down, climbing over masses of small, broken trees. It was at least a forty-five-degree slope. The great oak at the bottom was deeply gouged, missing a large chunk of bark about six feet off the ground, obviously where his car had hit. Very slowly, she turned and clambered back up the hill. The distance was about sixty feet from the road. She knew what he'd felt. It was terrifying. Jess stood looking at the road and tried to imagine the tire tracks as he had braked. She sat in her car for a long time, thoroughly shaken.

Why was he heading to the stables at six-thirty at night? Surely if he'd worked all day, he would have left work before three and gone home. Nothing was so urgent that it couldn't wait until morning. It didn't make any sense that he'd gone back.

Her phone rang. It was Carla. They met at the coffee shop in the mall. Jess was surprised to see Karen with her;

she was a casual member of their group and the wife of Andy's friend.

"How's it going?" Carla asked.

"I'm working through my to-do list. Andy's not home much these days, but it makes it easier for me in a lot of ways. How about you?" Jess replied.

"Only three weeks to go and I'll be home. I'm so excited." Carla said, a big smile on her face.

Jess looked at Karen. "Good to see you. How are you?" she asked, just pleased she'd come.

"I'm doing fine. I wanted to check up on you. Just because I'm married to one of Andy's friends doesn't mean I'm going to stop seeing you," Karen replied.

"You have no idea how much I appreciate that. So often friends lose touch when there's a breakup. I'm sure sooner or later, Andy will show up to one of your parties with the new girl. I just don't want to create awkward scenes and, to tell you the truth, I'm not sure how I'd react at this point."

Karen stayed and chatted with them, but a half hour later looked at her watch and said she had to go. Jess still had the impression she was pulling away somehow.

"Jess, have you thought any more about the vacation?" Carla asked.

"I'm going to say that I will definitely come. I just don't know when; the house has to sell. Tentatively, I'm thinking February. I've still got to get my passport. I'll let you know. I've got your email address. Maybe I'll book an Airbnb. It would be a lot cheaper than a hotel."

"I can keep my eye open for one, no problem. I'll try and find something close to my family's apartment and the dance studio. I'll let you know," she said.

"Do you know a Señor Diaz who owns a racing stable in Argentina? He bought a couple of fillies from the O'Connells. I'd like to see them when I'm visiting you."

"Actually, he lives on a huge estancia about thirty minutes from where I live. Small world, isn't it? He's a very important and respected businessman," she replied. "What's on your agenda tonight?"

"I've only got about six boxes of Dad's stuff left to sort out, then I'll search for my marriage certificate and birth certificate for the passport application. I'm also thinking of putting a résumé together. I don't know how much longer I can tolerate working at O'Connells."

"Is Ryan giving you a hard time?"

"Yes. He seems to think that because I'm getting divorced, I'd be available. He got close and personal, but I told him straight up what I thought of that. He's damned persistent. I'd probably get fired if I told him he's a disgusting, perverted idiot, but I can't afford to lose my job right now."

"Will you look for the same type of work?"

"I was thinking about applying to the feed company, but maybe working for one of the bloodstock agents would be a better fit. I just don't know yet. If I'm going to be visiting Argentina, I'd better learn some Spanish. You talk to me in Spanish, and maybe I can learn a few phrases while you're still here," Jess said.

"I'll get you a Spanish–English phrase book. It's simple and handy. I'm putting as many hours in as I can, so I'll have more money to go home with. I'm working the afternoon shift so I've got to go. Adios, amiga," said Carla, laughing.

Later Jess picked up groceries, went home, then headed downstairs to finish sorting. Most of the boxes contained her father's tools. She decided to get herself a small metal toolbox and just keep a few basic tools plus a box each of nails and screws. She had no use for the circular saw, the grinder, and the hand saws. She thought of several contractors who would probably be able to use them, so she carried the boxes upstairs and loaded them into her car.

Finally, she was finished. The man cave with its huge television looked spacious and bright, but it didn't look like anyone lived there. Upstairs, she ate her supper and watched television, much too tired to be bothered with paperwork.

*   *   *

JESS SPENT SUNDAY MORNING GOING THROUGH HER FILING cabinet, shredding a lot of unnecessary paper. She found her marriage certificate and birth certificate as well as all her graduation certificates. She filled out the passport application form. She'd have to drop it off to Dr. McMurray's office sometime to get his signature. She made a copy of the marriage certificate for Andy and kept the original for herself.

Around one o'clock, she phoned the police station. Detective Peterson was in the building, so she quickly drove over there. She asked the desk sergeant if it was possible to speak with him, then took a seat on the bench. She found it fascinating to watch the comings and goings.

Two officers brought in an inebriated, hand-cuffed individual who was giving them a hard time, cursing and swearing. A little old lady reported her dog stolen; several teens were sitting there looking apprehensive and glum, glued to their cellphones, and a thin, disheveled man with a black eye was being released. Eventually a plain clothes officer emerged from one of the rooms. He looked vaguely familiar to her, triggering the memory back to the night of her father's death. The sergeant spoke to him and pointed to her. The officer, who looked to be in his late forties approached her. He was the cop, who'd investigated her dad's accident.

He introduced himself as Detective John Peterson. "You wanted to talk to me?"

"I'm Jessica Coxwell. Brad Hollingsworth suggested I contact you. A couple of years ago, you were on duty when there was a car accident on the ravine road. The driver died at the scene. That was my father, Joe Hartford. I wondered if you could spare a few minutes to talk to me about it."

He glanced at his watch. "Mrs. Coxwell, I'm in the middle of something right now. Could you come back in about an hour?"

"Sure thing, I can wait." She went back to her car and passed the hour, sketching out the basics of her résumé: school and graduation dates, work experience, who she had worked for, the approximate dates she had been there, her duties at each one and courses she had taken. She made a list of people to use as references. It was going to be very awkward to get a reference from Ryan. She wasn't even sure he'd give her one since she hadn't been "cooperative."

Jess wandered back inside and sat on the bench. About twenty minutes later, Detective Peterson came out and ushered her into his tiny office. "Have a seat. Now what's this all about?"

"I'm moving and was going through all my dad's stuff. I guess I was too shocked when he died to think about things. Brad said you'd known him a long time."

He nodded. "Joe knew my father when I was in my twenties and he was my go-to guy after my dad died. I used to see him fairly regularly."

"Someone mentioned he was depressed or the accident might have been a suicide attempt, but his family doctor doesn't agree. Was there damage to the back of his car?" she asked.

He looked at her, as if deciding what to say. "Yes, there was damage, mostly on the driver's side. He took down enough trees to account for that. Not only that, but the edge of the culvert also scraped the whole side of the car on the way down."

"Did you take photos of the car and the skid marks on the road?"

"Yes, I did. Where are you going with this?" he said, with a puzzled look

"Could he have been rammed off the road?"

He paused for a few moments. "There were a few tiny pieces of red and white plastic and chrome up on the road, but they were close to the guardrail, which was consistent with the trajectory of the car."

"Was there any debris on the road, where the skid marks started? Would it be possible to have the plastic tested to see if it is from his make of car? They can identify vehicles that way, can't they? I'd like to see the photos, if possible. The pictures in the newspaper didn't show the back of the car."

"I didn't find anything like that on the road. I was thinking more in terms of him avoiding a deer. I'd known Joe for a long time, but I worked mostly up state."

"I think that at the time you were questioning his state of mind, because his office at the house was a mess and that was highly unusual. Why were you at the house?"

"Joe was obsessively tidy. When your brother Marty went to the house, he found it unlocked and the office and living room in a mess and he called the station," he said.

"Oh, Marty never told me that. I arrived later."

"The filing cabinet and the desk drawer were open and ransacked. It looked like someone had gone through the bookcase. There was no sign of anyone breaking in. The fact that the side door was unlocked was unusual, as Joe would have locked up before leaving the house. None of it made sense to me," Detective Peterson admitted.

"I was thinking today that it was really odd he was going back to the stable when he'd worked all day,"

"Go on," he said.

Did you read the coroner's report?" Jess asked.

"Yes, no drugs or alcohol were in his system. His injuries were consistent with the trauma. Nothing suspicious. The car's been scrapped, so any evidence has gone. The files are in storage. I'll see what I can do to find them and I'll give you a call. It might take a week or more to locate them, maybe longer." He took her number.

She realized that he might be reluctant to reveal what might be considered as a stain on his record or just plain not worth looking into as an old, closed case even if her father had been his friend..

Now there was another puzzle for her. Why had the side door been unlocked, giving access to the house? Certainly, robbery wasn't a motive. Her father's gun collection included a vintage Kentucky flintlock rifle displayed on the living room wall, which had not been touched. Her father had a house key on his key chain along with the car keys; Marty had one and so did she. There was no way he would have forgotten to lock the door.

She left the police station feeling hopeful that at least she could get to see the photos, at the same time dreading it because they'd be so graphic. Just walking down that gully had been mind-boggling. If Dad had been murdered, was she putting herself in danger? Had Ryan been in town? He could have hired someone. One word from her father that the horses had been switched and the Jockey Club would initiate an investigation possibly leading to the O'Connells being banned from racing. It was all conjecture.

It was so depressing. The black cloud of sadness enveloped her. She'd lost the two most important men in her life but for different reasons. Her pillars had crumbled. It was like sinking into an abyss. Andy didn't come home that night either.

Chapter 7

JESS SPENT MONDAY MORNING MODIFYING THE GRAIN ration for the pregnant mares and posted the notice in the grain room for the evening shift. Mornings were much cooler and she was thankful for her long-sleeved flannel shirt and quilted vest. The horses were starting to grow their winter coats, changing from sleek to fuzzy.

She knew herself well enough to know that sitting around moping was a really bad idea, and she needed something to keep her busy evenings and weekends. She was feeling sorry for herself and thought, *Get over it girl.*

Thinking about Andy, she knew deep down that she would at some point be able to get on with her life. Was she at fault? She didn't see how. Was she so boring than he'd opted for an eighteen-year-old? Had she not paid enough attention to him? The questions kept coming and she didn't have any answers. Doubt was creeping in about her value as a woman.

After work, she stopped in at the doctor's office and dropped off her passport application for him to sign. She then drove over the other side of town where she found construction crews finishing their jobs in a new subdivision. They were just putting their tools away for the day.

Jess picked out a guy in a hard hat, standing by his company truck so she offered him her father's tools.

"Sure, I've always got new apprentices who could use those. Thanks." He transferred the boxes from her car to his truck.

Jess stopped at the hardware store and purchased a small toolbox. She figured she'd just leave her tools in her car. Next stop was the grocery store where she bought a barbecued chicken and a bag of frozen veggies.

Andy was home but didn't say anything about his weekend. "Mark has another showing tomorrow afternoon. The place is looking good, so there's not much for us to do."

She offered him part of the chicken, but he'd already eaten. After supper, she went up to her office and started to think about what to do to keep mind and body on an even keel. She hadn't ridden for a while, so that was an option. It would be fun to learn some Spanish and maybe take some Latin dance lessons. Carla seemed serious about having her uncle teach her to tango and she didn't want to be a clumsy fool on the dance floor.

The rest of the week was uneventful. Mark called back to say that his client was looking for a bigger house, so that was a no-go. He was planning an open house on Saturday. Thursday, she got a message from the doctor's office with good news. All of her tests were negative and her passport application was ready to go. She booked an appointment with the passport office for Monday afternoon, to put in the application and get her mug shot done.

Friday was insane at the stables. All five stallions were getting bookings for stud service and Jess was amazed at the numbers. Ryan told her to call one of the local bloodstock agents to sell the three colts. Space was definitely going to be a problem.

As she was leaving that afternoon, she saw Laura crossing the driveway. Gone was the southern belle of gala night. Her hair was limp and hung in twisted uncombed strands; she wasn't wearing any makeup and there was a frown on her face. She was staring at the two rough-looking characters who were loading one of Ryan's classic cars onto a flat-bed truck. Ryan stood stone-faced beside the truck, his hands in his pockets.

Trouble in paradise. The big garage doors were open and she could see a couple of empty spaces; two weeks ago. that building had been full of antique cars. Jess wondered if the Mafia types were collecting on Ryan's gambling debts. Maybe she was wrong, but it reinforced her determination to find gainful employment elsewhere. After work, she drove over to Carla's.

"Here, Jess, I bought you a Spanish–English phrase book," Carla said, handing it to her.

They spent the evening snacking on nachos and going into hysterical laughter with Jess's pronunciation of even the simple Spanish words for "one, two, three."

"Try again. One is uno, pronounced *oono*; two is *dos*, three is *tres*," said Carla, giggling. "We'll keep working here on the basic stuff. In the meantime, you can work through the phrase book. It does show what to say and how to say it, but I think it would really help if you wrote it out as well."

Carla put on some Spanish CDs and they shimmied and boogied to the music, laughing the whole time. "My uncle would have a fit," Carla said. "He's a stickler for dancing properly."

It was after ten when Jess got home. Andy's car was in the driveway. She could hear him down in the den, watching sports as usual. She put the coffee pot on and called down to him, "I'm making coffee, do you want some?"

He yelled back, "No, I've got beer."

His words were slurred. She was surprised. Drunk? Curiosity got the better of her and she went downstairs. He was sprawled out on the couch, his hair tousled and clothes wrinkled. There was a twelve-pack carton on the floor but seven empty cans on the coffee table.

"I fucked up big time, didn't I?" he said taking another swig from the can in his hand.

Jess stood there for a few moments and didn't answer. In their entire six years of marriage, she'd never seen him drunk—this was wholly out of character. Unable to think of suitable reply, she said, "Don't forget we've got an open house in the morning. You'll have to clean all this up," and went back upstairs.

She took her coffee and went up to her room. Since she couldn't stay in the house during the showing, she decided to spend Saturday morning going to the dance studio and the local riding school. Sunday, she'd put the finishing touches to her résumé, and Monday was her passport appointment.

Jess lay in bed. She could faintly hear the television downstairs but Andy hadn't surfaced. She wondered if he'd fallen asleep. She could feel her mood spiraling down again into the dark place—that bottomless pit of anger and self-pity, that she was trying so hard to avoid.

Andy had made choices that had irrevocable effects upon her. If he had regrets, it was too bad and too late. Maybe the universe had other plans for her. Perhaps better now than when she was older. She curled up in a tight ball. The man she'd married was a mirage. He didn't exist anymore. Had he ever?

Chapter 8

SATURDAY MORNING, SHE HEARD THE SHOWER RUNNING; AT least Andy was awake. The downstairs television was off and the empty beer cans were in the case on the kitchen counter. That was good because she had no intention of cleaning up his mess. She put on her jeans and a sweater, gathered up her coat, her riding boots, a pair of dress shoes and gloves, then headed to the car.

The parking lot beside the dance studio was full, with parents either standing around talking, smoking, and sipping their coffee or waiting in their cars to pick up their children. She recognized some of them. She opened the front door and could see a large group of eight-year-old girls in their leotards, hair in tight buns, on their toes at the barre in the main room. The image reflected down the whole room-length mirror.

Strains of jazz music emanated from the second room where an elegant instructor put a class of teenage girls through their routines. Jess walked to the end of the hall and knocked on the door.

"Come in," a female voice called and Jess went in to find Jean Barry, the dance instructor, on the phone. She waved her over to an empty chair. Jess sat down and waited. Jean had been a friend of her mother's years ago.

"Jess Coxwell, I haven't seen you for ages!" Jean said with a warm smile as she put down the phone. "What can I do for you?"

"Sometime this winter, I'm going to Argentina for a vacation. I want tango lessons now, so that I don't look like a complete amateur when I get there. Is there any room in your schedule for some private lessons?" Jess asked.

"For you and Andy?"

"No. Andy and I are in the middle of a divorce. Just me."

"I'm sorry to hear that, Jess. I thought you and Andy were a good team. I'm sure Jim and I can find time for some private lessons. When are you available?"

"Weekends and evenings. I'm still working at the stables," Jess said.

Jean checked her calendar. "I can fit you in this afternoon at three-thirty. Does that work for you? Do you want the American or Argentinian style tango?"

"Three-thirty will be fine. It'd better be the Argentinian style. My friend's uncle is a dance instructor, and I hoping to hook up with him for lessons. I thought it was a good idea to get some practice here. It gives me something to look forward to as well. I won't just be sitting at home waiting for the house to sell. I'll see you this afternoon," she said and went back to the car.

It was a short drive to the Stattler stables and she hadn't ridden there for at least a year. John Stattler was a blood-stock agent but also ran a riding school for a wide variety of riding modalities—Western, English, as well as gaited—and he worked with all breeds. She could see Thoroughbreds,

Quarter horses and Arabs out in the paddocks. A couple of the training rings were empty and the oval track only had a few riders.

Seeing him could solve a number of problems in one visit. The best scenario would be if she could ride a horse, ask him questions about the bloodstock agent's job, and see if he could sell Ryan's three colts. No problem picking out John. The tall slim man wearing a Stetson, denim, and cowboy boots was riding a compact, muscular buckskin. Once he spotted her, he brought the horse to a halt beside her.

"Hi, Jessica. Good to see you. What can I do for you?"

"Hi, John. I'm hoping you can help me. I want to start riding again, at least once a week. I don't need lessons, just time on a horse. It's been a while," she said.

"You can start right now if you want. There are a couple of two-year-old Thoroughbreds in the barn. Both of them could use a workout. I've got potential buyers coming this week, and it would be nice to have these horses working better. I was going to ride them next, but if you want to that would be great. I never seem to have the time to get everything done."

"Sure. Tell me what sort of workout they need. I'd be delighted," she said putting on her boots.

He dismounted, tying his horse to the hitching post, and walked over to the stables with her. He showed her the horses in the far-end stalls and which tack belonged to them.

"Jess, the chestnut's barely broken, so basic walk and trot for him for an hour. The bay is a bit further along but the same basics for him. Thanks, I appreciate it." He turned and went back outside.

Jess gave the chestnut a quick brush down and picked out his hooves. He tried to avoid the bit by raising his head, but she slipped it into his mouth and got the cheek straps adjusted. He didn't fuss when she cinched up the girth or resist when she led him out of the stall. She quickly grabbed a riding helmet and strapped it on.

She led him over to an empty exercise ring where the footing was good, not wanting any other horses to distract him. He was quivering and eager, barely giving her time to get in the saddle. Reining him to a stop, she checked the girth, adjusted her stirrups while he stood there watching the other horses being worked. His ears swiveled like satellite dishes, picking up sounds from the barn and the track. Gently she gathered her reins and applied equal leg pressure to his sides to move him into a walk. He tossed his head, resisting the bit and tried walking sideways but she kept him moving. Eventually, he gave up fussing and started to pay attention.

For the next hour, she did circles, backed in straight lines and the halt. When he seemed to get the hang of it, she urged him into a trot. She loved the feel of him, the power of his long stride. She felt the very beginning of that subtle communication between horse and rider. His ears were now angled back, listening to her. Riding put her in that lovely bubble of calm, where the rest of the world was blocked out; there was just her and the horse, feeling the movement and the change in cadence as his rhythm smoothed out. His motion was a seamless flow of energy.

A dog barked close by. The horse skittered sideways, his ears pricked in the dog's direction. She slowed, then resumed the trot. When the hour was up, she walked him back to the barn, where she brought him to a halt. She made him stand still as she dismounted beside John, who was brushing down the buckskin.

"He went well for you out there," said John. "Do you want to ride the bay, now? I can brush this one down," he said, taking the reins from her.

"I have an appointment to go to. Could I come back tomorrow to ride the bay? I have a couple of things I want to talk to you about, if you have time."

"That would be great. Maybe around one o'clock tomorrow? What else?" he asked.

"What's involved with being a bloodstock agent? Is that a possibility for me?" she said.

"You're interested?"

"I'm looking at other job possibilities," she said. "The other thing is Ryan has three colts to sell. Do you want to take them?"

"I can't right now. I've got my hands full as you can see. Paul Wagner's been doing some European sales lately. He might be a good one to ask. I suppose you're swamped now you've got Arctic Cat in the yard."

"Yeah, it's crazy busy," she said.

"There are at least six bloodstock agents around here, and in all honesty, we are entirely different. Some do strictly sales. For example, I take different breeds and do both training and sales. Wagner just does Thoroughbreds and his sales are primarily in the US and Europe but occasionally worldwide. Hampton does Standardbreds only. Several others near Louisville work with Arabians. Some do insurance appraisals; others do pedigree work and advise on breeding. We all work on a five percent commission. You would have to have a decent amount of money to begin with—enough to have a working property and enough to get you by tide you over until you develop enough clientele to keep you going. With the experience you have, Wagner might be the better one to talk to."

"Thanks, John. I'll do that and I'll see you around one tomorrow to give the bay a workout," she said, heading back to the car.

Chapter 9

JIM BARRY WAS WAITING FOR HER WHEN SHE ARRIVED AT THE dance studio. She put on her dress shoes and hoped he wouldn't mind the slightly horsey aroma of her jeans.

"Jess, posture is one of the most important elements of tango. Your back should be straight and your head held high. This dance had humble origins, but it's become elegant and sophisticated. It depends on the style and the dancers themselves. We will work a basic form of the dance. The most experienced dancers are completely free form. For them there is no set pattern: he leads, she reacts, he reacts. Beautiful to watch."

Jim grasped Jess's right hand with his left and instructed her to place her left hand on his upper right arm, while his right hand rested on her left shoulder blade. "This is called the open embrace, or *abrazo abierto* in Spanish," he said. "Tango is based on a basic eight count, so we'll go through each step, one at a time."

For the next hour, they concentrated on getting the footwork right, shifting her weight with each step and perfecting the complicated move where her left foot scissored over her right foot. He put on the music and she followed his lead. The steps made more sense once she felt the rhythm of the music. Several times she had almost tripped over her own feet as she hadn't shifted her weight properly. She wasn't used to dancing in high heels.

"It doesn't matter if you make a mistake, Jess. Just keep going and follow. I think that's enough for one day," he said.

"Thanks, Jim. I've been watching some of the videos on YouTube; they make it look so easy."

"Just remember, Jess, those couples have probably been dancing since they were kids. They're very good. Come over to the office and we'll see when we can schedule another lesson."

She opted for a Thursday evening appointment; that would free her up for riding on the weekends. She felt tired, but in a happy, comfortable way. She stopped at the grocery store and picked up a couple of frozen dinners, plus fruit, and a salad. Arriving home, she saw the SUV and wondered how the showing had gone. She could hear Andy up in his office, working on the computer.

After putting all her groceries away, she made herself a coffee and went upstairs. She poked her head around the door to his office. "How did the open house go?"

"Mark had quite a few people through, and two couples are considering putting offers in. I'm keeping my fingers crossed," he said frowning.

Jess nodded. "I paid the electric and water bills yesterday. How's it going at work?"

"I'm just setting the mid-term exams. What have you been up to?"

"I went riding this morning and worked a two-year-old for John Stattler, then had a dance class this afternoon. Even though I'm around horses all the time, I didn't realize how much I missed riding. I'm going to ride every weekend if I can."

She popped a frozen dinner in the oven, still feeling the strangeness of not cooking for Andy. He had showered and was preparing to go out for the evening. She decided it was time to tackle the assignment Carla had given her and spent her time working with her little Spanish phrase book. Andy left just before six without saying goodbye, not that she expected it now. And he had his carryall with him. She assumed he wouldn't be back that night.

She sat in the living room and spread her papers on the coffee table. Reading out loud, she settled in to her lesson. Hello was *hola,* pronounced *o-lah.* She wrote that down. The "h" was silent. Good morning was *buenos dias,* pronounced *bweh-nos dee-ahs. Adios* was goodbye. At least she knew that one. She found that some phrases were familiar, like *de nada* (don't mention it) and *por favor* (please) where the written "v" became a verbal "b." In the numbers, zero was *cero,* but the "c" was pronounced as "th" as *theh-ro.* Half an hour of that was enough and she headed upstairs for a shower and went to bed.

She decided she'd give Paul Wagner a call first thing on Monday about Ryan's colts. It would probably be a good idea to download all her pedigree files onto a thumb drive for her own use. Then she could access her own information at home if she needed it. She had created them from scratch and accumulated quite a database over the years. They could be useful to her if she decided to become a bloodstock agent. It occurred to her that Ryan might get sticky about that. There was still no message from Detective Peterson about the photos. She knew deep down that it would be unlikely that she could prove her suspicions.

Sunday, Jess finished the résumé. She planned to call the feed company and talk to their rep. She sent an email to Marty and her mum:

> "Hi, so far everything's fine. We had a showing yesterday but haven't heard back from the real estate agent. Fingers crossed. I got all of Dad's stuff sorted. Most of it went to the thrift shop. Andy's not here most of the time, so I'm getting a lot done. I'm back to riding at Stattler's on weekends and getting some dance lessons with Jean and Jim Barry. Remember them? Until the house is sold, I don't know when I'll be going on vacation. Visiting Carla in Argentina sounds good to me. Anyway, I'm managing. Just me to cook for. Jess

The phone rang and it was Mark. "Hi, Jess. Is Andy around? I can't get him on the phone."

"No, Mark. He's out. I'm guessing he'll be back this evening. Did we get an offer?"

"Yeah, we actually got two."

"Great! Can you come tomorrow evening? If Andy comes home earlier, I'll let you know. I don't know where he is or when he'll be back for sure," she said and they hung up. That was exciting news. It was good to have two offers. Andy still wasn't back by bed time so she left him a note on the counter and went to bed.

*　　　　*　　　　*

MONDAY DAWNED DARK AND OVERCAST. THE TEMPERATURE was hovering just above forty degrees Fahrenheit. It was a day to wear her quilted jacket and gloves. Andy must have come in late; the SUV was in the driveway and the note wasn't on the counter. At the stables, the morning feed went without incident and Jess went to the office to get started on her paperwork. Annie and Becky were busy with stacks of paper. The breeding schedules were on the wall, quickly filling in, especially for Arctic Cat.

She managed to get hold of Paul Wagner around eight-thirty. "Hi, Paul. It's Jess Coxwell. We've got three yearling colts here that Ryan wants to move ASAP to open up some stall space. Would you be able to handle them for us?"

"Send me the pedigrees Jess, and I'll let you know," Paul said. "Any particular reason they weren't in the September sale?"

"They were late foals born in February or March so were smaller than the others. They're doing well now."

"Okay, send me the pedigrees then and I'll call you back," he said.

Jess hung up, photocopied the three pedigrees along with photos of the horses, and sent them off. Jess waited until Becky was out for her coffee break, then downloaded her pedigree files to her thumb drive. Since Becky sat behind her, she didn't want her to see what she was doing.

Two minutes later, Ryan walked in. "How far have you got with the yearlings?"

"I talked to Paul Wagner this morning and sent him copies of the pedigrees. He said he'd call us back shortly," she replied, thankful he hadn't walked in five minutes earlier. Ryan was in a foul mood as he walked back down the hall.

Paul called after lunch. "Jess, I've found a buyer in Chicago for the Whirlwind colt and he's willing to go sixty-five thousand. I'll keep working on the other two," he said.

"That's great, Paul. I'll let Ryan know."

She called Ryan. He grumbled about the price but okayed it. She called Paul back and gave him the go-ahead. She did the math. Paul had just made 3,250 dollars. Not bad commission for a morning's work.

After work, she headed to the passport office, had her picture taken, then put in her passport application. Her passport photo with her unsmiling face made her look like a reject from a criminal lineup. She decided that she'd spend the extra dollars and get the application expedited rather than waiting six to eight weeks for routine processing.

Arriving home, she placed the call to the feed company and spoke to their personnel department. The company was based in Louisville but operated in the four-state region of Indiana, Illinois, Kentucky, and Tennessee. She explained that she was inquiring about a position as a feed rep similar to Mitch Hadwin's role when he came to the O'Connell stable on his periodic visits. She wanted to know what credentials and training they required and explained that she had graduated from the Equine Management Program. They requested her résumé and said they'd be in touch. She typed up a cover letter and emailed the documents.

Andy arrived home around five-thirty, looking tired. Mark was on the doorstep about half an hour later, briefcase in hand.

"I've got two offers here," Mark said, handing the envelopes to Andy.

Andy opened both envelopes. "These people are offering 235,000 dollars, with a closing date of January and the other one is 240,000, with a closing date of February."

"Well, what do you think?" asked Mark.

Andy looked at Jess. "We want to sell this house as soon as possible. I'd be prepared to accept the higher offer at two-forty but with a January closing. The lower offer is much too low. We could send a counter offer of two-hundred and forty to the lower guy and see if he responds. Are you on board with that, Jess?"

She nodded.

"Okay, I'll run it by them and see what happens." Mark filled out the papers, which they signed. "I'll let you know," he said, heading out the door.

Andy seemed very moody and wasn't interested in talking, so she heated up her frozen dinner and watched the news. He took his plate of wieners and beans and a beer and went down to the man cave.

She watched a couple of programs, but didn't find them interesting. Jess was tired. She had done everything she could think of to prepare for the future and now her energy had bottomed out. She didn't feel like working on her Spanish lessons. It seemed a good idea to get an early night or read a book. It did occur to her to check with Mr. Ames to see if it was okay to go out of the country while the divorce was in progress.

*　　　　*　　　　*

THE NEXT FEW DAYS FOLLOWED THE SAME PATTERN. PAUL Wagner sold another colt. Arctic Cat's breeding roster was almost full despite the hefty seventy-thousand-dollar fee, with the other stallions getting booked as well. Ryan was looking less tense and Laura almost back to her usual self. *The infusion of breeding fees must be helping the finances*, Jess thought.

Her phone rang. It was Andy.

"Jess, I just had a call from Mark. The guy who offered two-forty has agreed to a January closing and he hasn't heard back from the other guy. Mark will be at the house at six tonight to sign the papers."

"I'll be there. I'll be so glad when this is settled," she said.

Later that afternoon, her phone rang again. It was Detective Peterson. "Hi, Jess. I finally found your father's file and I've looked it over. The damage was mostly to the front of the car from the impact and it was buckled all the way down the driver's side. I went over my report, and I don't see any inconsistencies. I'll leave copies of the photos and the coroner's report at the front desk. Just ask the desk sergeant for it."

"Thank you, I guess that's that then," said Jess. "I appreciate your time. It helps put my father's death in perspective." Regardless of what he said, she had a nagging feeling that the SUV might have been forced off the road. All she had for evidence were the photos, the mess at the house and the timing of the accident.

After work, she picked up the paperwork from the police station and looked at the pictures. The SUV was completely crumpled and twisted. It made her feel ill. She wondered if the driver of a truck had passed him and sideswiped him at the critical curve in the road, rather than rear-ending him. Since there hadn't been any glass or metal on the road, it seemed it was a mystery she was never going to solve. The coroner's report read just as Detective Peterson had said. From the drawings, the injuries had been massive. There wasn't one part of his body intact. She didn't bother picking up anything to eat. After looking at that, she wasn't hungry.

Mark arrived promptly at six and they sat at the dining room table with all the paperwork. It was simple enough: two-hundred forty-thousand for the house with closing on January 2nd. Jess and Andy signed the papers. Mark slapped the red "sold" on the lawn sign. Once Mark had gone, they sat there for a few moments in silence.

"Andy, who's your lawyer?" Jess asked.

"Lloyd Adams."

"I'll let Mr. Ames know. It is my understanding that two-hundred and forty-thousand will have deductions for the outstanding mortgage, real estate and legal fees, and the balance will be divided equally between us and deposited to our accounts. Am I right?" she asked.

"That's correct," said Andy looking annoyed. "You get more than you put in," his voice bitter and accusing.

Jess felt anger flood through her. "Go to hell, Andy! Remember, I make less than half you do. I put money on that down payment too. I've bought groceries, paid the utilities, and done renovations here. Don't you damn well dare imply that I haven't contributed my fair share to the house. It's not like I'm asking you for alimony! I'll be moving out on November 6, once Carla's gone, so you'll have the run of the place. I'll leave you checks to cover the utilities for November and December, so you won't accuse me of not holding up my end of the bargain," she snapped back at him. "You created this mess. If you can't afford the girlfriend, then maybe she should get off her back and get a job!" she spat out. So much for taking Mr. Ames' advice to keep calm.

Andy glared at her and for a moment she thought it would escalate, but it didn't. They were inches apart. His face was white and she could see the rigidity of his jaw muscles as he gritted his teeth. Suddenly, he spun around and stormed upstairs, slamming the bedroom door.

Jess couldn't remember ever being so angry. She hadn't felt it build up inside her. It just erupted when he'd made that last comment. This was their first big fight and hopefully their last. She stood still for a few moments, taking deep breaths, but her hands were shaking. In his current state of mind, she didn't trust him not to retaliate in some way. He was lucky she wasn't vindictive. She had enough ammunition to destroy him and he knew it.

Her one prized possession was her father's Kentucky rifle. Dad had loved that gun and had driven to gun shows and Civil War re-enactments to display it. She took it down from the wall, gently fingering the gleaming tiger maple stock. She wrapped it in blankets, put it in her car, then drove over to the storage unit to keep it safe. She thought about the dining room suite. She really couldn't afford to rent the storage unit indefinitely. There wasn't any room at Mrs. Hibbard's. From a practical standpoint, she needed to sell it before she moved. She had money in her savings account earmarked for her holiday but that was it; there wasn't much to spare.

Chapter 10

TUESDAY, SHE LET MR. AMES KNOW ABOUT THE SALE OF THE house and asked if it was alright to take an out-of-country vacation with the pending divorce. He told her yes. She gave him her email address and her change of address so that he could contact her at any time while she was away. She called Mrs. Hibbard and said she was moving in on the sixth. She completed change-of-address forms at the post office and called the utility, internet, and phone companies to install service. She needed to find someone with a truck to move her.

After work on Wednesday, she met the girls at the mall for a coffee and was pleased to find most of the old crowd there. Karen gave her a big hug and sat next to her. Nothing was mentioned about Andy and she felt comfortable seeing everyone again.

"*Buenos noches, Señorita* (good evening). *Me llama Jess* (my name is Jess)," she said turning to Carla.

"Good evening to you too, Jess. You've been doing your homework," said Carla.

"Slow progress, but I'll keep at it. Does anyone know a couple of guys with a truck? I need my furniture moved on the sixth," Jess said.

Marg said her brother sometimes did that, and she'd talk to him. They decided to have a final send off for Carla on the fourth.

"What time does your flight leave, Carla?"

"I get an early flight to Houston leaving at seven-thirty, but there's a long wait for the Houston to Buenos Aires plane. Don't worry about me; I'll call a cab."

When Jess got home, Andy was sullen and didn't speak to her. That was fine by her and she avoided him. She decided to sell the dining room suite and called the local antiques dealer. He was available Saturday morning and the timing worked for her; she could ride in the afternoon. Finding some cartons, she cleaned out the filing cabinet and packed the clothes she wasn't using. The room was looking bare. Marg called her back to give her brother's phone number for the move. Still no call from the feed company. What other options did she have? She sat at her desk, making a list of possibilities.

She thought about doing pedigrees but it wasn't busy enough for full-time work. Not too many stables had feed managers, certainly none locally. She was qualified as a broodmare attendant but the pay was low and her education qualified her for more than that.

Bloodstock agent? Although she had some savings from her father's estate in her 401K and there would be money from the sale of the house, it wasn't enough to buy a stable and she didn't know the cost of the legal fees for the divorce. Stattler's place was worth several million, not even taking into account the cost of the horses and paying staff.

Vet assistant? There was a specific course for that and she didn't have it, although her Equine Management Course could work if the vet was willing to take her. The local vet didn't need anyone. She would have to see if out-of-town vets had openings.

Exercise rider? It didn't pay much, and she wasn't getting any younger. Young Thoroughbreds were physically demanding to handle, so the prospect for long-term work didn't fly.

She was qualified to teach at the college, but with Andy and Angel there, that was a no-go, unless he was no longer working there..

Insurance agent for horses? Maybe. She could become a claims adjuster specifically for horse insurance—now that might be a possibility. She'd call local agent Allan Colton for information.

Jess needed to talk to a travel agent to discuss costs, flights, and accommodation for Buenos Aires. She had never been outside the US, and only out of state for fairs and races. Andy had always taught summer school. They'd camped, but her vacation experience was limited. Jess had never even been to California to see her mum or Marty, not that she really wanted to go there.

Thursday evening, she phoned Marg's brother Greg and they discussed the move.

"Greg, I need to move on November 6." He gave her the basic hourly rate. It was reasonable. "That sounds good to me. If we start with the house, we can do a second run to the storage unit on Man O' War Drive," she said.

Greg agreed and suggested a nine o'clock start.

"That's good," she said. All she wanted was to get everything settled and make life normal.

Later, she went to her dance class. To the strains of *El Poeta,* she managed to follow Jim. It was easier to dance with music—the rhythm of the bandoneon accordion, guitar. and violin took over.

"Follow me, Jess," he said holding her in the open embrace. "Keep your head up, and don't worry about your feet." He stuck to the basic eight count but started to add extra patterns. Jess was getting used to his style and he led well, even if she didn't know what she was doing. Several times, she got totally mixed up but he didn't seem to mind and they both laughed. Maybe by the time she got to Argentina, she wouldn't be such a klutz. The music and rhythms calmed her, allowing her to obliterate all the chaos and confusion of her week. It felt good to be in a man's arms with no fear of involvement.

Saturday morning, the antiques dealer came promptly at nine and they haggled for a while before settling on a price Jess knew was ridiculously low, but the suite had to go. That money could go towards her holiday. She watched the truck pull out of the driveway, with the table and chairs swathed in padding, seeing another important piece of her life disappear.

Jess called Walden's insurance and talked to the personnel lady. "I'm seriously considering a career change and was thinking of maybe a claims adjuster position for horse insurance." Apparently, courses were required as well as licensing. Taking full-time courses was out of the question right now. She'd consider that later.

*   *   *

JESS HAD A GOOD RIDE ON THE BAY HORSE, INITIALLY working him in the exercise ring, then moving him to the dirt track. He was bright, alert, and full of himself. He kept her sharp. It was like straddling a keg of dynamite, but it was a good ride. She brushed him down, put him back in his stall, the saddle back on the rack and the bridle below it. She stopped at the house, before going back to her car.

"Hi, Jess," said John. "How did he do?"

"Really well. He doesn't know much but he's willing. I wouldn't be giving him to any beginner, that's for sure. Do you need me to ride tomorrow?"

"Yeah, sure. Take the chestnut out again. That will work."

"Good, see you tomorrow. John, could I use your name as a reference? I'm putting a résumé together," she said.

"You sure can."

"Thanks," she said, changing into her runners. It had been a good ride and she liked the way it made her feel. When she got home, she looked at her room. Nothing left to pack. She washed a small load of laundry. One more week and she would leave the house with all its memories of Andy. Carla would be gone. Life was going to be different. She would have to adapt.

Chapter 11

MONDAY, JESS HAD A CALL FROM PAUL WAGNER. HE'D FOUND a buyer for the last colt, but she knew Ryan wouldn't like the price. She called the house to see if he was in.

"Hi Ryan, Paul's got a potential sale for the colt, but I'd like you to talk to him about the price," she said.

"How low is it?" he said.

"They're offering thirty-five thousand for him. Considering the breeding, it should be higher than that, but I know you've got to move him." She gave Ryan the phone number and hung up.

Ten minutes later, her phone rang. "I got him up to forty thousand," said Ryan. "It's still too low, but I need that stall space. He'll pick up on Thursday." With that, he hung up.

Jess prepared the paperwork, then passed the word on to the girl looking after the colt, to have him ready for transport Thursday. She took the papers to the house for Ryan to sign, meeting Laura in the hall. Laura was wearing a turtle neck sweater and skin-tight jeans. She looked tired. They spoke for a few moments. Jess noticed a fading bruise on Laura's neck that the turtle neck didn't quite cover. That didn't look good. She wondered if Ryan had hit her. Her opinion of him couldn't sink much lower.

When she knocked and entered, Ryan was sitting at his massive mahogany desk working at the computer. She placed the paperwork on his desk.

"I hear a rumor you're planning on leaving us," he said quietly, the look on his face deceptively benign.

She sat down, mentally scrambling to give him a calm and acceptable answer. "Ryan, that's a decision I haven't made yet. I'm finding it very difficult to live in Lexington, now Andy and I are divorcing. I'm thinking about the options I have. If and when I do come to a decision, you'll be the first to know. How much notice do you need?"

"Give me a month. You'll need to train your replacement," he said staring at her.

"Well then, I'd better get back to work," she said, rising and leaving the room. Walking back to the barn, she let out a deep breath and wondered who had told him. She fervently hoped he wouldn't fire her in the meantime. A full-time paycheck was critical for the next few months. She needed a good reference from him. It made her think of the horse photos in her safety deposit box. Did Ryan know she had them? The thought crossed her mind that she'd better do something about them to safe guard herself.

That night at home, she did some serious thinking. The most ethical decision would be to hand the photos over to the Jockey Club, creating complete chaos. The O'Connells would be banned from racing. Any foals from 2015 on would have to be declared ineligible for registration or ineligible for any races they'd won. It would be catastrophic for the owners who'd invested in those horses. Since Arctic Cat and Wing Commander were full brothers, it didn't change the bloodlines. Present offspring were winning on the track.

Neil, and Ryan wouldn't have the money to refund the stud fees. People would sue.

Jess wondered again how Neil managed to switch the DNA sample. Could he have bribed someone in the lab? How could the current sample be valid?

The issue came down to her own safety. The only thing she could think of was to write an explanatory letter to Marty, and leave it in her safety deposit box along with the photos. That made sense to her. If she tried to act on her own, it could place her in a precarious position. She typed out the letter detailing her father's suspicions and the fact that he had been to Ireland and seen both horses. She wrote on the outside of the envelope, "Marty, if I die of unexpected or suspicious causes, this letter as well as the horse photos are to be sent to the British Jockey Club and American Jockey Club. If there is no problem, simply destroy it."

Jess went to the bank the next day and felt relief just locking up the sealed letter. While she was there, it occurred to her to give Andy his explicit pictures when the divorce was finalized. She'd have to ask Mr. Ames to destroy his copies. They would serve no useful purpose then and were certainly not something she wanted to keep.

Thursday was Carla's farewell do at The Keg. All the girls showed up and they had a fabulous evening with a good meal and many toasts. They parted with hugs, good wishes, and more than a few tears. Jess promised to keep in touch and demanded that Carla send pictures of her January wedding.

By the time she got rounds done at the stables on Friday morning, Jess thought of Carla, well away on the first leg of her journey. Tomorrow would be moving day for her. As usual, Andy had disappeared before supper.

Saturday was hectic. Greg and a friend arrived at nine o'clock and started loading the truck. She ran up and down stairs leaving boxes in the hallway for them. It was obvious they'd have to make a second trip.

Fortunately, Mrs. Hibbard was home and had let the electric company in to turn the power on. No sign of the television people yet. She directed Greg to place the desk, filing cabinet and dresser on the back wall. The television went on the left-hand wall, with the book cases either side. They moved the sofa bed into the middle of the room facing the television and started stacking the boxes in whatever floor space was left over. They returned to the house for the second load. Jess left an envelope containing post-dated checks for the November and December utilities on the kitchen counter. It seemed bizarre to be closing the door for the last time. She left the key in an envelope in the mailbox.

Their last stop was the storage unit. They emptied it with room to spare in the truck and went on to the apartment. She canceled further use of the unit and returned the key. That was a sixty dollars monthly savings. She couldn't believe they'd done the move in just four hours. She thanked them and paid them cash.

Now to unpack. The television and phone crews arrived late in the afternoon and hooked everything up. Five o'clock found her utterly exhausted. Jess was far from finished but she'd unpacked most of the kitchenware. It was strange to be using the familiar dishes with their old-fashioned pattern. It brought back all sorts of childhood memories with her parents. She unpacked both the canned food and dry goods, made herself a coffee, and sat on the sofa surveying her domain. It looked like home already. The lamps were on the side tables, and the television was sitting on the coffee table against the side wall. It was bright, cheerful. and comfortable. There was room over the television to hang the Kentucky rifle and some of her father's photos.

There was a knock at her door. When she answered it, she found Mrs. H. standing there with a tray of goodies and a potted plant.

"Come in. Welcome to my world," she said, accepting the gift.

"I thought you'd had a very busy day so I've brought you supper and a little plant to brighten things up."

"Thank you so much. Most of this stuff was my father's, so it feels like home already. I've still got books to unpack, pictures to hang, plus clothes and linens to put away. I might have room for another dresser. The dinette set doesn't take up much space." She placed the plant on the table and its bright green leaves and pink-petaled blossoms looked delightful with the light streaming through the front window.

"Well, I think you timed it well. The forecast is for snow by the end of the week, but we never get much. You'll be snug and warm in here. Maybe if you're not busy after work some night, you could come over for supper. I get lonesome sometimes," Mrs. H. admitted.

"I need to pick up groceries tomorrow. Do you need anything?" Jess asked.

"No thanks, Jess. I've got plenty." With that, Mrs. H. left.

She opened up the bed and made it. She found the pillows and fluffed them up, then spent the evening stretched out on the bed watching TV. Supper was a delicious beef and vegetable stew with two slices of garlic bread and a piece of pumpkin pie for dessert. It was decadent. She couldn't find her bottle of wine. Ah well, she'd look tomorrow. She wondered if Andy would bring Angel back to the house that night. There had been no mention of him from any of her friends. He was obviously keeping a very low profile and certainly not parading Angel around to his acquaintances. Far too risky. She'd never bothered to look the girl up on social media; she had no interest in doing so.

Sunday morning was overcast with dense, steel-gray clouds that heralded snow. She folded up the bed, made herself breakfast, showered, and headed to Stattler's for a ride. This time, she worked a Hanoverian dressage horse in the arena. Dressage wasn't exactly her forte, but the gelding was very responsive to leg aids and she got a lovely extended trot out of him as they crossed the arena on the diagonal. John seemed pleased.

She stopped in the grocery store to pick up milk, bread, and fruit plus more canned goods. Hamburger was on sale, so she bought two pounds, plus some sausages, and pork chops. She selected potatoes, onions, and carrots. It was time to start cooking proper meals again, instead of grabbing store-made ones that probably weren't particularly healthy. Cheaper too.

After lunch, she set up her computer and put the files in the cabinet. She broke down the boxes and tied the bundles with string, placing them outside for pick up. Getting her tool box from the car, she grabbed the hammer to nail up picture hangers and put up a couple of brackets so that she could hang the rifle there. It looked great—a real museum piece. It was going to be a tight squeeze to hang her clothes in the one closet. Most of the towels and face cloths fit in the bathroom cupboard. She'd need to figure out where to stash the pillows, but for now she left them on the recliner. She sent an email to Marty and her mum.

Hi, folks:

I moved yesterday. Am still unpacking boxes but I think it's going to work out well for me, even though the place is small. The land lady is sweet. She brought me supper and a lovely potted plant. I've got all your dishes and cutlery, Mum, so it reminds me of being a kid. Lots of memories.

Ryan knows there is a possibility of me leaving for another job. I still haven't decided what sort of job I want. I've been riding quite a bit, and taking tango lessons. Am also trying to learn some Spanish. No trouble keeping busy.

Carla has gone back to Argentina now. She'll be preparing for her wedding. I intend to take up her offer for a vacation there. February is a possibility. So far, so good.

Love Jess.

The rest of the week passed uneventfully. Mrs. H. invited her for a potluck supper on the Wednesday evening, saying that she had a group of ladies coming over, she thought Jess might want to meet. Jess was happy with that and told her she'd bring a salad and pickles.

Wednesday evening came. Cars started arriving around six o'clock, so Jess went next door carrying her contributions.

Most of the women were older, but there were a couple of younger ones too. Introductions were made. The women were friendly, and interesting. After supper, they sat in the living room drinking their coffee.

"How do you ladies know each other?" Jess asked.

"We met at a bereavement seminar and have stayed in touch ever since," a lady named Jean said.

"A bereavement seminar?" said Jess, puzzled.

"After my husband died, I was totally lost," Mrs. H. said. "I felt so lonely. We'd been married for thirty years. I'd never had anyone else. The funeral home put on a seminar about dealing with grief. We all attended and have been friends from then on. We meet at someone's home every two weeks for socializing and a little grief work."

Ellie was one of the younger ones. "My husband, Luke was in the military and was deployed overseas. An IED exploded and although he survived, he lost both legs. He never got over that. Last spring, he committed suicide. There wasn't a thing I could do to help him. These ladies saved me. I've a three-year-old to raise, and it's tough."

"Do you find it helpful to talk about it?" Jess asked.

"Support means a lot," Ellie replied. "Nobody judges me. Sometimes I just need someone to listen. Everyone here has been through bad stuff."

Jess heard their stories and felt her heart go out to them. Her own problems seemed minuscule in comparison. One elderly woman in her mid-seventies recounted that when she was diagnosed with breast cancer, her husband of forty years left her for another woman. "He told me I was damaged goods."

There was silence for a moment, then Jess spoke and told them she was divorcing Andy, but she wasn't ready yet to discuss the why with them. She spoke of being angry and doubting herself. She wondered if she would ever trust another man or have another relationship.

Mrs. H. spoke very quietly. "Jess, we've learned there are five stages in the grief process. Some experts say there are seven. They are denial, anger, bargaining, depression, and acceptance. You will go through all of these over a period of time until you are able to let things go and get on with life. It is really important that you work your way through each one. Remembering and forgiving are crucial in moving forward."

After the other guests had left, Mrs. H. looked at her. "I hope I wasn't putting you in an awkward position, Jess. You looked so overwhelmed the first time I saw you and you don't have any family here to help, so I took the liberty of asking you to come and meet them. It is entirely up to you if you want to come back. Just let me know," she said, handing Jess some literature.

Jess gave her a hug and went back to the apartment. She found her little place calming and comfortable—her cave, her refuge. She quickly got on the computer and sent Carla an email.

> Hi Carla:
>
> Hope you had a good trip home and are getting used to a whole new life in Argentina. Are you running the stables now? The move went well. I still have boxes to unpack but this place is mine. Mrs. H. is a real sweetheart.

Somehow Ryan found out I'm considering another job. He was quiet—that's unusual and somehow more disturbing than if he'd yelled or something. I still haven't heard back from the feed company and am considering other options.

Have you gone for your dress fitting? How is Mateo? He must be glad to have you back home. Love Jess.

She spent half hour working on her Spanish. My *nombre* (first name) is Jess. My *apellido* (last name) is Coxwell. *Me llamo* Jess Coxwell (my name is Jess Coxwell.) My *nombre de soltera* (maiden name) is Hartford. She really wished she could find someone locally to help her with her Spanish.

Chapter 12

THE FIRST SNOWFALL AND PLUNGING TEMPERATURES LEFT Lexingtonians scrambling for their snow shovels. Jess cleared the driveway for Mrs. H. The snow was light, fluffy stuff and probably wouldn't last long. At the stables, the horses were looking distinctly furry and were blanketed when they went out to the paddocks. Mares waiting to be bred were under the lights in the evenings, to bring them in heat at the right time for the breeding schedule.

Jess's phone rang.

"Jessica, this is Frank Whitley. I'm the personnel manager for Wainright Feeds. I received your job application and résumé. Sorry for the delay getting back to you. We are undergoing a major reorganization and expansion in the company, so it's taking a while to sort out what jobs will be available. We'd like to interview you," he said.

"That's great. I'm definitely interested. What date did you have in mind?" Jess asked.

"How about the fifteenth at ten?" he asked.

"I look forward it," she said, pumping her fist, thinking, *Yes!* She was in a good mood for the rest of the day.

Her evening tango lessons went well too, with Jim adding new steps. She was starting to feel more confidence with the dance. Reviewing some videos that evening, she watched again, recognizing the steps she was learning. Of course, she didn't have the elegance, grace, passion, or extended leg positions the professional dancers did. Practice, practice, practice.

Friday morning, she noticed that Ryan's car was gone, so she went to the office and talked to Laura.

"Hi Laura, it looks like Ryan's not here. I wanted to speak to him about taking the fifteenth off. "

"He told me that you're looking for another job," said Laura.

"There's not much holding me here in Lexington with Andy out of my life. The rest of my family are in California, but I don't want to go there. I'm not sure what I want, to tell you the truth. It's all been so sudden," Jess said.

"I don't blame you for wanting to leave. I wish I could myself, at times," Laura said, looking sad. "Go ahead, Jess."

"Thanks, Laura. I appreciate it," said Jess, and watched Laura making a note of it on the day planner. "I'll ask Brenda to oversee the others. Ryan's assigned her to cover me on other occasions when I've been sick or on holidays. I'm expecting it to be quiet that day; no deliveries are scheduled and there's nothing else on the agenda with the horses."

*   *   *

IT SEEMED TO TAKE FOREVER FOR THE FIFTEENTH TO COME around. Jess looked at the clothes in her closet. She'd never had a formal job interview. Jess had been hired at the stable because her father had worked there, recommending her. She didn't have clothes suitable to wear. She needed to up her game with something business-like—not feminine or frilly—a classic power suit. Her competitors, customers, and coworkers would likely be men. She was going to have to prove herself as a practical and knowledgeable candidate for a job. Selling herself as a suitable candidate was her first priority.

She looked up Wainright Feeds on the internet. The website gave a history of the company, details on its operations in the four states, and the fact that it was a farmers' co-op. Apparently, they produced feed for horses, cattle, pigs, and poultry. If she got the job, she might be driving around the countryside, presenting the feeds processed by Wainright Foods, and assessing livestock. The clients would be hard working, practical farmers, and managers.

She headed to the mall and chose a high-end clothing store, where she normally wouldn't have shopped. When the shop assistant asked her what she was looking for, Jess replied "I'm going for a job interview so I want a classic suit." The woman led her past the slinky dresses, directly to the rack at the back, displaying the conservative suits. Winter colors of navy blue, black, dark brown, or a light gray were offered. The light gray one appealed to her. It was a heavy-weight linen finish with lapels and two pearly buttons on the front.

She needed a long-sleeved blouse and sorted through the racks for something to contrast with the gray. One caught her eye. It had a gather at the left shoulder that draped the material across her chest, with a boat-shaped neck line. It was pretty, in a random pattern of blue tones. She tried the clothes on and liked what she saw in the mirror: classic, conservative. but feminine at the same time. The blouse softened the plainness of the suit.

Next, she hunted for a pair of black leather shoes with low heels. There was a black leather purse on the sales rack that went well with it. The price at the checkout almost made her put them back, but she didn't. It might make a dent in her budget, but she needed to project the right image. It would be worth it. What to do with her hair, that was the next question. Leave it loose, put it in a ponytail, braid it? She'd play with the look when she got home.

The fifteenth: she planned to be on the I-64 promptly at eight o'clock for the eighty-mile drive to Louisville. She opted for arranging her hair in a bun. She applied a very light smoky gray eye shadow, brushed her brows, added a little mascara, and a soft touch of lipstick. She almost didn't recognize the face in the mirror, so seldom did she dress formally.

She slipped into her winter coat, keeping her fingers crossed that the predicted snow would hold off. She took her snow boots just in case. Frank's directions were straightforward. She found the Wainright building and a parking space with time to spare. Purse in hand, she entered the building with what she hoped was a quiet confidence. She checked the directory on the wall, then took the elevator to the fourth floor. Despite being twenty-six, she still found elevators a novelty.

She approached the receptionist. "Hello, my name's Jessica Coxwell. I have an appointment at ten o'clock with Frank Whitley," she said and was directed to have a seat while the woman placed the call. Jess looked around. The pictures on the walls dated back in the thirties: fifty-horse teams, side by side, cutting wheat in endless flat fields, old silos, early views of the original store complete with old-style pickup trucks, tractors and wagons, progressing to modern times.

She was so engrossed in looking at the pictures, that she almost jumped out of her skin when she sensed someone behind her. It was a fiftyish man, graying at the temples, wearing a suit and tie.

"Sorry to scare you, Jessica. I'm Frank Whitley," he said, shaking her hand. "Come on in." He led her down the hall to a light-filled office. She hung her coat on the coat rack. "We're using the conference room," he said ushering her past his paper-strewn desk to the inner room.

Four other men were at the table. One of them was Mitch Hadwin, her area rep. He arose from the leather swivel chair with a big smile on his face and shook her hand. Jess had never seen him in a suit before.

"So glad you could make it," he said. "I'd like you to meet Ben Edwards, the rep for Tennessee, Jonathan Davies from Idaho, and Gary Anderson from Illinois."

Jess shook hands with everyone and took the chair beside Mitch. She removed the notepad from her purse. She'd written down a list of questions. Frank took over the meeting.

"Jessica, we've looked over your résumé thoroughly. Tell us a little about yourself and what expectations you have, if you are hired here," he said.

Jess paused for a moment, then began. "I became involved with race horses when I was a child, mainly through my father, Joe Hartford. He was a stable boy, an exercise rider, and finally the feed manager at O'Connells. I graduated from the Horse Management Program at the college. From there I worked at O'Connells as a broodmare attendant, then took over Dad's position two years ago after he died. I have worked with Mitch here, who has taught me the finer details of feeding broodmares, foals, and stallions."

"Are you familiar with other breeders in our four-state area?" Ben Edwards asked.

"I'm in contact with breeders, trainers, bloodstock agents, and vets in my job. I've met many out-of-state owners through O'Connells galas and some are families of my classmates in college," she replied.

"Would it be a problem to be on the road a lot of the time?" Frank queried.

"No. I don't have any family commitments, so I'm flexible."

"What attracted you to Wainright's?" Mitch asked.

"Working with you, mostly. We've worked together for two years. You've educated me on many occasions for feeding the horses. We've discussed things like crop management and pasture rotation. I do have a basic knowledge of farm economics." Andy's lecture notes had come in handy.

"What are you specifically looking for in a job?" Davies asked.

"I've come to a point in my life where I want to expand my horizons. I have extensive experience with horses. I want a job that allows me to be part of a bigger picture and I want long-term employment. Your company offers that. Horses are my specialty but I know you provide feed for cattle, poultry, and pigs. I would need training for them. I'm a practical farm-girl type of person."

There was a pause then Frank responded. "As I said, we are reorganizing the company. Ben is planning on retiring in the spring and Mitch would like the opportunity to move into the Tennessee territory to be closer to his family, so we've got some shuffling to do. I like your credentials and experience. Here's a sample job description for the rep's position," he said passing a document across the table to her.

Jess looked it over. "Frank, I also want to know where you get your scientific research from, for formulating your feeds. I think it's important to know the research behind the product I'd be promoting, so that I'm not just selling feed, but improving the farmers' bottom line," she said.

"You mentioned research. We have a research division for all our formulated feeds. They're right down the hall. Any other questions?" he asked.

Jess briefly glanced at her notebook. "I know nothing about co-ops. Could someone please explain to me how a co-op works?"

Jonathan Davies informed her about the producer-based system, how each farmer had a share of the business, and the group consultation process. Gary explained that Wainright had two divisions, one for the agricultural products and a second one for formulated feeds and research.

Frank spoke about the many different jobs within the organization. "Now for a state rep, the duties are split between head office and their territory. They can be on the road three days a week, working either with producers or visiting feed suppliers. The other two days are here in the office. Sometimes, they represent the company at agricultural fairs and trade shows, some are out of state, which involves substantial public relations. The starting salary will

vary depending on the job. We do have a six-month probation period. If we are satisfied at the six-month mark, then
the job is permanent and there are paid benefits. What do
you think, Jessica?"

She paused for a moment before answering him. "It
has definite possibilities. I like the scope of this and the
flexibility it would give me. There's a lot to learn, but I'd
enjoy that."

"Well, I think that wraps it up," Frank said. "We appreciate you coming in and we'll be in touch with you in a
couple of days."

"Thank you, gentleman, for your time," Jess said, rising
from her chair, acknowledging each man by name as Frank
walked her out of the room. He closed the conference
room door.

"Well, Jessica. Will it work for you?"

"Yes, I think it could. It depends on what job you're
offering. As I said, there is room here for me to grow and
establish myself. I like the fact that it is multifaceted. I have
the advantage of knowing a lot of people socially, which
could be an asset. If I do get hired, I will need to give the
O'Connells a month's notice so I can train my replacement,
if that has any bearing on your time-line."

Frank helped her get her coat on, then walked her to
the elevator. There was an attractive young man at the desk,
talking to the receptionist. Frank paused for a moment, then
took her over to reception. "Jessica, I'd like to introduce
you to Todd Wainright, our accountant. His grandfather
started the company and his father is our CEO. Todd has an
independent accounting business but takes care of all of our
accounting needs.

"Todd, we've just interviewed Jessica for the rep vacancy, pending our reorganization decisions."

"Pleased to meet you, Jessica," he said, his hazel eyes thoroughly examining her.

Jess didn't find it offensive but more about curiosity, unlike Ryan's examinations.

She thanked Frank again and said goodbye to both men before taking the elevator down to the main floor. She had no idea how she'd done. All the men had been pleasant and informative, but she didn't get any definite feeling that she'd nailed the job. At the moment she didn't even know what job they could offer her.

It was snowing lightly when she crossed the parking lot. She sat in her car for a few minutes and happened to glance up at the fourth floor. A single figure was visible, looking down at her. The strawberry blond hair of Todd Wainright was unmistakable.

Chapter 13

THE FOLLOWING TUESDAY WAS POT LUCK NIGHT FOR THE bereavement group. Jess debated whether to go. It was a sad group in one way but at the same time it often put things in perspective for her. She decided to go, taking a tray of veggies and dip.

As soon as the cars arrived, Jess went next door and immediately recognized many faces, although remembering their names was a challenge. She took one look at Ellie and knew the girl was in trouble; she looked awful.

"I'm sorry folks, but I've had a bad week. Someone made a comment to me and I can't get it out of my head. All I've done is cry," the girl said burying her face in her hands.

Mrs. H. immediately sat on the couch beside her, cradling her arm around her shoulders. "Ellie, what happened?"

"I met some of Luke's old friends. The wife wanted to know how I could stand being married to a coward who committed suicide. I lost it and screamed at her to go away. It's all I can think of now," she said in a quiet hoarse whisper.

A collective groan went through the room at the callousness of the remark. Jess shook her head. How could she help Ellie? Much to her own surprise, she found herself on her knees on the floor, grasping Ellie's hands.

"Ellie, stop! There are ignorant people in this world, and that bitch is one of them. I think you've got it all wrong. You've described your husband as a member of an elite military unit, an expert marksman. From what I've seen on the news, those men bond like brothers. There is no way on the planet Luke was a coward. Yes, he committed suicide, but surely it was out of love for you and the child, not out of fear."

The room went completely silent. Jess felt tears welling up in her own eyes. Ellie just stared at her, raising one hand to her mouth. Mrs. H. continued to cradle her. It took a few minutes, then a red-eyed Ellie blew her nose and looked at Jess who was still kneeling on the floor.

"Thanks, Jess," she whispered. "That puts a different spin on it."

Jess got back on her chair, now feeling awkward. "You're damn right it does," she said, surprised by her own emotions. She thought about Luke—in a wheelchair—no job, probably no prospect of one either and a wife and child he couldn't support.

The food was demolished quickly after that; even Ellie ate a bit. It was a short meeting. Everyone seemed to go inward. After they went home, Mrs. H. gave her a long hug and looked up at her. "Jess, that was powerful."

Jess went back to her apartment but lay awake for a long time. It had been deeply disturbing. No wonder people were so screwed up, with the horrible things that happened to them. How would anyone ever get back to normal?

*   *   *

SHE THOROUGHLY ENJOYED THURSDAY'S DANCE CLASS. IT was good exercise, a lot of fun and she was finally getting the hang of it. Jim suggested they run through other Latin dances such as the samba and cha-cha, expanding her repertoire. She loved the guitar rhythms.

Friday morning, while she was working on time sheets, her cellphone rang. It was Frank. "Jessica, can you come in this afternoon when you get off work? We've got a job offer for you. I'd prefer to talk to you in person, not over the phone."

"Okay, Frank, I get off work around two o'clock, so I'd probably be there about three-forty-five, depending on the roads. Does that work for you?"

"That's great. See you then," he said and hung up.

She decided she'd go home immediately after work to change out of her grubbies and into her suit. She was elated, ready to burst. Even Ryan of the lecherous hands wasn't going to upset her today. She slithered out of his reach when they were in the hallway and kept right on through the door. He didn't look happy with his failed grope.

By two thirty, she was home and changed, then was back on the I-64. The roads were wet from the light snow. Truck traffic threw up sheets of gritty gray spray that kept the wipers busy. One section of the highway was down to one lane for a mile due to an accident, but other than that she made good time, pulling in to Wainright's parking lot at three-forty.

This time she knew where she was going and went straight up to the fourth floor. She didn't need to introduce herself as the receptionist immediately picked up her phone. "Mr. Whitley, Jessica Coxwell is here."

She sat down, feeling the excitement coursing through her. What will they offer her? Would it be enough for her to support herself?

Ten minutes later, Frank came out and waved her into his office, much less formal this time.

"Let's use the conference room," he said, taking a map and a pile of papers. He opened the map showing the four-state area. "Here we go. Wainright would like to offer you a representative's position for the state of Kentucky with home base here in Louisville. You'll basically be doing the same job as Mitch, dealing with all the animal products we have: cattle, horses, poultry, and pig feed. That will require extensive training, which we will provide in this building."

She got the job!

"The job will commence on March first and the probationary period will end on September thirtieth. Salary is thirty-five thousand to start, rising to thirty-eight when you pass probation. There is a benefits package for full-time people. I'm not sure whether there'll be a company vehicle for you yet, but we will pay mileage if you are using your own car for client visits. You will also be doing public relations at fairs and shows. If you work a weekend at a fair, you will get the Monday and Tuesday off. Here's a new job description," he said, handing it to her.

"We'll also slot you in for some time in the research and development department since you'd expressed an interest in the scientific end of it. Does that work for you?" he said with a broad grin on his face.

"Yes!" said Jess almost bouncing with enthusiasm. "Now I can give notice to Ryan, effective the end of January. I'm planning a holiday to Argentina for February, but I'll be back by the end of the month."

"Congratulations, Jess. Welcome aboard. It's a good company to work for," he said. "Here's your official offer letter."

"Just one other thing. I will need a day off probably in April or May when my divorce gets finalized. I don't have a confirmed date yet."

"Sorry to hear that. I wasn't aware there was a problem. A day off can be arranged," he said.

"So far it's pretty straight forward. Hope there aren't any glitches," she said as she started filling in the paperwork including her social security number for tax purposes. She couldn't believe she'd landed a job with Wainright.

On her way out of the building, she saw Todd Wainright coming out the back entrance with his briefcase and a box of papers. He called out, "Wait, Jessica," and stashed everything in the back seat of his SUV.

She paused and waited for him. He strode across the tarmac and extended his hand.

"Congratulations. I hear you got the job," he said, with a broad grin on his face. "Would you be interested in grabbing a coffee with me, before you head home?"

"I don't know anything about you, other than you're an accountant and your family started the business," she said, taken aback by his boldness. Inwardly she groaned—not another Ryan.

"Sorry, Jessica. My enthusiasm got the better of my common sense but we can walk right across the street to the diner. They know me," he said.

"Okay, but I'd like to keep it short. It will be getting dark soon and the I-64 can be nasty on a Friday night with truck traffic and even light snow." A few flakes were still descending.

They sat in a booth. Jess watched his interactions with the couple running the diner. The older woman automatically put two mugs of coffee on the table. The older man was obviously the cook. There was an easy rapport between them. Todd was familiar too with most of the other patrons, calling them by name as they bantered back and forth. She felt shy but decided she needed to quickly establish the ground rules.

"Tell me about yourself. Are you married?" she asked.

"No." The hazel eyes looked at her. There was a hint of amusement on his face. "I'm five-ten, weigh a hundred and sixty-five pounds, enjoy bike riding and hiking, don't smoke, like the occasional bourbon, have my own house, and visit my family frequently. Mum and Dad have a farm on the next concession. I'm their youngest. They raise Herefords, wheat, hay, and sometimes oats and barley. I have two brothers and a sister, all married with kids. We get along great. I have had girlfriends, but none that I'd want to spend forever with. I'm a certified public accountant and have my own business; Wainright is my major client. That's the short bio. Now what about you?"

Jess laughed. "I did say to keep it brief, didn't I. Well, my bio reads like this: born and raised in Lexington. Father was a stable hand and exercise rider most of his life, then feed manager at O'Connell's stable. Mum stayed home. They divorced ten years ago. She remarried a Thoroughbred trainer and moved to California. I have one brother; he's older than me and he's an IT guy in California. I graduated from the horse management program at the U of K, and took over the feed manager position after my dad died in a car accident. My husband and I are in the middle of a divorce. I'm not interested in dating at the present time. I want a new beginning and that starts with a new and interesting job. I have a one-room apartment in a converted garage. I don't smoke, I enjoy a glass of wine, I love riding, and am taking tango lessons because I'm going to Argentina in February to visit a friend. End of story."

He thoughtfully stirred his coffee, then looked at her. "Message received, loud and clear. You need time to work through things. I won't rush you, but I'm interested. I hear Ryan O'Connell is a difficult man to work for, especially with the female staff."

"Todd, that's a conversation I don't want to get into. I won't talk about the man, period."

"The tone of your voice says a lot."

"If I don't say it or imply it, then I can't be sued, can I? Thanks for the coffee, Todd, but I think I should be heading home," she said, slipping her jacket back on. He walked her to her car.

She watched him in her rearview mirror as she pulled out of the parking lot and joined the bumper-to-bumper traffic trying to merge onto the interstate. She thought about Todd. His manner was straightforward and she liked that in a man but she didn't want anyone in her life yet. She hadn't dealt with the one she had. Her shattered heart needed time to heal. What had Mrs. H. said? Ninety percent of problems in future relationships were based on unresolved issues from the first one.

On the way home, she thought about her future. Would it be in her best interest to move to Louisville, so she wouldn't have the hour's commute? No. Better to stay at Mrs. H.'s until the end of the probation period. That would also put a little space between her and the gung-ho Mr. Todd Wainright, not that he wasn't a nice specimen of manhood and he seemed very pleasant, but it was far too soon, even if it was a little boost to her ego.

Saturday morning, she headed to the mall to see the travel agent. They discussed the trip and like Carla, she chose the Lexington to Houston to Buenos Aires route. It jogged her memory that she hadn't received her passport yet. The airfare was a whopping three thousand dollars! That was going to put a huge dent in her savings account. She left with a handful of literature.

Bumping into Karen at the mall was sheer luck. They sat and had a quick coffee before to she drove to Stattler's. Her phone rang. She pulled into a parking lot and picked it up. It was a message from Brad Hollingsworth. She called him back.

"Hi, Brad, I got your call. What's up?"

"Just thought I'd let you know I was talking to John Peterson and something interesting is going on at the penitentiary."

"Oh?"

"A snitch overheard another inmate bragging about how he'd been hired to kill a guy by running his car off the Rapids Road, a couple of years ago, so he reported it."

That got her attention.

"Anyway, the long and short of it is, they're interrogating the guy. There've been a lot of accidents on that curve but only a few fatalities and the timing's right for your father. The guy's not saying a word at the moment. He's an old junk dealer in town. He was arrested for an unrelated break and enter after your father's death. Remember you asked John Peterson about the pieces of broken taillight? He sent all the glass off to the lab."

"Thanks, Brad. What's the inmate's name? I might know him from work."

"Will Harper's his name.

"I do know him! He was an older guy, maybe fifty, wore grubby clothes. He used to pick up junk from Ryan and Laura and take it to the dump. He had an old rusted out silver Chevy truck. He used to live over on the east side in one of the old war-time houses," she said.

"I'll tell John. Jess, leave it to the police. Don't you go poking around. John would need a warrant to search the place. You'd be trespassing and you might destroy evidence. Do you understand?"

"Oh yes, I fully understand. I have no intention of poking around, but I'm curious now. The door to my dad's house was found unlocked and the house was a mess, like someone had searched it. Will would have quite capable of picking a lock, wouldn't he?"

"I wasn't aware the house was unlocked," he said.

"Detective Peterson knows. Maybe Harper broke into the house looking for something. Dad wouldn't have forgotten to lock up. He was a neat freak. He'd never leave the house in a mess like that."

"If the house was broken into, what was Harper looking for?" Brad asked.

"The bigger question here is who hired him to do the job? I've never figured out why my dad was going back to the stable when he'd worked all that day and would've gone back the following morning. My guess is that someone at the stable called him. That would have set him up for the accident if Harper was waiting for him."

"If someone called from the stable, old phone records would show it. It's long distance there," Brad said.

Jess thought about it. "Please keep me informed, Brad."

"John's very thorough; he'll work it out but it's a slow process. It can take weeks to get results from the lab. I'm sure John will keep in touch," Brad said and hung up.

Wow! What were the chances of that happening, after two years?

*　　　　　*　　　　　*

JESS WORKED A COUPLE OF HORSES FOR JOHN STATTLER, returned home and spent the evening going over the Argentina information. She pulled up articles on history, politics, polo, and Thoroughbreds. When she opened her email, Carla had sent preliminary pictures of her lacy wedding dress. There was a lovely photo of Carla's mother holding up the dress, obviously excited and very happy. The woman was short with black hair pulled back in a bun and had the same mocha-toned skin, very much like Carla.

Jess answered the email back, giving the full details about her new job and the dates for her flights. She hoped three weeks wasn't going to be a bother for Carla's family and asked her to look for an Airbnb in a safe area. She definitely couldn't afford a hotel with the price she was paying for airfare. She reminded Carla about the Diaz fillies too.

She called her mother and had a long chat, telling her about her new job, but left out all the tidbits about the police investigation. Her mother wouldn't have been interested anyway.

It was after six, so she made her supper, and spent an hour working on her Spanish. *Quiero un vaso de vino blanco, por favor* (I'd like a glass of white wine, please). *Quiero mi bistec bien hecho.* (I want my steak well done.)

She had a quick shower, pulled out her bed and fell asleep with the television still playing.

Sunday morning, she sat down and after many attempts composed her letter of resignation.

> To: Ryan and Laura,
>
> After serious consideration, I have accepted a position elsewhere and will be resigning as your feed manager as of January 30th. I shall train my replacement, as you requested.
>
> I appreciate the opportunities you have given me and for allowing me to assist with your social events. It has permitted me to meet many people and learn more about Thoroughbred horses than any course could ever have taught me.
>
> Lexington has been my home, but personal things have changed and I want to start over.
>
> Yours truly,
>
> Jessica Coxwell

Chapter 14

MONDAY MORNING AFTER PREPARING THE FEED, SHE TOOK her letter of resignation to the house. Ryan's car was parked in front of the garage, so he was home. Part of her was anxious to move forward, but right now she was scared. If Ryan was responsible for her father's death, she was walking into the lion's den.

The house was quiet and nobody else was around; there was no sign of Laura or Mrs. Porter. She knocked on Ryan's office door. "Come in," he said. She entered. He frowned as he watched her place the envelope on the desk. He motioned her to sit, which she did. He tore the envelope open, read the letter, and threw it on the desk. Spinning around in his chair, he stood up and stared out the window, his hands on his hips.

Jess sat motionless, watching him, waiting for the volcano to erupt. It seemed like forever when he turned towards her and leaned on the desk, staring at her.

"You can send Brenda up to see me. She'll be your replacement. I'll advertise for someone to replace her, someone with experience. We've got foaling coming up." Then he sat down, without looking at her.

Considering herself dismissed, she left the room closing the door behind her. It felt like she'd dodged a bullet. She crossed the quadrangle of stalls and found Brenda.

"Brenda, Ryan wants to see you now," she said, shooing her up to the house.

By late afternoon, it was general knowledge among the staff that she was leaving and Brenda was taking her place. David and Inga, two of the stable attendants had called some of their friends to apply for the now open broodmare attendant position. After work, she went to Mr. Ames' office.

"Hi Jess," he said. "How are you doing?"

"Very well," she replied. "Any glitches with the house?"

"No, everything's on track. Lloyd has all the divorce prep done too. Everything should be finalized sometime in April or May."

"With regard to your copy of Andy's photos, I would like you to destroy them. I'm going to give the originals back to him. I've no intention of ever using them. I've never told anyone else about that situation. That's his business."

He pulled her file from the cabinet, found the copy, and put it through the shredder.

"Thanks, Mr. Ames. I've got a new job with Wainright Feeds, starting in March. I'm going to be away in Argentina in February. I will keep my apartment here in Lexington until at least September next year. You've got my email address if you need to contact me."

"That's a smart move, young lady. Get on with your life," he said.

On her way home, Jess thought about finding a safe place for her safety deposit box key. She didn't want to leave it in the apartment while she was away. She took a piece of duct tape and affixed the key to the underside of the upper tray of her toolbox in her car. Not likely anyone would find it there.

*   *   *

SEVERAL INCHES OF SNOW HAD FALLEN OVERNIGHT. IT TOOK a few days to adjust to winter driving. Some drivers were stupid, not leaving enough stopping room, resulting in long traffic tie-ups as the cops dealt with rear-end collisions. At work, she found the two faxed résumés she'd been expecting; one was David's male friend and the other was Inga's roommate, Tina. Both candidates appeared well-qualified. After morning rounds, she took the papers to the house. Ryan's car was gone. She didn't see Laura's either, so she gave the résumés to Mrs. Porter.

Jess went back to organizing her list of chores—the body scoring system, pasture rotations, each horse's file with all the data and the changes in diet throughout the year. Then there was all the information on the feed—what she ordered, how much, delivery details, and amount of surplus to have in stock. Next came a list of all the contact people—Mitch for Wainright, the bloodstock agents, the blacksmith, the vet, transport companies, and contacts at the airport for long-distance shipping. She'd have to show Brenda how to do a pedigree from scratch as well as pulling one up on the Jockey Club website. Other tasks including making out work schedules as well as checking payroll sheets before she took them up to the office each week.

Jess wasn't sure what Laura was going to do for the social end of things. She had no intention of playing hostess again; she was merely Wainright's rep.

She took a look at the horses. The stallions were in fine shape and just slightly overweight. Breeding season would be hard on them, especially Cat who was scheduled to service two mares a day. Big bellies were starting to show on the mares. Foaling was only six to eight weeks away. There were twenty of their own mares due to foal and right after New Year's there would be a daily stream of trailers bringing outside mares in for breeding. Most would go back home with their owners; others would stay for several days in the south barn. Their own mares could be re-bred on foaling heat. The teaser stallions were looking good too. Jess felt sorry for them. *They must get so frustrated, checking out the mares to see if they're in heat but never being allowed to breed,* she thought.

Jess was glad this year that she only had January to contend with. She loved seeing the foals born, but the yard was chaos. It was pretty much a production line. Everyone had to be right on their game for keeping track of horses and paperwork. She reminded herself to show Brenda where she kept her camera and how to take proper photos of the foals, plus starting a new file on each one when they were born.

On Wednesday, Ryan hired Tina to replace Brenda. That was no surprise. She hadn't expected him to pick the male applicant, even though the man had more experience. Brenda and Jess slowly started going through all the routines. "If anything's not clear, please ask. Any invoices for feeds go to Annie or Becky."

Her dance lessons on Thursdays and her Saturday rides kept her sane. She was pleased with her progress in the tango. She wasn't doing any of the fancy steps yet like the caresses, where she was supposed to rub her leg up and down her partner's leg. For the past week or so, she hadn't done any of her Spanish lessons. She needed to get back into that routine. She also needed to maintain contact with Karen and the other girls for a quick coffee at the mall, at least once a week.

Sunday was her usual day to either call or email her mother and brother but there was little news to report at the moment. December seemed to fly by. Winter storms came and went, never leaving more than an inch or two of snow. She got her exercise shoveling the driveway and sidewalk. The backyard was sometimes blanketed with snow so she bought bird seed to fill the feeders for the chickadees, sparrows, juncos, nuthatches, blue jays, and mourning doves who came in droves. The neighbor's yellow-eyed cat often prowled the top of the fence in hunting mode, but never seemed to catch anything.

The bereavement group canceled meetings until January as it was simply too busy with Christmas for everyone to get together. Lately, Ellie had been in a better frame of mind. The girl's strength was inspirational.

Mrs. H. invited Jess over for Christmas dinner, along with a couple of the other single ladies. Jess was happy to accept. She thought it might be nice if she brought two bottles of wine, a poinsettia and maybe a basket of cheeses and fruit cake for Mrs. H.

She didn't have much shopping to do; just a gift card for her mother for her favorite clothing store and checks for Marty and his family. She found herself looking at things that Andy would have wanted, but now there was no need. She hadn't seen him since she's moved. She had a few Christmas cards to send to Carla, Jim and Jean Barry, John Stattler, and the staff at O'Connells, but wasn't going to send one to Ryan and Laura; they were out of her sphere now.

Her passport finally arrived. She laughed out loud at her photo. The unsmiling face really didn't look like her at all. Five more weeks to vacation time, her first plane ride and first out-of-country holiday. It was exciting. In many ways it was an escape, a total change of venue, somewhere to let herself start again.

She was in contact with Carla, every week and received updates on all the wedding preparations. It sounded like a really big deal—fancy church wedding with over three hundred guests. Her father owned the Mercedes dealership in Buenos Aires, so was well known in the community.

Hi, Jess:

The horses are keeping me busy. I'm working for a local stable three days a week.

Mateo's playing polo in his spare time. We're between team games but he still goes to practice. By the time you get here, you'll be able to see a real game. I've found a good Airbnb for you near my parents' apartment. If you complete the application on the Airbnb website for Buenos Aires, you can book it and leave a deposit. Have the final fitting for my dress today. Adios. Carla

There was no more news from the police regarding the investigation into Will Harper so Jess let it go. She had done all she could at this point and unless forensics could nail down something definite on the vehicle, it wasn't going any further.

Christmas was a very quiet affair. After lunch, she talked to her mother and Marty and later went next door for the gathering. They were a sweet group of ladies. Mrs. H. had cooked a small turkey, complete with stuffing; even the smell of it made Jess salivate. She came home later with a doggie bag for her lunches.

The following day was quiet. She sat down on the couch and decided it was the perfect time to go through her dad's photos, which were still in two boxes on the shelf beneath the television. The photo albums were the old-fashioned kind made of black paper and had the little sticky corners to fix the photos in place. Fortunately, he had penciled the names of the people on the back of each photo. Many were black-and-white dating back to the nineteen thirties. She'd bought new albums and put all the photos in chronological order.

There were pictures of her dad, as a child with his parents and grandparents. She had never met them. Somehow contact had been lost. There were others showing him as a young man, usually with a horse. There were photos of him in his army uniform before and after the war, even one of him riding a motorcycle. He'd cut quite a dashing figure. She laughed at the early pictures of her mother as a very slim young woman with the long pageboy haircut and weird hats. Marty's baby pictures were hilarious. There were later ones of him playing football as a six-year-old. It was hard to imagine how fast time had passed and so much had changed. The last photos were his Ireland trips. The ones taken at Neil's stable showed Arctic Cat but the infamous scar wasn't evident from the angles those photos had been taken.

Ryan, Laura, and family had flown to Miami for the school break between Christmas and New Year's, so she felt she could do her work without interruptions. Work was genuinely pleasant. The mares were so round they looked like they would burst. Everyone was on the alert for signs of imminent foaling.

Chapter 15

JANUARY 2ND, THE SALE OF THE HOUSE WAS FINALIZED, much to Jess's relief. Two mares foaled that day. Mums and babies were doing well. Jess supervised, making sure Brenda was present for both deliveries and the attendants got some hands-on experience. Watching the foals nurse was really satisfying. It never failed to amaze her how quickly they found their footing with their long wobbly and very collapsible legs, instinctively nosing around for their first suckle.

It was almost six o'clock when she got home. She was ravenous and threw a frozen pizza in the oven. No phone messages or emails. Carla was getting married on Saturday. Jess studied the Spanish version of days of the week for an hour. Just three weeks to go.

Thursday after work, she drove straight to the studio, arriving with minutes to spare. Jim put her through her paces for an hour, changing from tango, to samba, rumba, and cha-cha. She was keeping up with him. Considering the short period of time, she'd been dancing, she was pleased with her progress.

"Jess, now you've got the basics on the footwork, we need to work on style. I want to see arrogance and attitude in how you place your feet and turn your head," he said.

She pretended she was haughty and looked down her nose at him, her head high and back straight. He nodded and they kept moving. As long as she concentrated on following his lead, she was okay. Improvising wasn't an option yet.

Jess went home and made wieners and beans for supper—not exactly gourmet fare. She lay in bed thinking that there was a world of opportunities open to her. She'd always worked with horses. What talents did she have? She'd never tried other things to even see what she was capable of. She had taken the feed company job mostly to escape the O'Connells and to support herself. Just like the dancing, she would see if it worked for her. The six-month probation was definitely a good thing.

She thought about Todd Wainright. Her contact with him had been brief. He seemed pleasant and was willing to keep things casual. She appreciated that. He was nice but didn't exactly spark any fires for her. Much too soon for that.

The rest of the week remained busy at work. Three outside mares arrived and were assigned their stalls. Two O'Connell mares foaled. It was starting to get hectic. Rounds were made more frequently. Other mares were starting to arrive for breeding to the stallions, so there were horse trailers coming and going in the yard. Names were being penciled in on the available stall sheet that was quickly filling.

Saturday morning presented with two inches of blowing snow. She was very thankful she didn't have to drive. Her thoughts were with Carla in a hot, sunny Buenos Aires. She could hardly wait for the wedding pictures. She was quite content to get groceries, clean up the apartment and have a coffee with the girls. Aah! Holidays just a few weeks away.

She paid the outstanding amount on the Airbnb rental so that was finalized.

*   *   *

FOUR WEEKS WENT BEFORE SHE KNEW IT. BRENDA WAS FULLY participating with the foaling and had a solid, practical head on her shoulders for dealing with staff, horses, and owners. Tina had some experience with brood mares and seemed to be fitting in well. Finally, it was the end of the month and Jess's last day. She said goodbye to all the stable and office staff. Ann gave her a big hug. There was no sign of either Ryan or Laura which didn't bother her in the least.

When she got home it was hard to believe that in the morning she'd be on a plane. She hauled out her suitcase and started packing: bathing suit, shorts, T-shirts, shoes, dancing shoes, her Spanish–English book, raincoat, camera and battery charger, passport, tickets, notebook, toiletries, and laptop. Had she forgotten anything?

Jess looked down at the gold wedding band she still wore and very gently twisted it off. She should have taken that off long ago. How long it would take for the groove in her ring finger to disappear? Putting the ring in her jewelry box, she closed the lid. It was the last symbol of her marriage, the symbol of love and loyalty, the final acknowledgment that it was well and truly over. She really couldn't explain why she hadn't removed it weeks ago. It wasn't as if she was going to change her mind. Maybe this was part of the acceptance thing.

Still deep in thought, she continued her packing. According to the weather channel, the temperature in Houston was in the high sixties and in Buenos Aires was nearly eighty degrees with rain, so she set aside a carry bag for her winter jacket. Mrs. H. had offered to water her plants, pick up her mail, and drive her to the airport for the first leg of her trip. Jess was happy with that. She fired off a quick email to Carla, who should have returned from her honeymoon by then.

Jess had a long chat with her mother and promised to keep in touch. She was so excited, she had trouble sleeping. She'd set her alarm clock for four but was awake earlier. Promptly at five-thirty, Mrs. H. knocked on the door. Jess took one last look around, locked the door and gave the apartment key and car keys to Mrs. H. It only took twenty-five minutes to get to the Lexington airport.

"Thank you so much, I really appreciate this," Jess said.

"You have a good holiday. Just be careful. Bad things can happen to visitors in these foreign countries," Mrs. H. said, with a look of concern.

"Don't worry. I'll be with friends and I'll be careful," Jess replied, as she closed the car door, waved goodbye, and headed through the doors of the glassed-in terminal building. There was a lineup at the check-in area for United Airlines. Jess got her bearings and looked up at the departure board. Flight 319 was scheduled to leave at eight.

An odd thought passed through her mind. She remembered her fortune cookie from way back in the fall. *You are going on a journey. Your lucky numbers are 3 19 24 37 45.* Now she was on a journey and her flight was 319; her seat number was 24. That was a good omen! Her suitcase was tagged and disappeared on a conveyor belt. Jess moved through the security check point then to the departure lounge for flight 319. She got herself a coffee and took a seat overlooking the runway. There were still traces of snow on the grassy areas of the airport, but the runways were clear. Flags were snapping in the stiff, cold breeze. The ground crew were transferring luggage from the luggage carts to the plane. At least half the seats in the waiting area were full. Most of the passengers looked like business men.

By seven, the lounge was full. At seven-fifteen, the desk staff arrived. She patiently got in the lineup and when it was her turn, handed over her boarding pass and ID. She followed the others down the passenger boarding bridge and was welcomed by the flight attendant. Jess followed the numbers and found seat 24, an aisle seat and stashed her carry-on bag containing her laptop in the overhead compartment. An older man was seated at the window, making a few last calls on his cellphone. There were quite a few empty seats.

Jess was curious about everything. The seatbelt light came on and she strapped herself in. Flight attendants started to give the safety lecture indicating the exits and the overhead oxygen masks. She found the laminated set of instructions in the front seat pocket and read them, identifying the exit doors. Powerful engines roared to life and they were pulsating, throbbing, and loud. Her seat position was behind the wing, limiting her view but she could still see some ground activity. Slowly, the plane began to move. It taxied away from the building to the threshold ready for takeoff. She watched another plane on the runway moving at speed, its nose pointed upwards. Then there was that moment when it became airborne. Jess watched it move out of her line of sight, phantom vortices swirling behind.

She felt and heard the engines revving to maximum power then the plane gathered speed along the runway. It was an awesome moment when the vibrations increased and the plane became airborne. She found herself gripping the arms of the seat for dear life and felt her stomach drop. The plane climbed, rising through the clouds, as Lexington shrank to a mere dot. The wing dipped as the plane curved south. For one ear-popping moment, she wondered if she would fall out but of course she didn't. She caught glimpses of the snow-tipped green hills, then they were above the clouds into sunshine. How could something as heavy as a plane fly?

The captain came on the overhead speaker. "Welcome to flight 319. We will be cruising at twenty-nine-thousand feet and arriving in Houston in two hours and thirty-five minutes. Temperature there is sixty-nine degrees. Their time zone is one hour ahead. Enjoy your flight." The flight attendants began pushing a snack cart down the aisle, dispensing potato chips, chocolate bars, and drinks. Jess took a ginger ale and sat back, watching everything around her.

Two hours later, the descent into Houston airport terminated with the roar of brakes and a solid thump as the plane touched down. It taxied to a halt at the passenger bridge and soon everyone was out of their seats, opening the overhead bins and grabbing their carry-ons. Jess was in no hurry to disembark. There was a long wait for the second leg of the trip. Outside it was bright with sunshine. Jess took off her winter jacket and stuffed it in her carry-on bag. She found the departure gate for the next flight, then wandered around finally finding a mystery book to read. She spent the next four hours people watching, reading her book, and munching on junk food to pass the time.

As departure time got closer, the lounge began to fill. Half the passengers were business types but there were dark-haired couples speaking Spanish. Finally, the desk opened and she joined the lineup for flight 702. This time she had been allocated 38, a window seat. She enjoyed having an uninterrupted view. An elderly woman beside her plugged in her ear phones and was listening to a Spanish station. Once again, the flight attendant went through the safety routine in English but repeated it in Spanish, fluently bilingual. The plane departed on time. At least now Jess knew what to expect.

Once the plane was airborne, the captain announced they would be flying at thirty thousand feet and were expected to arrive at Aeropuerto Internacional Ministro Pistarini (otherwise called Ezeiza Airport) in six-and-a-half hours. She calculated that would be roughly eight in the evening. The temperature there was seventy-eight degrees.

She could hardly wait to see Carla again and had high expectations for the trip. Some people watched a movie, but she pulled out her novel and read until the evening meal was served. Later, the flight attendants dispensed forms to fill out which were in Spanish.

"Do you have a camera, gifts, a computer, any jewelry or anything of value to declare?" the young woman queried when Jess asked for help.

"Yes, I have a camera and a laptop," Jess said and was shown where to add those items.

"Are you carrying any meat or fruit? Are you carrying more than ten thousand dollars in cash?"

"No," she said and signed the form.

When the elderly lady got up from her seat, Jess took the opportunity to stretch her legs. She found the washroom. She got back to her seat as the seat belt sign came back on when they hit a patch of turbulence that lasted ten minutes. She double-checked to see where the barf bag was and found it in the front pocket. She didn't feel sick but it was handy if she needed it. It wasn't until the captain's voice announced that they were coming into land, that she realized she'd been asleep.

The plane descended through the clouds into a rose-tinted evening, the sun sinking on the western horizon. Below she could see the brown waters of the Rio de la Plata mixing with aqua water along the Atlantic coast. The city sprawled for miles. Buenos Aires was named by the Spaniards in the 1500s for its fair winds.

Chapter 16

IT TOOK A WHILE FOR THE LUGGAGE TO DESCEND ONTO THE carousel. She grabbed her suitcase and joined the straggling line of passengers following the signs *Aduano* (customs). She gave her passport to the officer on duty. He examined it and asked, "What is the purpose of your visit?" in perfect English.

"My first holiday to Argentina," she said with a big smile on her face.

"How long is your trip?"

"Three weeks," she said.

He scanned her passport, stamped it, and gave it back to her. "Enjoy your vacation."

"*Gracias, Señor.*" She towed her suitcase behind her and followed the corridors. Finally, she saw the glassed-in area and hundreds of people waiting in the main terminal. The doors opened automatically and she followed several others out. Uniformed armed security personnel were everywhere. She scanned the sea of faces, looking for Carla and finally saw the sign "Jessica" being waved above the heads of the crowd by a dark-haired young man. She headed for it and suddenly found herself in Carla's arms. It was hugs and laughter.

"Señora Santos, I'm so happy to be here," Jess said. "You look great!"

"Jess, this is my husband Mateo," Carla said slipping her arm around her husband, obviously very much in love and proud of him.

He shook Jess's hand and gave her a light kiss on the cheek. "Welcome to Argentina," he said. He was short, only a few inches taller than she was but slim, wiry, and attractive.

Jess followed them out to the parking lot where the truck was parked. It sported a trailer hitch no doubt to haul the horse trailer to polo matches.

The two women talked nonstop as Mateo drove on the main thoroughfare heading north.

Jess was amazed at the size of the city.

"What's the population of Buenos Aires, Carla?" she asked, looking at the streets pulsing with colorful neon lights. Towering apartment buildings loomed in the northeast with poorer districts to the southwest. The highway was bumper-to-bumper traffic. "Is it always this busy?"

"I think it's around thirteen million now. It's pretty typical for the evenings to be busy. You'll find supper is served at ten in the evening and bars and restaurants don't close until three or four in the morning. We're night owls," Carla said.

Carla told her all about their honeymoon. They'd been away for a week up at Iguazú Falls in the far north of the country. "The falls were so beautiful but we had to come back, Mateo has polo practice on Saturday. I thought you might like to come," she said. "Sunday we will go to the old cathedral with my parents."

"I'm so looking forward to seeing a polo match. That's on my to-do list."

"I got hold of Señor Diaz. We'll be going to his estancia in the morning to see the horses. It's only about a thirty-minute drive from our house," she said. "What else is on your list?"

"I want to have a dance lesson every morning at your uncle's dance studio, then go sight-seeing. I want to see the Plaza de Mayo, San Telmo, a football game, the art gallery, the opera house, the old cemetery, and just about anything else I can cram in. I want to see the tango dancers mostly," she said. "Oh, I almost forgot, I want to try your famous wines and go to an *asado* for a properly grilled steak."

Mateo burst out laughing. "I take it you're not someone who lays around the pool sunbathing."

"No," said Jess. "If I wanted that I could have gone to Florida. This is my first trip to a foreign country and I want to learn about the culture and the history, enjoy the differences, maybe ride horses, and do a proper tango. My dance instructor at home taught me the basics but this is the real thing."

Jess stared into the descending darkness as they continued on the highway; four lanes dropped down to two. They were leaving the city behind as night closed in on them. In the glare of the headlights, she could see smaller towns, fences, and more open space. Most of the road signs were just a blur. They were on Highway 9 but soon turned off onto Highway 8. She didn't understand most of the Spanish she'd heard, as the people had spoken too quickly. She felt reluctant to use the little Spanish she did have. Maybe she'd become more proficient as the trip went on. Luckily the most important people around her were bilingual.

As soon as she started to relax, she felt incredibly tired, hardly surprising as she'd been up since three o'clock in the morning. Finally, the truck pulled off into a lane way, the headlights revealing a stucco-and-brick bungalow with a red tile roof. Mateo carried her suitcase and she followed them into the house. It was lovely inside. The walls were white stucco with burnished red-brown floor tiles. Colorful patterned pillows adorned the highly polished, dark wood furniture. Horse pictures hung everywhere, many with Mateo astride a galloping horse, swinging a polo mallet. Carla gave her a quick tour then showed her to her room, where she'd stay for the next few nights before going to the Airbnb.

Carla offered her a coffee, but Jess politely declined. "Sorry Carla, I'm beat. I was up really early to get my first flight. What time do you get up in the morning?"

"Usually at six. Mateo has to drive into the city, so he leaves about seven-thirty. I figure we'll look after the horses then head over to Señor Diaz's estancia about nine o'clock."

Jess gave her another big hug, said goodnight to Mateo then headed to the bathroom to clean her teeth and have a quick wash. As soon as she climbed into bed, she fell asleep cocooned in a single cotton sheet, bathed by the warm breeze from the open window. No snow!

Chapter 17

MELODIC BIRD CALLS WOKE HER. HIGH IN THE DARK GREEN foliage outside her window, two birds were singing, hidden by the lush greenery. Further away a horse nickered. Filtered sunlight flooded the room. She lay there for a few moments and listened to the house. The muted voices of Carla and Mateo came from the kitchen as well as the lovely aroma of fresh coffee. Jess stretched and climbed out of bed. It was seven o'clock and hot already. She closed the shutters to keep the room cooler and unpacked her suitcase. She chose a light T-shirt, jeans, and sneakers.

She went into the bathroom for a shower and heard Mateo drive away. Refreshed and ready to go, she braided her hair into one large plait and bounced into the kitchen where Carla was washing the dishes.

"Good morning, Carla."

"Hi, Jess, how did you sleep?"

"Like the dead. This is sooo exciting. What can I do?"

"Pour yourself a cup of coffee and I'll make breakfast. I've asked my cousin Felipe to join us. He's a photographer and an artist. I hope you don't mind. I'll tell you about him later. He should be here by the time we finish checking the horses, then we'll go to the Diaz estate." Carla pulled a tray of croissants out of the oven. "We usually have a very light breakfast, then something more substantial for lunch."

Jess savored the coffee and the flaky pastries, licking her fingers afterward. "Where does Mateo work?"

"He's a financial adviser at a city bank. He plays polo during the polo season and practices at least twice a week, year-round. Let's go out and see the horses."

The nine-acre property was divided into three fields. Jess could see the area nearest the house contained an open-sided roofed structure with a water trough. The horses were out in the field, their shiny coats shimmering in the sun. A large horse trailer was parked at the end of the driveway along with Carla's small Ford.

"The shed gives them shade in the afternoon when it gets hot," said Carla as they strolled among them. The animals were in beautiful condition and were soon clustered around them, nosing their pockets for treats. Carla handed her a few alfalfa cubes and soft whiskery lips gently took them from her hand.

"What's their breeding?" Jess asked.

"Thoroughbreds or Thoroughbred crosses," Carla replied.

"I read somewhere about cloned horses. That's legal for polo ponies isn't it?"

"It is. You might see some at polo practice tomorrow. One of Argentina's best polo players, Adolfo Cambiaso, cloned a number of his horses. It's pretty amazing really, but very expensive. He's part owner of a cloning company in Texas. It's way out of our league," she said.

"A lot less work with no stalls to clean," Jess said, eyeing the setup. The countryside was an almost flat and empty expanse of green to the horizon with only a few trees and country homes. Fields on neighboring properties were showing crop growth. "I thought the pampas was just grass. Are they farming it more now?"

"Yes. Farmers are putting cattle in feedlots. They can make more money raising soybeans, corn, and wheat, even rice in some areas. I work part-time at a racing stable just down the road, Monday to Wednesday. Juan has ten horses. Ah, here's Felipe."

Jess watched a white sedan pull into the driveway. The man who got out was in his early thirties. He had a short, tight, and stocky build and was casually dressed in cream-colored shirt and slacks. The thick mass of wavy black hair was down to his shoulders and he hadn't shaved in a few days. The dark shuttered eyes under thick black brows had a hooded, brooding quality. He scrutinized her for a few moments, but his facial expression remained aloof.

Carla made the introductions. "Jessica, this is *el primo* Felipe, my cousin Felipe," she said.

He spoke English with a deep resonant voice and welcomed her to Argentina although Jess got the impression that while he said the words, the eyes weren't that welcoming.

"*Gracias, Señor,*" she said, feeling awkward.

They went back in the house for a few minutes to wash their hands and pick up their purses. Jess had brought one with a long chain strap, so she could wear it across her body, leaving her hands free for her camera. As she got in the back seat of the car, she noticed his camera and long-distance lenses in his camera bag.

"What can you tell me about Señor Diaz's estancia?" she asked.

"He comes from one of the old families that were given land grants very early in our history, so he has about twenty thousand acres," Carla said.

Jess was astounded. "I can't even imagine what twenty thousand acres looks like!"

"Me neither," said Carla. "He has broodmares and about twenty horses that he runs at the race track in Buenos Aires. He's into many different businesses."

"I'm really interested to see how the two fillies are doing," said Jess, aware a pair of serious, dark eyes monitoring her in the rear-view mirror. "Felipe, with your photography, are there certain things that appeal to you?"

"No, not really: birds, landscapes, people in cafes, old buildings, textures and light," he said. "I always carry my camera. I never know when I might find a scene that interests me."

The car slowed and turned into a gated, landscaped entrance way with an overhead arch sporting a running horse. The bungalow beyond was the same style as Carla's but triple the size, having a broad shaded porch across the entire front. Paddocks bordered the road with stables to the left. Jess could see the oval of an exercise track out back and several riders working horses. There was a four-bay garage containing two Mercedes, a pickup truck, a blue Kia Sorento as well as several horse trailers parked nearby. She noted security cameras on all buildings.

"Wow, this is quite the setup," she said as Felipe stopped close to the house. No sooner had they exited the car, then the front door of the house swung open and Señor Diaz appeared. He looked the same as he had at the O'Connells but was wearing a casual short-sleeved shirt and slacks. He welcomed them and led them past the paddocks to a large field where a herd of horses were grazing. Felipe had his camera around his neck and was in conversation in Spanish with the older man.

Carla nudged her. "He just introduced himself and asked permission to take photos of us and the horses. Felipe is quite well known for his photos and for his paintings. He's not painting right now. It's a long sad story. I'll tell you later when we're alone."

Jess said, "Okay." She switched her attention to the herd out in the field and immediately picked out the bright chestnut coat of Charmer. Full Moon was harder to spot as there were several dark-coated horses out there.

"Señor Diaz, may I call them? I don't know if they will still come to me. It's been four months."

He nodded and watched her. Jess gave her camera to Carla and asked her to take some photos. She opened the gate, slipped into the field, and placed her fingers on her lips, emitting a piercing whistle. Immediately two heads popped up; one was chestnut and the other dark brown. She whistled again and watched with delight as the two fillies separated from the herd, moving from a trot to a full gallop towards her. She walked towards them oblivious to everything but their sheer majesty. It was almost like slow motion; the background faded, manes and tails streamed with their movement, necks flattened, legs extended, and nostrils flared. Charmer reached her first, coming to an abrupt halt not three feet from her. Full Moon was not far behind.

Charmer sniffed her and nickered. Jess laughed and pulled an alfalfa cube from each pocket as she got frisked.

She stood still with Charmer's forehead against her chest and caressed her ears. She ran her hand along her neck and over her back and legs. "I can't believe how much she's grown. Look at her; she must be close to seventeen hands." She surveyed the depth and width of the chest. The filly was lean but well-muscled and full of herself, totally feminine yet a powerhouse.

Jess switched her attention to Full Moon. This filly too had grown but in a totally different way. Jess gave her a head rub and got nuzzled. "Señor Diaz, she's not what I expected. She's more compact, shorter back, not as tall but the width of chest is even greater than Charmer's. Are they in training?"

"Si, Señora. Charmer is the speed horse; Full Moon not so much."

"You know, if you go further back in her pedigree, a couple of generations on the sire's line, there was an Italian horse called Trojan Warrior. He was a stayer, a distance runner, and won a lot of races in Europe, but didn't do much until he was four. Maybe she's a throwback to him. She might take a bit more time to mature."

Jess walked back to the fence oblivious to the cameras. "That was beautiful, seeing those girls run like that," she said, eyeing the two fillies now placidly grazing their way back to the herd.

She was about to turn around when she heard a voice behind her, a male voice she knew well. Jess momentarily froze in her tracks. Carla looked at her and both of them turned around. There was Neil O'Connell talking to Señor Diaz and further back beside the Sorento was Duffy, his driver-cum-body guard.

Jess caught her breath and tried to look normal. She caught a glimpse of Felipe's face; he seemed to have picked up on her confusion, one eyebrow raised.

"Ah, you know each other of course," said Señor Diaz. "Neil's been staying with us for a few days to look at some mares in the area."

"I'm surprised to see you," said Neil, pouring on the Irish charm, looking his usual suave attractive self in a short-sleeved open-neck shirt, light-colored slacks, and sandals.

"I can't believe I've traveled thousands of miles and the first person I run into on my vacation is someone I know," said Jess shaking her head. Coincidence? She politely asked him how things were going. He told her that everything was fine and he'd be taking Arctic Cat back to Ireland in a month's time.

"Ryan tells me you'll be working for Wainright Feeds," he said.

"I'm really looking forward to trying something completely different." How did Ryan know that?

"Do you miss us?" he said, in that challenging way he had, with all kinds of innuendos in his voice, giving her his usual head-to-toe assessment.

"I only left yesterday so I haven't had time to miss anyone," she said, dismissively.

Señor Diaz brought Felipe over and introduced him to Neil, so Jess took the opportunity to step away from the line of fire and watch them. Neil made a comment about seeing one of his paintings in Barcelona a few years back. The men talked for a few moments but it had the prickly atmosphere of two alpha dogs facing off.

How famous was Felipe if his paintings to have been on display in Barcelona, for Neil to know about him, or for Neil to even go to an art gallery? When the men had finished talking, Jess approached Señor Diaz, thanking him for allowing her to visit the horses. "I was there the night Charmer was born," she said. "It's amazing how the scrawny little thing has grown into such a beautiful animal. It's breathtaking," she said.

The visit was over and Felipe ushered them back to the car. Within minutes, they were on the road to Carla's house. Jess was silent for the most part, still a bit stunned by the latest encounter and what it could mean. She was aware of Duffy, standing just behind Neil the whole time, a small smile on his face and eyes that frequently had been on her.

Carla prepared a pizza for lunch. "It's one of Argentina's most popular dishes because in the late 1800's, generations of Italians emigrated here for work."

While they were sitting at the table munching through the thick crust, Felipe looked at her and asked. "What is your relationship with that man Neil?"

"He's the senior partner in the stable where I used to work in Kentucky. Technically, he was my boss," she said.

He grunted and went back to eating his pizza.

Carla made coffee, then Felipe decided to go home. As he was leaving, he kissed Carla on the cheek and turned to Jess. "When you are in the city, come and see my studio," he said then left.

Jess took a look at the pictures Carla had taken and several of them were really good, showing Charmer with her head against Jess's chest and checking out her pockets. There was a nice head shot of Full Moon as well.

"That's great Carla. Thank you. Could I use my computer to email my mum so she knows I got here safely?"

"Sure," Carla said

Dear folks,

Long flight to Buenos Aires—took about six and a half hours from Houston. It's eighty degrees and humid. Everything shuts down in the afternoon as it is so hot. I'm told the city comes alive after dark.

We visited an estancia this morning to see two fillies O'Connells sold last fall. They looked great and still came to me when I whistled. Great natural grass here year- round. They don't have to worry about hay.

Tomorrow, Carla's husband Mateo is practicing polo, so I will get to see a match. On Sunday, we will be heading into the city and spend the day with her parents, going to church, and later a family barbecue. She has found accommodation for me near her parents, so that I will be handy to all the sightseeing venues. Fortunately, most of her family speak at least some English, which is a good thing. My limited Spanish isn't going to be enough. I'll keep in touch.

They sat down on the patio in the shade. "I'm curious about your cousin. I was surprised when Neil mentioned he'd seen his paintings in Spain. Is he famous?" Jess asked.

Carla looked at her. "He's a very talented artist and was just starting to get known outside Argentina when there was a terrible car accident and his wife was killed. Actually, today was the most communicative I've seen him in a long time. I try to get him out every once in a while, just to keep in touch. Occasionally, he phones me."

"You said, he was your cousin. How is he related to you?"

"My father had a brother named Tomas. He died a while back. Felipe is Tomas's son. The accident that killed Felipe's wife, happened about five years ago. Felipe's never been the same. He keeps to himself and never goes to church, rarely to family functions either. He seems angry most of the time."

"Well, I'm glad you told me. I picked up on his mood. I thought I'd done something wrong or it was a nuisance for him to take us there," said Jess.

"Sadly, he stopped painting. He has always been a keen photographer, so he makes a living by selling prints of his photos in a little shop in San Telmo. He took quite a lot of pictures of you with the horses this morning," she said. "I'm surprised he asked you to visit the store. Usually he's not that sociable. He didn't like the way Neil looked at you," said Carla with a grin on her face.

"Good thing he hasn't met Ryan then," said Jess, dryly.

"How are things going with your divorce?"

"I'm expecting to get the paperwork finalized sometime in April if everything proceeds as it should. I haven't seen Andy since I moved out, right after you left. I'm getting used to living on my own. Mrs. H. is a pet, such a nice lady. I have supper with her once in a while. She said to say hello."

"I think of her too. She was so kind to me when I was there. What's your new job going to be like?" Carla asked.

"It will be interesting, and I've got a lot to learn about the various animal feeds. The salary's decent. I don't know if it will be my forever job. I'll be traveling all over the state, so I'll get to meet new people. Some of my horse contacts will be useful. I'm sure I'm going to run into Andy and his students at the fairs but I think I can handle it now."

"Do you still go for coffee with the girls, like we used to?"

"I try to keep in touch with Karen and the others once a week but often it's just for a coffee, not supper like we did. It'll be harder to do that when I'm working in Louisville. I've been to a couple of Mrs. H.'s bereavement meetings and I can see I've got work to do. First, I need to understand the impact it's had on me. I've no idea what my capabilities are. I don't want to be a sad and miserable person the rest of my life. It's just going to take time. The bereavement group has been useful for that. Hearing about other peoples' troubles helps me as well. She's like a surrogate mum."

"She was for me too, always making cookies or just dropping in," Carla said.

"There's a nice guy at Wainright's who seems interested in me, but I'm not at that point yet. I don't trust anymore and I don't want to date anyone. I like being my own boss although it's scary at times and I do get lonely."

"I don't think I could live alone. I've always got family around. Jess, you're braver than I am. Would you mind if we spent the afternoon cleaning tack?" Carla asked.

"Not at all," said Jess and they spent a pleasant afternoon sitting in the shade, cleaning bridles and saddles, organizing saddle pads and leg wraps, and talking about everything under the sun.

Mateo arrived home from work around six o'clock. Jess sat in the lounge chair with a large glass of sangria, quite content to leave the love birds alone. It had been a good day, except for Neil's surprise appearance. It was perfectly plausible that he was shopping for horses. She really hoped that was the true reason for him being in Argentina. Duffy had almost seemed friendly.

Cousin Felipe was a strange man. She didn't know what to make of him. She understood the grief end of it, but couldn't grasp why he'd stopped painting. As the heat of the day settled on her, her eyelids drooped and she nodded off to sleep.

It was much later when Carla woke her up for supper.

"I don't believe it. I've slept two hours. It must be jet lag," said Jess.

"Mateo's going to fire up the barbecue. On Sunday, we'll have a proper Argentinian barbecue at my parents' place with all the family. Here it's called an *asado* and it's an absolute art form. It's not just a matter of turning on the gas barbecue and grilling a steak. You'll see how it's done. The cuts of beef are not the same as you're used to either and we eat our beef well done."

"I like mine *bien hecho* (well done) too," Jess replied, doing a quick rewind on her Spanish homework. "I'm understanding a little bit of what people are saying, but most of the time they're speaking too quickly."

"Keep trying; the more you use it, the easier it gets," said Carla. "Sunday, you'll meet Uncle Sebastian, that's *Tio* Sebastian; he's the dance instructor. We'll get you set up for lessons. I'm working Monday to Wednesday. I might get a ride into the city with Mateo on Thursday, then you and I can go shopping. You said you needed a dress or two. That way we can have lunch together and I can come home with him when he gets off work," Carla said.

"Sounds good to me," said Jess.

Supper was excellent. The steak was thick, juicy, and dripping with flavor. Mateo told her all about the red wine they were drinking. "We're lucky to have excellent growing conditions for grapes. Most of what's grown is consumed in Argentina; not much is exported." He proceeded to explain about the Argentinian economy, which was now diversifying, instead of relying on the traditional beef exports.

"I hadn't realized the Thoroughbred industry was so big here," Jess said.

"Historically most of the breeding stock came from Europe, but more horses now are being bought and sold with the US as you probably know," he said. "We've got a few more race tracks in the city. It's very popular, although not as much as football."

It was after midnight when they finally went to bed. Saturday was going to be a busy day with polo practice.

*   *   *

JESS HEARD THEIR ALARM CLOCK GO OFF AT SIX O'CLOCK AND within the hour, they had three horses loaded onto the trailer plus all their gear. Carla had packed a picnic lunch, stowing the hamper in the truck bed. Minutes later they were hauling the trailer southbound on the busy highway to Buenos Aires.

The city amazed her. The highway system was complicated with multiple lanes converging and exiting like a tangle of snakes. The thought of thirteen-million people in comparison to Lexington's four-hundred-thousand was hard to grasp. There were skyscrapers fifty stories high, glass and steel office blocks, factories, subdivisions, and malls. Many historical churches were grand stucco or stone edifices with lovely arched wooden doors, red tile roofs and bell towers like she'd seen in old Westerns. The poorer parts were also very evident with two or three-story concrete slums, looking crowded and shabby.

"It's about sixty miles across," said Carla, pointing out different areas of the city as they passed. Traffic was building by the time they arrived at the polo field. Gaps between buildings showed the southern Atlantic, some of the port structures, with enormous cranes against a backdrop of cargo and cruise ships dotting the harbor, all the way to the eastern horizon. Jess was mesmerized.

The polo field was huge, bigger than two football fields with the open goal posts at either end. There were twenty to thirty trailers, many horses, and a large group of riders already mounted. Jess and Carla unloaded the horses and equipment while Mateo changed into his polo gear. Jess brushed the horses down while Carla wrapped their tails and legs. Quickly, he was out on the field cantering his horse in a warm-up session, swinging his mallet.

"He sure looks good on a horse, doesn't he," said Jess, eyeing his slim, lithe figure and laughed at Carla's exaggerated leer. They stood in the shade of the shed watching the skirmishes. Jess was fixated on the footwork. The riders reined left-handed, the mallets in their right. The horses, mostly mares, were agile and tough, jostling each other shoulder-to-shoulder, ears flattened, at a full gallop or instantly changing direction on cue to possessively pivot over the ball so that no one else could claim it. The riders were cueing their mounts with weight shifts and leg aids. She was amazed no one got hurt. It definitely wasn't a sport for the faint of heart.

Meanwhile, the riders were skilled enough to lean over, swing the mallet, sometimes leaning right under the horse's neck to strike the ball at impossible angles. With every goal, the teams changed ends and continued. The only comparison Jess could think of was a strategic game of chess at thirty miles an hour—soccer on horseback.

Mateo and the other riders took turns on the field. Carla had the second horse ready and continued to give Jess a running commentary on what was going on, who had the right of way, plus pointed out a couple of horses that were clones. Jess looked at them carefully. They were the same color and general shape, but their markings were not identical. That fascinated her and she made a mental note to look it up online. She was pretty sure that cloning of Thoroughbreds was illegal in the US, at least as far as Thoroughbred racing was concerned.

"Mateo's hoping that he'll get good enough to make the national team," said Carla. "I don't know if his job will allow him to have the time off and the cost of the horses and transport is prohibitive. The polo season is usually from mid-February to May, then September to December. It'll be standing room only then. Argentina really does well, and several of our very best players are on international teams.

Today is the last chance for him to practice before the series starts."

By lunch time, all three horses had been ridden hard. Jess and Carla brushed them down after Mateo was finished with them. Carla watered them, then both women sat in the truck and ate their lunches while Mateo was off talking to other riders. There were probably several hundred spectators watching the workouts. The heat and humidity were increasing, so Jess stayed in the shade, her pale skin starting to turn pink.

"You can imagine what this field is like during a game. There will be thousands of people here," said Carla while Jess took photos. "Some of the games are played at night when it's cooler."

By one o'clock it was too hot to play, so they all packed up, reloaded the horses, and headed home. Outbound traffic was relatively light so Mateo made good time. When they arrived home, the horses were released in the paddock and Jess helped put the equipment into the storage room.

She had a quick shower and changed into shorts, to be greeted by Mateo bearing a tray with three large glasses of dark red wine. They all settled onto lounge chairs in the shade of the porch, toasted the wine of Argentina, and discussed the day.

Later, Jess started to read her guide book, trying to decide which venues to see in the city during the next few weeks. A lot would depend on her dance schedule. She felt herself start to relax, probably for the first time in weeks if not months. She was on holiday and was determined to enjoy it. No more tension over Andy, lawyers, the new job, the apartment, and the lingering mystery of her father's death. She felt the tension ebb away and sank back into the cushions, away from her need to keep busy, so she didn't feel the loneliness, the insecurities, and the dark place.

*   *   *

SUNDAY MORNING, JESS AWOKE AND PUT ON HER ONLY dress, a simple light cotton one she'd had for years and a pair of heeled sandals. She was a little nervous about meeting Carla's family as her Spanish was still very limited.

"Jess, there's nothing to worry about. My parents entertain a lot and are quite comfortable with Americans. My father, Emilio, owns the Mercedes dealership and meets foreign nationals all the time. Mum's name is Olivia. They live in a high-rise building in the Palermo district. It's quite lovely and they have a view of the river and the ocean. I don't know if Felipe will be there today. He has his own studio and upstairs apartment in San Telmo. San Telmo's closer to the waterfront and a little bit south," Carla said as both of them searched the city map for the location.

"I warn you now that there will be at least thirty of us for the asado tonight, possibly more. Everyone has big families here. They often bring their friends too. I have three brothers, Enzo, Gabriel, and Lorenze, and one sister, Luisa."

"So, the game plan is to meet your parents at the church, then afterwards take me to the Airbnb to drop off my luggage before going back to their place for the asado?"

"I'm not sure how it will work out. If we get into the city by eleven, we'll be able to meet them at the church.

After that we'll play it by ear and see what happens. Remind me to give you our phone numbers. Did you bring your cellphone?"

"No, I didn't. Should I buy a cheap one?"

"That would be a waste. I think Mateo has a spare one. I'll look around. Then we'd just need a new SIM card. Take mine for now. I've already checked the water tank for the horses, so I don't have any other chores this morning."

"There's certainly less maintenance for the horses with your climate. They can graze to their heart's content and not be cooped up in a stall," said Jess, looking over the landscape and thinking of less manure to shovel, no need to order shavings, minimal disposal issues—just pasture rotation.

"Well, it allows me to get our horses done quickly, then head off to my job. I do enjoy having my own car and money and not having to ask Mateo for an allowance."

"Your apprenticeship qualifications must come in handy."

"They sure do. For one thing, the Fitzgerald stable has an excellent reputation and having them as a reference allows me to access people here, who would normally be out of my reach. Sometimes I get to know people because they buy a car from my father. Being qualified helps me get past some of the traditional female role bias too. Contacts like that might be helpful for Mateo. Who knows? My boss is going on a two-week holiday soon and when he is away, I will be in charge of the stable. That's huge! I don't know any other woman who does that. Because I'm bilingual, they sometimes call me if they need an interpreter," said Carla.

"So, the trick for you then is to expand your role, in keeping with your Catholic religion and your Argentinian male-dominated culture," Jess said.

Carla nodded. "My mother thinks I'm a rebel. If she had her way, I'd be pregnant and not working. Things are different these days from how she was raised. I like the freedom to drive, buy what I want and I really enjoy the horses, just like you do. Mateo wants to be a professional polo player, but he can't do that on his bank salary alone. He wants to have children too, but not right away."

They were on the road by ten and met Carla's parents at the cathedral. Jess guessed Emilio and Olivia were in their late sixties or early seventies. They were immaculately dressed. Emilio wore a fine lightweight silk suit and Olivia was in a subtle, classic dress—a classy couple with good taste—no flaunting the wealth like Ryan. They had the look of affluence about them without the bling and attitude. Both had darker complexions, their black hair streaked with gray and were short and compact. Carla made the introductions. Jess shook hands with Emilio and thanked them both for the invitation to Buenos Aires.

Olivia took her by the hands, looking up at her from her five-foot frame, with a wise, loving face and intelligent dark brown eyes. "You are more than welcome. We want to thank you for being Carla's friend when she was apprenticing. I was so worried about her being on her own in a foreign country. She's a very determined young woman and seems quite prepared to take risks that seem unthinkable to me. You took good care of her and we are grateful. Now I've got her back home, she's a wife and hopefully will be a mother soon. Good things, good things," she said, patting Jess's hands.

They were standing on the steps of the church as the other people started to go inside.

"Carla, you know I'm not Catholic," said Jess. "Is there anything I need to do other that sit and be quiet?"

"No, you'll be fine. Visitors are welcome. Sit beside me."

Jess followed them in as they made their way down the main aisle towards the altar. The church was large and lavish with marble and mosaic floors, classical oil paintings, and multiple statues of Mary, Christ, and the saints. One statue of Mary showed the classic vivid blue dress, trimmed in gold while another was in a bronzed gold. A subtle fragrance of incense lingered on the air. People were seated in the front pews and, from the strong resemblance, she guessed these must be Carla's brothers and sister with their children. This was confirmed when Emilio and Olivia joined them.

She gazed at the columns which drew her eyes to the vaulted ceilings. The dome at the far end had a stained-glass window allowing the sunlight to illuminate the altar area. The building was old but well cared for. All the wooden surfaces showed the high patina from centuries of polishing. She could hear the quiet shuffling as people settled in their pews behind them. The next hour was filled with prayers, the sermon, communion, and hymns, all in Spanish. The language had a lovely cadence to it, even if she didn't understand it. She thought about the history and the ritual which must be the same the world over, regardless of the language and she was quite content to feel the blanket of calm about her.

When the service was over, they walked out of the building into the sunshine. Mateo pointed out the high rise where Emilio and Olivia lived, then made a ninety-degree turn and pointed to another building, perhaps six blocks away. "That's where you'll be staying," he said. It took less than ten minutes to negotiate the busy streets and enter the parking lot. Jess counted twenty-five floors. All the units had balconies and she could see a fenced pool.

"I think you're going to like this," Carla said as they parked the truck. Mateo pressed the button beside the name Ortiz and a woman's voice answered and buzzed them in.

"This is a lovely building," Jess said, admiring the glass and marble foyer. If she had marveled at the Wainright elevator, this far exceeded it. Mateo pushed the button for the fourteenth floor and they zoomed quietly upward. The doors opened to a wide hallway painted in a cream tone with light blue carpet; the door to 1418 was open with a young woman waiting to greet them.

Mateo and Carla entered first, with Jess tagging along behind. There was a rapid exchange of Spanish. A man welcomed them in. Jess estimated the couple were in their late twenties.

"Welcome to Buenos Aires, Jessica. My name is Leonardo and this is my wife, Emilia," he said.

"*Meucho gusto* (pleased to meet you)," replied Jess, figuring this was as good a time as any to try out her Spanish. "My Spanish isn't very good yet. I'm so pleased you can speak English. That makes it much easier."

They were shown around the apartment which Jess considered high end. It was spacious, modern, and spotlessly clean. There were three bedrooms, a kitchen, dining room, and bathroom. Off the main living area were glass doors leading to the balcony, which blossomed with potted plants. Jess's room had a double bed and lots of space. She rolled her suitcase beside the closet. A set of color-coordinated towels were on the dresser for her. "I have my computer with me.

Do you have Wi-FI here, so I can connect to your service?" She had noticed a computer in their second bedroom.

"We can do that later this evening when you get back from your asado," Emilia said, giving her the key to the apartment.

Jess noted that Emilia had a much slower pace of speaking English, with a strong Spanish overtone and hesitated with the words. Still, Emilia's English was better than her Spanish.

"I know you from somewhere," Leonardo said to Mateo as they were standing there talking.

"I play polo and sometimes that's televised."

"No, it was an article in *Ole* a while back," Leonardo said and the two men fell back into rapid-fire Spanish.

Emilia took her onto the balcony. The fourteenth floor gave them a good view of most of the old city but it seemed so high, Jess was leery of looking down. From that vantage point, she could see the private swimming pool at ground level.

"We've got a private gymnasium as well with exercise machines," said Emelia.

"I'm going to Santoses' asado this evening. Is there a particular time you would prefer I come back?"

"No, Jess. We stay up late on the weekends so it doesn't matter. Here, "ll write down our telephone number in case you need to call us."

Jess put it in her purse, thanked Emilia, and followed the Santoses back down to the truck. "They seem like really nice people. I think this will work out great. How'd you find them?"

"They were on the Airbnb website. My parents know them too, so that helped. At least I knew they were reliable," said Carla.

It was a short drive to the other apartment complex. Jess watched the streets, trying to remember the names. Mateo slowed the truck down, as Carla pointed out the dance studio where Jess would have her first tango lesson the next morning. Jess fixed the location in her mind, looking upward at the towering office block beside it. That was her landmark. She also saw one of the tourist offices. Banks seemed to be everywhere.

"Does it matter which bank I use?" she asked.

"No, any one will do, but not all of them have English-speaking tellers. You should be able to access the banks, with your credit card, either with a teller or the ATM's. The banks near the big hotels certainly have bilingual staff," Mateo replied.

He had trouble finding a parking space for the truck, so dropped them off at the front door.

"We may as well go up," said Carla. "It may take him a while. Most families get together on Sundays."

Once again, Jess found the opulence overwhelming. There were towering glass doors and windows, plants, a small marble fountain with a gilded statue and paintings of gauchos adorning the lobby. Carla opened the door with her key and they took the elevator to the penthouse floor.

"One really nice thing about this apartment is the roof garden, so we can have our asado right there and don't have to go out for supper."

"Do all of your family come every Sunday?" Jess queried.

"Not all of them every Sunday, but we try to get together as often as we can. Sometimes there could be seventy of us. Tio Sebastian is the dance instructor and he's preparing Enzo's two children, Diego and Julia, for professional dancing. They always do a dance demonstration."

"That sounds great. What an interesting family."

"With you being on your own and nobody close, you must find it strange to have so much family activity," Carla said.

"I like my privacy for sure and quiet time, but I guess it works both ways. You must have found it difficult to be alone when you were in Kentucky," said Jess.

"That's true. You and Mrs. H. were a big help there."

Getting off the elevator, she found the hall bright, wide, and silent. There were only two doors. Carla headed for the left one; Jess behind her. The door was unlocked and Carla just walked in. The first impression was of light and space— high ceilings, soft white walls and bright vivid colors in the draperies and cushions. Olivia was in the kitchen putting the finishing touches to trays of sliced fruit and cheeses. Queen of her kitchen. The sound of voices and laughter filtered in from the shaded patio through the open doors. Probably twenty people were already there.

"Oh, Carla, this is beautiful," she said, looking at the pergola, covered in a canopy of luxuriant vines with large fragrant pink and yellow flowers, shading the deck from the still scorching sun. Beyond the pergola, there was the broad vista of the Rio de la Plata and the ocean, in gorgeous shades of turquoise, greens, and blues, tipped with flickering sun-tinted gold. Benches and wooden chairs lined the perimeter of a large wooden dance floor that looked more than forty feet long.

"There's the barbecue set up. The grill is called a *parrilla,*" said Carla pointing to a huge metal grating on an adjustable frame, over an eight-foot-long brick fire pit loaded with wood and charcoal. A rake and a shovel stood nearby, propped against a pillar beside the outside water tap. A chef was preparing trays of meat: steaks, sausages, and other cuts. Jess was amazed at the amount of meat. It looked like half a cow.

Mateo came in a few minutes later, giving his mother-in-law a kiss on the cheek then sought out Emilio. Jess watched the family interactions with interest. There was a constant circulation of people familiar with each other. What particularly struck her was that all the women were wearing dresses. Back home most of the girls, particularly the teenagers, would have been in jeans.

"I hope you don't expect me to remember everybody's name," said Jess, looking at the crowd varying from tots to teens, right up to one very elderly lady who was holding court across the room.

"That's my grandmother, Mum's mother. She's over ninety. I'm not sure anyone really knows how old she is; she won't tell. She had four children, Emilio, Tomas—Felip''s father, Sebastian, and Sofia. Tio Tomas passed away about ten years ago, so Felipe only has his mother and brothers now."

"Do all of your family live in the city?" Jess asked.

"Oh yes, but in different sections, like distinct small towns within the bigger city. Over in the corner, those two children are Diego and Julia. They're Enzo's children; they're eleven and thirteen. You'll see them at the dance studio. They've won championships already in the junior division dance competitions," said Carla.

Jess looked at Diego. He was younger and shorter than his sister, but had the look of a professional dancer with the slicked down hair, a white shirt with full sleeves, tight-fitting black trousers, vest, and shoes. He moved like a cat, light and graceful with the formal straight-backed posture.

Julia had her black hair in a tight bun. She had a lean, immature body molded into her tango dress. The girl's haughty look and imperial stance made Jess smile. She had never been able to maintain that attitude without breaking into laughter when Jim had told her to do it. Obviously, if she was going to learn tango, she'd have to find a way to hold the persona.

Carla made the rounds, greeting family members and introducing Jess who somehow found the courage to start trying out her basic Spanish. Thankfully, most of the people spoke some English. They all had a good laugh over some of her mistakes. She met Felipe's mother, Maria, a gentle and shy lady and wondered what his father had been like, or if his brothers had the same personality he had.

Jess finally met Tio Sebastian. He questioned her about her dance experience and who her instructor was. He'd never heard of Jim Barry. "Come to the studio at nine-thirty, then we'll make a schedule for you. My son Antonio will be your instructor. Do you know where the studio is?"

"Yes, it is only a few blocks from the apartment where I'm staying," she said.

It became apparent that the dance exhibition was going to happen, so everyone sat down and Tio Sebastian sorted through CDs for the music. Jess sat between Carla and Mateo on one side and Emilio and Olivia on the other. All eyes were on Diego and Julia. With the click of Sebastian's remote, the air was filled with the notes of bandoneon accordion and guitar, distinctly Latin. The two youngsters assumed their formal position and began.

Jess was mesmerized. Diego led with the air of an adult drill sergeant, extracting precision from his partner. Julia followed, her foot placement precise, sophisticated, and equally as challenging, with beautiful extensions of her elegant, slender legs. Jess had never seen anything like it and suddenly realized how unrealistic her expectations were. Five months of dance and three weeks of instruction here was not going to get her far. But there again, she couldn't expect to do what it had taken these young people years to accomplish with an expert instructor. It would be better just to improve her skills and enjoy herself.

The dynamic duo danced a few more dances, then Sebastian seemed satisfied. Everyone gave them a huge round of applause, the music changed and conversations resumed. Other couples got up on the dance floor including Emilio and Olivia, as well as Sebastian and his wife Sofia. Jess watched them too. This was not competition style tango but the tango of the people. Everyone was snuggling in close and comfortable but the dance was sensual none-theless, regardless of age. She found it quite touching to see the older couples nestled in each other's arms, head-to-head, never missing a beat.

There was a tap on her shoulder and she looked up to see Felipe. He glanced toward the dance floor, then back at her. She nodded, getting up to join him. Carla had told her that men didn't openly ask a woman to dance but used their eyes. If a woman wasn't interested, she looked away. This was called *cabeceo*—no awkward refusals. He led her to the floor, clasped her in the closed embrace then immediately started to move. She felt a moment of tension, took a deep breath, and let go. They danced several tangos, then a samba. He was easy to follow and kept it simple. She had the impression he hadn't danced for a while.

"*Gracias, el Primo* Felipe (Cousin Felipe). I suppose you were brought up with the dancing too," she said as he escorted her back to her seat.

"Oh yes. Everyone in the family is indoctrinated early. It really wasn't one of my talents. I may be Carla's *el Primo*, Señora, but definitely not yours," he said quietly with a tiny smile that seemed this time to extend to his dark, probing eyes.

"I'll remember that. What day would be convenient for me to visit your studio?" she asked.

He paused for a moment. "I close the store from twelve to four most days, but Wednesday would be good. I just had an idea. I'll get back to you," he said as he turned and walked back to his mother's table. There was another man sitting there, an older version of Felipe. Jess guessed he might be a brother.

The music changed as the adults sat down and the teenagers got up to the pulsing pace of modern Spanish songs and their music idols. Carla had Mateo on the dance floor but it was obvious to Jess that he preferred the polo field.

Jess watched the chef clean the grill with newspaper, then light the charcoal. Once the charcoal burned, he raked the smoldering embers until the entire length of the pit was glowing. He placed thick steaks on the rack and lowered it. Soon there was the sizzle, smoke, and the wonderful aroma of cooking meat. Olivia was supervising several of her young nephews who were filling wine glasses at each table. Jess was mind-boggled by the amount of organization required to feed the clan. The thought of doing it weekly seemed daunting.

She watched the chef turn the meat only once then shift smaller cuts to the right side of the grill as they were cooked. He then added links of sausage, racks of ribs, and some unrecognizable parts Jess could only guess at. Drops of fat fell on the coals and sizzled.

Mateo turned to Jess. "How do you like your steak, Jess?"

"*Bien hecho,*" she replied with a smile.

He joined the lineup at the grill, returning shortly juggling three plates, each with a large steak. Fresh bread and bowls of salads supplemented the meal. They sat and ate. The big patio went relatively quiet with everyone eating rather than talking.

"As soon as we finish eating, we'll head home. We'll drop you off at the apartment. It's a work day tomorrow," Carla said.

Jess couldn't finish the steak. It was simply too big but it was delicious and full of flavor. Grass fed probably. They started to say their goodbyes when Felipe walked over to them, accompanied by Diego.

"Diego and Julia are at the dance studio every day, now they 're on their summer holidays. So, on Wednesday when they are finished their class, Diego will bring you to my studio and show you how to find your way around the city," Felipe said.

Jess introduced herself to the boy and thanked him for helping her out. "I look forward to seeing you both on Wednesday then," she said with a big smile. Diego smiled and nodded, looking back to Felipe who had a tiny trace of a smile and a twinkle in his eye. She made sure to thank Olivia for the lovely meal. The lady was gracious.

It had been a great day. It pleased her to see Felipe in a lighter mood that took away the brooding look, transforming him into a much more attractive man. That in itself was a bit disturbing. He looked the flamboyant artist, with the ruffled wild hair. His eyes were something else—alarmingly seductive.

After Carla and Mateo dropped her off, she let herself into the building and took the elevator to the fourteenth floor. Glancing at her watch, she saw it was ten o'clock, so she let herself in quietly, not sure if Leonardo and Emilia would be up but there they were sitting on the sofa, eating their supper and watching TV.

They briefly chatted about their day, but Jess was tired and excused herself. She had a quick shower, set her travel alarm for seven-thirty, and snuggled into bed. She was asleep as soon as her head hit the pillow.

Chapter 18

JESS AWOKE WITH THE ALARM, THANKFUL SHE'D HAD A GOOD solid sleep. She plotted the dance studio and the tourist office on her map, memorizing the streets and tucked it in her bag along with her capris and high heels. From the noises in the kitchen, Leonardo and Emilia were already up. She wasn't sure if they both worked. Peering through her door, the bathroom was clear, so she quickly washed and cleaned her teeth. She braided her hair. From looking around yesterday, she'd noticed that many of the younger women had their hair cut short and looked really smart. It occurred to her for the first time ever, that maybe she should cut her hair. She'd talk with Carla on Thursday about that. She put on her black bodysuit, the covering blue skirt and sandals, then went out to the kitchen.

"Good morning, Jess. Have a seat. Did you sleep well?" asked Emilia.

"Yes, the bed's very comfortable."

"What's on your agenda for today?" Leonardo said.

"I'm going to the Ramirez dance studio for my tango lesson. I want to dance every weekday morning, then I'm going to the tourist office for some city tours. I've got a whole list of places I want to see."

"Sounds like you've got it all figured out. Don't forget the pool downstairs."

"I'll probably use that in the afternoons when it's too hot to do much. I'd like to find a place nearby where I can get lunch and supper. Is there one you'd recommend?" said Jess.

"There's a nice little restaurant called "The Gaucho" two blocks south of here. They're open from ten in the morning until two a.m.," Emilia said while she prepared fruit and toast plus coffee for breakfast, which suited Jess just fine.

Breakfast finished, Jess stacked her dishes in the dishwasher. At eight o'clock, the couple left for work. Jess exited the building half-an-hour later, making sure she locked the apartment door and put the keys in the inside pocket of her tote bag. The traffic was bumper-to-bumper; it was noisy, the air full of fumes, and the sidewalks crammed with people in suits and dresses. *This is a very sophisticated population*, she thought. Jess followed the streets, keeping her eye on the landmark office tower. It took her twenty-five minutes to reach the studio at a steady brisk pace. That worked out well.

She took a seat in the foyer and waited, listening to the music in one of the rooms down the hall while she changed into her high heels. Near nine-fifteen she heard footsteps down the hall. It was Tio Sebastian. He greeted her with a warm smile.

"I see you found us. Come this way," he said, leading her down the hall to a smaller room at the end. A slim, dark-haired young man greeted them. "This is my son, Antonio," Tio Sebastián said. "He'll be your instructor while you are here."

"I want daily lessons for two weeks. How much are they and how do I pay you?" Jess asked.

"Credit card would be fine," he said naming a price. "See me after your class and we can take care of that."

Jess was pleased; the lessons were cheaper than Jim's.

"Antonio," she said, "I'd like you to work me really hard. I have so much to learn and you're the best teacher I can get, so I want to make the most of it."

"Right then," he said. "I'll start with basic steps to find out what you can do, then we'll take it from there. I don't want to limit you solely to tango. The other Latin dances will also give you the opportunity to learn the rhythms and steps. Don't worry, I will work you hard,"

With that he put on the music and they began. Jess found him easy to follow. They danced nonstop so she was blindly following wherever he stepped. There was no set pattern; he led—she followed.

At the hour, they stopped and sat down. "Well, what do you think?" she asked.

"You have a good basic training, but it's time for you to expand your repertoire. I can help you to the next level. Most people start dance at an earlier age. Don't get me wrong; I'm not saying you're old, but the earlier you start the better, as you can see with Diego and Julia. We only have a couple of weeks and a lot of work ahead of us. What will you do with this once you go back home?" he asked.

"That's a good question. I'm not sure. I haven't really thought much beyond getting here and enjoying my holiday."

"How do you keep so fit?" he asked.

"I've worked at Thoroughbred stables most of my life and I still ride on weekends."

"Just like horse-crazy Carla. That makes sense. She told us you worked at another stable when she was in the US," he said, shaking his head.

She went back out to the foyer where a young woman was at the main desk. Tio Sebastian appeared from the studio where she could see Diego and Julia working a routine.

"Ah Jessica. How did it go?" he asked.

"Very well, I think. Antonio promised to work me hard and he did. I have so much to learn. So, nine-thirty every morning for the next two weeks?" she said, pulling out her credit card. The girl punched in the numbers and Jess completed the transaction. She slipped into the washroom and changed into her capris. Next stop, the tourist office.

*   *   *

IT TOOK JESS ABOUT THIRTY MINUTES TO REACH THE TOURIST office. The place was packed mostly with Americans, but she could see other groups as well including some French, Germans, and Italians. There was a large tour bus parked outside. She browsed through the pamphlets, picking out ones on her list and venues for tango exhibitions, several art galleries, and theaters. She joined a lineup for the service desk, whiling away the wait time by scanning the brochures. Finally, it was her turn. She sat down and explained to the young woman what she wanted.

"I want to start with a city tour, preferably a bus tour. Are the tours in English?"

"Most of the tour leaders are bilingual. There's an afternoon minibus tour at one o'clock, and the bus is air conditioned. That would be a good one to start with. Here's the pamphlet for it," the girl said.

"That sounds good. I see the Recoleta Cemetery and the Plaza de Mayo are on that one," she said, buying a ticket for it. Two items to cross off her list. "The other thing I'm interested in seeing is the schedule for the theater, the port, the nature reserve, and horseback riding. Where's the nearest bank?" she asked and was directed to one two blocks away that was open until three o'clock.

"Be careful. Don't be flashing large amounts of money around," the girl advised her. Jess came out with a handful of pamphlets, which she stuffed in her bag and went to the bank. She didn't want to look like a tourist but that was probably obvious from her pale skin and being dressed as she was.

She was just about to go into the bank when she glimpsed a man not forty feet away who really resembled Duffy. She slipped through the door then spun to the right to look through the window. The man continued walking. It was Duffy. Coincidence? Not likely. Was he following her? Had Neil sent him? She used the teller and received brightly colored bills marked with Argentinian pesos. She asked what the exchange rate was.

"One US dollar is forty-nine pesos this week," she was told.

So roughly fifty pesos to the dollar. Tucking the bills in her wallet, she headed back out the door and looked around. Duffy was nowhere in sight.

She made her way back to the tourist office, pausing now and then to look in a store window, taking the opportunity to look at the street in the reflection. No sign of him. She went into a small cafeteria, read the menu and was glad that she at least had a few basic Spanish words. The simple burger and coffee were delicious and really hit the spot. The bill was less than ten dollars. With lunch out of the way she was back at the tourist office by twelve-thirty and waited for her tour to start.

She was one of ten passengers booked for the tour. The guide was an older man who drove the small bus and gave a running commentary of the sights along the way. The first stop was the Recoleta Cemetery (*Cementerio de la Recoleta).*

After parking the bus, he led them past the nunnery and the Basilica of Our Lady of Pillar, "built in 1732" and through the Greek-columned gateway. The vista exploded into a panorama of thousands of above-ground marble and concrete vaults, crammed together. "This cemetery is fourteen acres of land and contains four thousand, six hundred and ninety-one graves, some going back to the early 1800s. Many of them are still in use. Once it was on the outskirts of the city. Now you see it surrounded by high-rises and office blocks. Please feel free to walk around and meet me back at the bus in an hour," he said.

Jess wandered the narrow, paved lanes of magnificent, sculptured marble crypts; some depicting the Virgin Mary, others with portraits of the interred, yet others had angels, or their horse or dog with them, all carved in stone. No two were alike. A few had beautiful wrought-iron railings. Most were less than twenty feet high. The occupants had been presidents, military leaders, scientists, and the well-to-do. She took a lot of photos, including several of Eva Peron's black marble edifice with the cross on the doors, where someone had placed fresh-cut roses. Identifying brass plates on the vaults were polished and still bright. The workmanship of the sculpting was unbelievable.

It was a relief to get back in the air-conditioned bus. The heat was oppressive. Next stop was the Plaza de Mayo. The bus traveled south to the Avenue de Mayo, a wide divided roadway with three lanes in each direction and a boulevard in the middle complete with jacaranda trees.

Parking the bus, their guide explained, "This is the center of the city (*El Centro*). The concrete obelisk you see here between the roads is 221 feet high. It commemorates the four hundredth anniversary of the founding of the city in 1536 by the Spanish. If you are interested, there is a stairway to the top." No one on the bus volunteered for the climb.

Wow—1536! She wasn't interested in walking up the hundreds of stairs either. From the bus she could see the nearby La Casa Rosada, the pink presidential palace, complete with blue-uniformed guards. She couldn't imagine standing at attention in the heat. Many of the buildings were from the colonial period and several needed restoring. Also along that boulevard were the Metropolitan Cathedral, the municipal offices, and the Congress building. Further exploration was warranted, but it would have to be another day.

In the dense traffic, it took over an hour to get back to the tourist office. The driver was good to point out other venues. Jess felt she had quite enough for one day and walked back to the apartment. She changed into her bathing suit, put on her wrap, and headed down to the pool. After a quick swim in the very warm water, she slathered herself in sunscreen and set her watch alarm for thirty minutes, stretching out on the poolside lounge chair. The alarm woke her. She wasn't the least bit surprise, she'd fallen asleep. It had been a busy and active day. She reset the alarm and lay on her belly. She figured she'd get in a swim and some sun every day and avoid getting a burn.

By the time she went back up to the apartment, Leonardo and Emilia were home from work. She changed clothes and opened her computer, sending emails to her mother and Carla. On a whim, she typed into the browser, "Felipe Ramirez, artist."

Wikipedia revealed a photo of a younger, wilder Felipe, looking like a wild-haired 18th-century buccaneer and showed several of his paintings. The colors were flamboyant with broad brush strokes, mostly city scenes—the craggy faces of old street vendors in the market, football players in action, activists marching in the Plaza de Mayo, and beautiful girls sunning themselves near flowering jacaranda trees. It mentioned that he now concentrated on photography.

She spent about an hour looking through her pamphlets and decided she'd visit the Museum of Modern Art in the morning and other arts venues if she had time. Juan Navarro Carrizo, a Spanish guitarist was playing at the Colon Theater the following week. She wanted to hear him.

"What's the best way to get to the museums?" she asked Leonardo and Emilia, when they'd finished their supper.

"You could go by bus. Here, let me show you on the map," said Leonardo, spreading it out on the table. Emilia mentioned the number of the bus and the nearest bus stop. "You can get a bus pass too," she said.

Maybe Diego could help her with that on Wednesday. She'd never been on a bus or a subway train in her life.

It was eight o'clock so Jess walked to The Gaucho and was lucky enough to find a small table at the back where she had a great view of the diners and the street. Spanish music blared from amplifiers behind her. The sidewalks were full of couples out for the evening or tourists like herself. Several locals were just sitting there, people-watching, others were on their laptops or cellphones. She was having difficulty adjusting to eating so late. She ordered a steak and a glass of deep red Malbec and sat there sipping, quite aware of being watched by a number of men in the room. It seemed to be a national past time. She definitely needed to buy new clothes, as everyone dressed so well.

When she left, she headed back to the apartment at a quick walk. No one followed her as far as she could tell. She turned into the driveway of the building when a blue Kia with a blond driver pulled out of a parking spot across the street and disappeared into traffic. She had her key out and bolted into the main foyer. There was no doubt in her mind now; Duffy was tailing her. Why?

She spent a restless night, trying to decide what to do about Duffy and there wasn't a simple answer. Hiding in the apartment and not going out defeated the whole purpose of the trip. Maybe she should just confront him if she ran into him again. Perhaps it was better he was visible. He wasn't making much effort to hide from her and with his training he could become invisible if he wanted to. His light skin and blond brush cut certainly made him stand out in the Latino crowd.

When she checked her email, Carla had responded.

Hi, Jess:

I'm looking forward to seeing you Thursday morning. Will come into town with Mateo and meet you at the dance studio. Do you really want to get your hair cut? I'll take you to the salon where I get my hair done. Was talking to Mum and she is expecting you to attend the Sunday asados but I think you can skip coming to church if you want to. If you get to their place around two o'clock that should be fine. The horses are doing well. We have a game booked Saturday evening if you're interested. Wish I could spend more time with you but it's so busy. Love Carla

Jess promptly replied:

Hi, Carla:

I'm doing fine. Leonard and Emelia are very good. It's great they speak English. That sounds good to me for Sunday. I'll have to let you know about Saturday. There's so much to see here. I haven't figured out yet what I want to do. Went to the Recoleta Cemetery today and did a tour of the city center. Today I'm going to several art galleries including the Museum of Modern Art. It's great to have the pool here. Do you know of an estancia where I can ride either an Andalusian, a Pasa Fino or even a Creolo? Antonio's working me hard, which is good. I think you'll see a difference in my dancing. See you. Jess

Chapter 19

TUESDAY MORNING BEGAN WITH THE USUAL ROUTINE, UP early, breakfast then to the studio. After a quick warm up, Antonio showed her how to do the caresses and adjust her balance so that she could rub her leg up and down his. That wasn't easy in heels.

"I never wear heels at home, so I'm still a bit clumsy. Now when do I do the caress? Do you cue me or do I just do it when I want to?"

"For now, wait until I cue you, but when you are comfortable and trust me, you can initiate it yourself," he replied. "I'll feel your cue."

They spent about half an hour on the tango, then he switched the music to cha-cha and samba where she got to shimmy and sashay her hips. That had her giggling, much to his amusement.

"You enjoy this, don't you?"

"Antonio, I love the music and the rhythms. When I dance, it makes me feel good. I'll never win a dance competition, but for me that's not why I dance. It puts me in a completely different head space, just like riding a good horse." It didn't hurt to dance with a nice-looking guy and feel like a woman either.

"Knowing how you feel about horses, I will take that as a compliment. There's no shame taking second place to a stallion," Antonio said with a laugh.

They both giggled.

"Would it be possible for me to watch Diego and Julia having their lesson?"

"I'll check with my father first," he said, slipping into the next room. Less than a minute later he stuck his head out the door. "Come in."

She sat on a chair against the wall and watched.

Sebastian was strict and exacting with them. He allowed no errors; every step, every nuance had to be perfect. Jess wondered if the two children had ever had a normal childhood, like playing with their friends or watching TV. Her exposure to children had been minimal, mainly with Marty's kids before they moved west. When the lesson was over, Sebastian left the room.

Jess walked over to them. "You dance beautifully. How long has he been teaching you?"

Julia looked at her. "I began dancing when I was four but it wasn't until I was six that Diego joined me. Then Tio Sebastian started to train us." The child had the proud and slightly arrogant countenance, emulating adult dancers.

"Your foot placement is exquisite. May I watch your lessons? I think I could learn a lot from seeing what you do." Seven years of lessons with Sebastian. No wonder they were good.

"Certainly," said Diego with a hint of mischief in his eyes.

Jess thanked them then went to the change room for a shower. She rinsed out her body suit and left it hanging in the locker to dry.

"Where are you off to now?" Antonio asked as she was leaving.

"I'm heading to the Museum of Modern Art and a couple of other galleries. That should be an adventure. Enjoy your day," she said and walked out into the sunshine. A quick scan didn't find any signs of Duffy. Jess thought about taking the bus, then chickened out. She would leave that until tomorrow when she had Diego with her. She flagged down a taxi giving the driver the slip of paper with the name and address of the museum.

It took about forty minutes of bumper-to-bumper traffic to reach the museum. The taxi fare was more expensive than the bus would have been, but it was less hassle and she still got to see the city. Jess wandered around from room to room looking at the different styles. She realized she'd never taken an interest in art at home so she now took the time to browse. Most of the artists were contemporary, from Argentina or Brazil. Some paintings were totally abstract, just blotches of color or simple designs of shapes. That style really didn't appeal to her. She checked the artists' names on the signs just in case any of them were Felipe's work but couldn't find any. She definitely had a preference for tradi-tional art rather than modern.

The next gallery was in a mall close enough to walk to. It didn't seem to matter what time of the day it was, the streets were full of people. She saw a couple of paintings she liked. They were seascapes with beaches and sailboats. Another painting that took her fancy was a bright blue and yellow macaw on a background of leaves and branches, so real you could almost feel the feathers. The six-hundred-dollar (US) price tag nixed the idea of buying that one, but it was beautifully done.

There was one more gallery to see, before she stopped for lunch. It was in an old colonial house and was dedicated to artists from Buenos Aires. It was cooler inside, to her relief. There were many small rooms with gorgeous old woodwork on doorways, window frames, and baseboards. Jess peeked in one room and there on the wall was Felipe's painting of the street vendors that she had seen online. She double checked the brass plate and the signature on the painting which read a very flamboyant "Felipe Ramirez" in the bottom right corner; no price was given.

The background had been done with a bold yellow sunshine against stone walls, striped canvas stalls with fruit, textiles, and other goods but it was the faces that drew her. The eyes and expressions on the men's faces seemed to come alive. It was like meeting them in person. They looked like real characters—a deeply lined face with hooded eyes peering out under the brim of an old fedora, a face with a sly look, a cigarette dangling from the lips, soiled hands with dirt under the nails—men of the streets. Felipe had a real gift. The last time she'd done any art was probably in grade school, with crayons.

Jess left the gallery and found a small restaurant. She looked at the other diners to see what they were eating and was tempted by an egg dish that was being consumed at a neighboring table. She scanned the menu looking for "*huevos*" and found Huevos Benedict.

The waiter took her order. "Eggs Benedict with roasted potatoes, mixed greens, and toast with your choice of beverage. Dessert is extra," he said in perfect English, apparently picking up her rudimentary accent. Sitting there sipping her coffee, she looked at the street and saw a Japanese restaurant, a French restaurant, and several other small cafes. She glanced at the menu and saw no lack of options and prices were amazingly reasonable. The supper menus were considerably more expensive. It might be better to have a hefty lunch and a light supper. Eating a pound of beef at nine o'clock at night threw her right off. She didn't even have time to digest it before going to bed.

It was an excellent lunch and she left a good tip. Flagging down a taxi, she headed back to the apartment. It was time for a swim and a siesta. When she went down to the pool, she met two other girls who were in another Airbnb in the building. They were British and in their early twenties.

Jess did her laps and felt quite modest in her one-piece suit. The buxom Brits fully filled their skimpy bikinis, their skin even paler than hers. She had to stop comparing herself to them. She stretched out on the lounge chair and soaked up the rays, cooking evenly on both front and back for an hour before slathering on the sunscreen.

"We're going out on Friday night to the tango clubs. Do you want to come with us?" the girl named Sandee asked, flicking water from her hair.

"I'd love to," said Jess. "It's risky to go out alone in a city like this. Tourists are targeted. I'm in 1418. Where are you?"

"We're in 802. Why don't we meet in the lobby say nine o'clock Friday evening and we can share a cab?" said Ann, the taller of the two.

"That sounds great. Should be a lot of fun. I'm taking tango lessons every morning, so I would like to see the pros," she said. Maybe if she was with other people Duffy would leave her alone.

*   *   *

WEDNESDAY STARTED OFF WITH THE SAME ROUTINE AS usual. After her lesson with Antonio, she watched Diego and Julia's lesson. When they were finished, Julia went home but Diego stayed behind and Sebastian went to teach another lesson. Diego walked up to her.

"I'd like to dance with you, if you permit it," he said in a very formal voice.

"I would like to but would it be okay with your uncle?" she asked. "I wouldn't want to spoil your performance."

He acted like a miniature version of his uncle. "I'm sure he wouldn't object," he said. Walking over to the CDs, he selected one and turned the volume down.

Jess took off her shoes to reduce the five-inch height difference. Tango music filled the room. He stood for a moment, positioned himself appropriately, head up, spine straight, with that aloof and arrogant expression and held her in the starting posture. For the next fifteen minutes, she forgot he was eleven. He was very light on his feet, but he led well, fully extending his steps to match the strides of her long legs. He was smart enough to keep the steps simple. but just like Antonio, he didn't allow errors, repeating a sequence if she got the footwork wrong.

After four dances, he walked her back to her chair. "I thank you Señora. You have improved a lot even in three days. I've been watching you. I'd like to continue dancing with you while you are here. It gives me a chance to dance with someone other than my sister."

"Okay," Jess said, looking at her watch. "I think it's time we go to San Telmo. Will we be going by bus or train?" she asked.

"Bus is easier," he said.

"I'd like you to help me with the tickets and the money. I took a taxi yesterday because I wasn't sure of myself. My Spanish isn't good enough yet."

"No problem," Diego said with a grin that showed glimpses of the eleven-year-old. He changed into his sneakers.

It was like having her own personal tour guide. He explained everything. They walked to the bus stop and joined the lineup. When they got on, he told the bus driver where they wanted off and gave the correct change. They were fortunate to find a seat and like a professional teacher, he explained to her what to say in Spanish, enunciating slowly, getting her to repeat it, then explained the money, making her count it out, again in Spanish.

"A bus pass would be practical for you, so you don't have to have the correct change all the time," he said.

"That sounds like a good idea. This is my first time on a public bus. I've never been on a subway train either."

"Never? How do you get around?"

"I live in a small city back home, less than four-hundred-thousand people. There are buses but I work out in the countryside, so I have a car. It's not a fancy car like Tio Emilio's, but I drive everywhere myself. There is no subway in Lexington."

"You drive a car." He paused as if considering that a novelty. "Perhaps we should take the train home this afternoon, so you can have a ride and see what it's like," he said.

"Sounds like a good idea. I've driven since I was sixteen years old," Jess said with a smile. For a boy so young, he was good company. The bus passed through the Plaza de Mayo and continued south to the San Telmo area.

"This is the old colonial part of the city." Diego pointed out the streets of narrow shops with apartments above. "The waterfront is to the east and there is a large nature reserve with footpaths; it was originally swamp."

Ten minutes later they got off the bus and walked down a busy side street. This was obviously a tourist area, with tiny shops selling arts, crafts, specialty wines, and clothes. The one with the bright yellow facade said "Estudio Fotografico," displaying framed photos of Buenos Aires. The closed sign was on the door. Diego knocked.

Felipe only took a few moments to open the door and welcome them in. He looked cool and casual in a long-sleeved shirt and pressed slacks. The walls were covered with hundreds of photos, both color and black and white. He locked the door behind them.

"I'm closed from twelve to four, then re-open from four o'clock to eight. That's the best time to catch the tourists. Have a look around, then I'll show you my work shop."

Some of the photos were amazing. She particularly liked a set of six black and white shots taken in the harbor where huge cranes were unloading cargo ships. The gray shadows and the angles created interesting shapes. Some of the color ones were night shots of the downtown streets with streams of neon, the lights of moving cars, theaters, shops and cafes, and the human figures shadowy and blurred. Another spectacular picture was from the rooftop of a glass-walled high-rise office tower. The shot angled down over the street, showing an overhead view of the streets and a panorama of the business district. Felipe must have been hanging over the roof edge like Spiderman to get that shot. Jess was totally engrossed in looking at the pictures hearing only a low-level discussion in the background and was completely unprepared when there was a loud crash followed by Felipe shouting and screaming.

She sprinted into the studio to find a horrified Diego sprawled flat on a paint-splotched floor with paintings strewn about him. The open can of yellow paint was still rolling. Felipe's face was unrecognizable—it was a purple mask of rage. He was bent over the fallen child, shaking his fists, and bellowing in Spanish.

Jess pushed her way between them and braced herself. A venomous cloud of invective gushed over her like a pyroclastic flow from an erupting volcano but she stood her ground not saying a word, her eyes firmly fixed on his. Felipe was so intense, she felt he was seeing right through her and so close, mere inches away, that pellets of spit hit her face as he yelled. Diego was getting to his feet behind her. Slowly the storm abated and Felipe finally stopped and stood there, his chest heaving, fists opening and closing.

"Are you finished?" she asked.

For a moment, she thought he was going to hit her, but he didn't. She turned to Diego. The polished pre-teen had vanished. Instead, there was a terrified boy looking totally lost, struggling not to cry. She immediately saw the cause of the problem. An extension cord crossed the room and

Diego must have tripped over it, knocking the pictures and the can of paint from the desk.

"Diego," she said as calmly as she could muster, "Would you please go to the other room and sit on the chair. Wait for me. I want to talk to Tio Felipe."

Diego stood, still looking very uncertain, avoiding any eye contact with his uncle. He nodded so she gently grasped him by the shoulders and steered him past Felipe into the other room. "Is there a washroom where you can clean up?" she whispered, looking at the yellow paint smeared over his leg.

"Si, Señora," the child said and fled down the hall.

Jess slowly walked back into the studio. Felipe hadn't moved. He was standing, contemplating the destruction. The sheet which had covered the pictures, had been pulled off with the fall, revealing the canvasses. She started to pick up the paintings and stack them on the desk. Several were torn. Most were small eight by tens. Looking at them she was startled to see they were self-portraits done in grays and blacks, depicting a man squatting on the floor of a deep dark cave. He had his head buried in his hands, the epitome of despair. All of the paintings were the same image, painting after painting. He had created a dark gray world with no sun, no light, and no way out. They were so different from his picture at the museum. He'd very vividly captured the dark hole, that place she'd occasionally fallen into herself, in her grief over Andy.

"You haven't left yourself any way out," she said aloud, holding the painting and looking directly at him. He was standing there, his head bowed. She didn't even know if he heard her. Jess put the picture on the desk and went back into the store.

Diego was sitting on the chair staring at the floor. She didn't have a clue how to handle kids. He looks devastated. She sat beside him, put her arm around his shoulders, wondering what to do next.

"Are you okay? I know you didn't mean to do that. It was an accident," she said.

"Si, Señora, I tripped over the cord and put my hand out to stop myself, but pulled everything down," he said leaning into her.

They sat quietly for a few minutes. "Diego, I need you to be very brave. Artists are very temperamental people. That's what makes them good artists but sometimes it gets out of control. Do you think you're brave enough to apologize to him? He's not angry any more, just sad. I'll come with you."

Diego sat for a moment thinking then nodded. "Okay," he said, tentatively. He stood up, straightened his clothes, took a deep breath, and started walking towards the workshop like a rookie bull fighter facing his first opponent. Jess walked behind him. Felipe was sitting on the stool. He looked up as they walked in.

"Felipe, Diego has come to apologize." She looked over Diego's head at Felipe and raised an eyebrow to him, thinking, *Make a move, man, you're the adult here.* Felipe opened his arms and Diego ran to him, burying himself against Felipe's chest. She could see the tears welling up in Felipe's eyes. She turned and walked away. It was a very sensitive moment and she didn't want to intrude. It looked like there was a possibility of salvaging the situation. Best to let them be.

Carla had told her Diego thought the world of his uncle. This event was nasty. She'd been scared when he was raging right in her face, but she couldn't risk him hurting the child. Felipe had been out of control. Talk about volatile!

She sat on the chair and waited. A short time later, Felipe walked out, his hand on Diego's shoulder. The boy sat beside her, looking a bit more composed. Felipe crouched down in front of them.

"I apologize to both of you. What can I say? I lost it. No excuses. I have treated my nephew and my guest abominably. My behavior was completely unacceptable. I said things I didn't mean, should not have said, and I am deeply ashamed. A grown man should be able to deal with things properly."

"What do you think, Diego? Do we accept the apology?" she asked.

Diego looked first at Felipe, then at Jess. "I think so."

"Well, maybe you say an extra prayer for him at church on Sunday. He needs all the help he can get," said Jess. "Diego, I think now's a good time for us to go home, don't you? I think we'll get a taxi and do the subway another day."

Felipe called a cab and unlocked the door. Nothing further was said. When the cab pulled up outside and honked its horn Jess and Diego departed, leaving him standing on the doorstep.

Diego's parents, Enzo and Angelica had a modest apartment in a good but not over-the-top building. Jess escorted Diego up to the eighth floor, wondering what she was going to tell them. They looked askance at their son, usually meticulously dressed, his clothing still splattered in yellow paint.

"What happened?" Enzo demanded.

"I think Diego had better explain it," Jess replied as they hovered over the boy.

Diego recounted the story in Spanish with his mother looking on in horror. Enzo's face was like stone. Finally, the old Diego began to resurface, more composed, and sure of himself. "She defended me," he said, looking at Jess.

Jess suddenly found herself engulfed in Angelica's arms, being kissed on the cheeks.

"Angelica, Diego was very brave and apologized for damaging the paintings. Felipe did apologize to both of us for his behavior. I just wanted to make sure Diego was safe."

"Please stay for supper with us. Felipe hasn't been right since his wife died, so moody, so angry," Angelica said, wringing her hands. Enzo still looked like thunder.

Jess didn't get back to her apartment until after ten. The evening had been very pleasant with a lovely meal, more red wine, and time with both Diego and Julia. Angelica had hand-sewn all of the girl's dance dresses and they were beautiful. Julia had proudly shown them off.

"Diego was such a help to me today. He showed me what to do on the bus and give the right money. I'm really looking forward to him showing me the subway sometime next week with your permission." She watched his face light up. His parents nodded in agreement.

"I'm going shopping with Carla tomorrow, so I won't be dancing with him until Friday." Jess explained to his parents that he had danced with her earlier in the day, correcting some of her errors. They did not object.

When Jess asked if she should be paying him for his time, Angelica shook her head. "No, but you could buy him lunch that day."

She lay in bed thinking about the whole episode and really didn't understand Felipe's outburst. The paintings were depressing and ugly and, if anything, a blob of yellow was, in her mind an improvement of sorts. For some reason, an image of Todd Wainright floated into her head. Cool, calm, and patient Todd was the absolute antithesis of Felipe.

Chapter 20

IT WAS RAINING WHEN SHE WOKE UP THURSDAY MORNING but it eased off by the time she arrived at the studio. Antonio was already there and started her routine immediately.

"There's only so far I can take you with the amount of time we have, Jess. There are a few more things I want to teach you, then we'll concentrate on polishing your technique."

They worked on the tango for the whole hour, learning the side-by-side promenades and pivots where Jess strutted around him. When they were finished, she looked up to Diego and Julia peeking into the room, obviously critiquing her style. She went over to talk to them for a few minutes. Diego seemed to be back to his normal self. Kids were so resilient.

She didn't see Carla in the waiting area so she quickly showered and changed into street clothes. She pulled her hair back in a ponytail and walked out of the change room and there was Carla. It was like old home week. Had it only been four days since they'd seen each other? So much had happened.

Together, they walked out of the building, talking non-stop and waited for a bus. Carla told her what was going on at the stable where she worked, about Mateo's polo schedule, and the horses.

They arrived at a mall with Carla directing her to the salon. They went through a stack of hair style magazines to get ideas. Eventually she found what she wanted. The cut was short all round, tapered at the neck and around the ears, with her hair one length from the crown down and bangs across the forehead. Carla held the picture up beside Jess's face, brushed the bangs more to one side.

"I like this Jess. I've only known you with long hair. This is sharp and sophisticated and it suits you. It will be really easy to look after too, just wash and go. Are you ready for this?"

Jess looked at it again. "Let's do it," she said. "If I don't like it, I can always grow it out." The next thing she knew, she was sitting in the swivel chair, a plastic cape around her shoulders, and Carla directing the stylist. The young woman looked at the picture, looked at Jess's reflection in the mirror, and started cutting. Jess had no recollection of having her hair cut, except trimming the ends herself. She had seldom had her hair styled except for both her own and Marty's weddings. It was shocking to see foot-long lengths of hair cascading to the floor.

Finally, the girl put down the scissors and ran the electric razor over Jess' neck. She took the mirror and held it behind her head to show off the back. With the cape removed, Jess stood up. She didn't look like the same person. Goodbye Kentucky country hick; hello city girl from Buenos Aires. Wow! She tossed her head, surprised at how light it felt. She hadn't realized how heavy her hair had been. It made her neck look long and elegant. She paid the stylist, tipping her well..

"Okay, worker of miracles, where to now?" she said to Carla.

"Exactly what style of dresses are you looking for?"

"I want three dresses: two simple stylish ones for daytime, then something dressier that I can wear for evening or dancing. Maybe a fitted top, but I want the skirt full enough that I can do the extensions."

"There are a couple of shops in this mall. Let's take a look."

Jess went through the racks and came up with several. One was a basic white with coral-colored flowers and green leaves in a polyester cotton. It had a soft draped neckline with short sleeves, a fitted bodice, and a slight flaring from the waistline to the hips. She looked younger, slimmer, and quite feminine. The other dress was in tones of aqua and blues, sleeveless with inch-wide shoulder straps and a padded bra top. Once again, the top was fitted and the skirt fell in soft folds. Jess liked both of them.

"How much are they?" Jess said.

"You work it out. What's on the tag?" Carla said.

"It's fifteen hundred pesos. One US dollar is roughly fifty pesos so we're looking at thirty dollars US."

"That's right."

"I think I'll take both of them and find some shoes. I don't want stilettos. They're too hard to dance in. I want maybe three-inch heels with a thicker heel so I can get my balance better."

They wandered around the mall looking at shoes and the elusive other dress. Carla took her to several shops, but Jess couldn't find anything suitable. She held up one plain black dress but the cleavage was too deep and revealing for her liking.

They enlisted help from the saleswoman who disappeared into the back of the store and returned a short time later, carrying three dresses. Jess rejected two immediately but took a serious look at the third one. The material was a crimson red silk with spaghetti straps, with the material crisscrossed over the breasts, then flowing from the waist band down to the soft, shapely, flaring skirt.

"Yes, yes, yes! I really like that. It's classy." She tried it on and loved it. Here she was, a jeans and T-shirt girl buying a classy evening dress, priced at 2,500 Argentinian pesos, fifty US. She knew it was an extravagance but she'd feel like a million bucks wearing it. It was beautiful. She walked out of the change room, posing herself and watched in amusement as Carla's mouth fell open.

"Jess, you look drop-dead gorgeous. Oh my God! You look like a model. What color shoes are you going to get to go with it?"

"Black, no—gold maybe."

"How about we have lunch then see what we can find?" Carla suggested.

They were sitting in the cafe, discussing all the places Jess had been to when Jess finally told her about the events of the previous day.

"I already know. Felipe phoned me last night and told me what happened. He hasn't been right since Francesca died. I think they'd had a big fight. She had a temper on her, just like him. The problem was that when the autopsy was performed, he found out she was six weeks pregnant."

"Oh, no. He lost his baby too."

"But it's worse than that. He told me they hadn't been sleeping together for several months and the baby wasn't his. Please don't repeat that to anyone because he thinks it was someone in the family. Promise me."

"I promise. No wonder he's so screwed up. Not only did he lose his wife but he found out she was cheating. He'll always wonder which relative it was. Mind you, I have trouble believing he'd be faithful for very long. His eyes are always on the women," Jess said, thinking about the way he'd looked at her.

"Listen, to change the subject, I've found a place for you to ride. Can you free yourself up next Wednesday? I'm can switch my days at the stables next week. I'll come in with Mateo, like I did today but I'll keep the truck and take you out to the estancia. I found an American couple who are own a stable and they have an Andalusian. I gave them your credentials. Only problem is that Felipe wants to come to take some photos. Are you willing to do that after what's happened?"

"Well, yes, I suppose so. You're going to be there. He was scary, Carla. I've never seen anyone lose control like that. I was afraid he'd hurt Diego. The paintings he's done are awful, all dark and depressing."

"I didn't think he was painting at all," Carla said.

"I doubt any of those would be for sale to anyone."

"He can borrow a car, like he did before and meet us out there. I'll give him the directions."

By the end of the day, Jess had found a pair of sandals that went well with the cotton dresses, but she was tired of shopping. She decided her old black dancing shoes would have to do for the silk dress. At the last minute, she bought some dark mascara and a smoky eye shadow. She'd had a terrific day and was happy with her purchases. She told Carla she wanted to see Juan Navarro Carrizo, the guitarist at the Colon Theater, if she was able to get a ticket. It would be an opportunity to wear the red dress.

Carla dropped her off at the apartment, then continued to pick up Mateo from work. Carla was such good company. Jess happily toted her bag of goodies up to her room and changed into her bathing suit. There were people in the pool she didn't know, but Ann and Sandee weren't there.

Later, she went for supper at The Gaucho and had a well-cooked beef brisket and her usual glass of red wine. After dinner, she was on her way back home when she spotted the blue Sorento parked down a side street but the car was empty. Immediately, she was on alert looking for Duffy but didn't see him anywhere. Not knowing where he was worrisome.

*   *   *

FRIDAY WAS THE USUAL ROUTINE. AFTER HER SESSION WITH Antonio, Jess shifted into the smaller back room and met with Diego and Julia. She had a suggestion for them. "I only have two Sunday asados left, then I'll be going home. You always do demonstration dances. How about you choreograph a dance that involves the three of us—something where you lead but Julia and I constantly switch places and dance with you throughout. It would have to be something relatively simple because I don't have your skill and experience. We could throw in a little flamenco, some paso doble. What do you think?"

She could see the excitement on their faces. They were immediately discussing it in rapid Spanish, gesticulating with their arms and hands so enthusiastically that it brought a smile to her face. They spent the next forty-five minutes trying things out. Jess suddenly realized that they'd never done any free-form dancing, no getting up on the dance floor to boogie to the music. She fervently hoped this wouldn't somehow upset their professional dancing careers with Sebastian. Already it was quite apparent that Diego was very pleased with the concept of having two female partners at the same time. He was going to be pure trouble when he became a teenager.

When the dance was finished, she said she'd see them on Sunday. Jess was looking forward to going out with Ann and Sandee that evening and felt a little lazy, deciding to spend the rest of the day by the pool. Her tan was coming along nicely, so she didn't look quite so much like a tourist. After looking at her dresses, she decided to wear the floral one. She checked her email and saw she had one from Mr. Ames. Quickly, she opened it.

Hi Jessica,

Hope you are enjoying your holiday in the sun. Typical February weather here with a few storms, daytime high around thirty-six degrees and just below freezing at night. You'll be pleased to know your divorce papers will be ready to sign on March 29th. Get in touch with me as soon as you get back, there are still a few things we need to discuss.

Scott Ames

Jess immediately emailed him back.

Hi, Mr. Ames:

It's eighty degrees and humid most of the time.
Thanks for letting me know. I'll call you as soon as
I get back. Jessica

She was elated. The final act of signing those papers was
the piece of the puzzle she desperately needed, to get some
sort of closure. Later in the afternoon, she slipped out to the
local deli and picked up two sandwiches and some canned
pop; one for lunch and one for supper. She spent the rest
of the time sorting through pamphlets on the remaining
venues that she hadn't seen yet. She wanted to go to the
polo game and somehow fit in a soccer game. People here
were football fanatics. She looked up the ticket price. One
hundred US seemed awfully steep. It was members only
for admission to the La Boca Juniors games, so that was
out. Maybe watching it on TV was an option. She'd have to
ask Leonardo.

Another venue that looked interesting was the *campanopolis,* fantastical houses that looked like a street scene from
a Harry Potter movie set. Perhaps that would be a good one
to go to with Diego. It was further away and would mean a
subway ride. She emailed Carla.

Hi Carla:

When is your next polo game? I could meet you at
the arena. Jess.

It was later in the evening, just before she went to bed that
she checked her email again and found Carla had replied.

Hi, Jess:

Next Tuesday. Meet us at the car entrance at six o'clock. I'm driving the horses down. Mateo will go there straight from work and meet us at the gate. Carla

WHEN LEONARDO AND EMILIA GOT HOME, JESS ASKED THEM about the soccer game.

"We watch it on TV. Tickets are expensive and thousands of crazy fans are too much, so TV works for us. There'll be a game on Thursday evening. River Plate's playing San Lorenzo. It'll be a good game."

"Could I watch it with you?" Jess asked.

"Certainly," he replied.

"I'm not used to big crowds like that, so watching it on TV is fine by me. Then, you can explain everything."

"Don't you have football at home, Jess?" Leonardo asked.

"Well, Americans have a different kind of football where they wear pads and helmets. Soccer is played but it's not as popular as the other one. I'm not interested in it but most American men are avid fans and wouldn't miss a game," she said, thinking of Andy. Somehow the six-month old memory of sitting in the living room with a beer, listening to him cheer on his team was distant and fleeting.

At nine o'clock, she went down to the lobby to wait for Ann and Sandee. Jess felt quite elegant in her coral-colored dress and heels. She had applied her makeup with care and was feeling good about how she looked. The short haircut really did make a difference, making her feel classy and sophisticated.

The elevator doors opened and the two girls strutted out, wearing tight provocative dresses that emphasized their cleavage. Both had left their hair long; Ann had pulled her hair behind her ears and used clips either side to hold it in place while Sandee had let hers fall in a dark wavy cascade to her shoulders. They had probably been into the wine already from the way they were laughing. Jess had no doubt they would attract a lot of attention.

The cab pulled up at the door and they all piled in. The tango club they had chosen was in a different part of the city, but it appeared quite lively already with flashing neon lights outside and was full of locals (*portenos*) when they arrived. It took them a few minutes to find a table where they could sit together. Latin music was blaring over the speakers and the dance floor was alive with couples swaying and dancing. Jess could feel the throb of bass rhythms pulsing right through her. Ann went up to the bar and got the first round of drinks. Soon there was a parade of young men passing their table and before long Jess was sitting solo, watching the girls charm the Latin guys.

She wasn't alone for long, as one suave young fellow, probably still in his teens gave her the look and she nodded. He was a good dancer and it pleased her immensely that she was able to follow him through the first dance. He seemed surprised that she could dance and upped the degree of difficulty on the next two numbers. He wasn't as good as Antonio but was good enough to test her. She thoroughly enjoyed herself. It seemed odd to be dancing for pleasure and not having a lesson. It felt good just to dance with a man, his arms around her, close enough for her to savor the fragrance of his musky aftershave.

The fourth dance was a tango and it was all she could have wished for. She paid attention to his lead and matched the fluid movement of his hips, placing her feet in a deliberate yet feminine manner. She curved around him on the turns, averted her eyes when they were in closed embrace but held off doing any of the caresses, which to her seemed a bit personal with a total stranger.

"*Gracias, Señor*," she said as he walked her back to the table where Ann was sitting. He smiled at her and walked away to join the other young men on the sidelines. Sandee was still on the dance floor cuddling up to an older man. Jess bought a round of drinks and sat down for a few minutes. The evening continued, with a constant line of young men indicating their interest.

Jess suddenly realized she'd been on the dance floor for quite some time and there was no sign of either Ann or Sandee. She headed for the ladies room but they weren't there either. Now she felt uneasy. They had left without her, more than likely with their partners for the evening and now she was by herself—just the situation she'd been trying to avoid. She followed some young women out of the club, hoping to seem part of their *portenos* group and scanned the street for a cab. None in sight. Fortunately, the streets were still crowded. She dodged from group to group. She remembered seeing a cab stand outside one of the hotels nearby and headed for it. She was passing an alley between two buildings when two strong hands grabbed her from behind and dragged her into the gloom.

She was too surprised to scream as she was slammed against the brick wall of the building dimly lit by shuttered upper windows, the wind knocked out of her. Hands groped her. Two muscular male bodies pulled her down to the ground. One slashed at her purse but his knife couldn't cut the light chain strap.

The other one shoved her dress up and grabbed her crotch. She kicked him hard and screamed. Suddenly, there was another figure in the alley, striding purposefully towards them, both arms extended. The faint light outlined the gun in his hand. Everyone froze. She felt her attackers release her and jump to their feet, backing away.

The man with the gun barked a few staccato commands in Spanish. Both attackers melted into the darkness. Jess scrambled. There was something familiar about the voice. *Oh my God, it was Duffy.*

"Jess, get up NOW," he said clasping her hand, jerking her to her feet but never taking his eyes from the two fleeing figures. She did as she was told, moving behind him closer to the street, pure terror taking over. She was shaking uncontrollably. He slipped the gun into his shoulder holster, his eyes constantly searching. He spun around and propelled her onto the pavement to join the crowds. They moved at a very brisk walk his hand gripping hers. She saw the Sorento parked near the hotel and they dodged traffic to cross the busy road to reach it. Drivers honked in annoyance as the couple darted between cars.

"Get in," he said unlocking the door, at the same time pulling the gun from the holster, looking at threatening,. dark shadows in the parking lot.

The gun was now six inches from her face and she froze, staring at it. "Duffy, please don't kill me," she begged, bracing herself against the frame of the car, afraid to get inside.

"What?!" he said. He shifted his attention to her face and saw her eyes fixated on the gun, so he slid it back in the holster. Jess started to sag and for a moment she thought she was going to faint. He caught her and swung her into the passenger seat. Getting quickly into the car, he started it and moved into traffic. He made a series of sharp turns, as if eluding followers. In a quieter area, he pulled the car into a parking space. Jess was quietly curled up against the passenger door as far from him as she could get, tears trickling down her cheeks.

"Good God, woman, why did you think I was going to kill you? I've spent the past week trying to protect you." He handed her his handkerchief and she wiped her face and blew her nose.

"I think Neil had my father killed," she said.

"I highly doubt that," he said after a long thoughtful pause. He pulled out his cellphone and tapped in the number. "Neil, I've got an emergency situation here. I'm bringing Jessica to see you right now. Sorry boss, but this can't wait."

Ten minutes later they arrived at the biggest, grandest, and most expensive hotel in the city. They crossed the lobby to the elevators and he stood beside her, his arm around her. She wasn't sure if he was protecting her or making sure she couldn't get away, not that she could run in heels anyway. It stopped at the seventeenth floor, the doors silently opening to a deeply carpeted hallway. Duffy's knock at number 1704 was promptly answered by Neil himself.

They'd obviously disturbed Neil's latest romantic encounter. There were two wine glasses and an empty bottle on the table, and the bedroom door was wide open, showing rumpled bed clothes. He was barefoot and bare-chested, wearing only his slacks. His dark hair hung in tousled locks. Under other circumstances, he would have been a dream; right now, he was a nightmare.

At that point, Jess didn't care, she was just too frightened and sank into the arm chair. She kept her eyes averted, trying to control her breathing, and wondering what was going to happen.

Duffy explained the situation and Jess's comment to Neil. "She thinks you ordered her father killed. She thought I was going to shoot her."

Neil stood looking at her for a few moments, then went over to the wet bar and poured hefty shots of Scotch into three crystal tumblers. He gave one to Duffy, then placed a glass in Jess's trembling hand, pulling a chair beside her. "Drink that."

She was too scared to refuse. The neat alcohol burned her throat. There was a lull until the trembling stopped and she glanced up at him. He was sitting patiently sipping his Scotch, watching. She couldn't read his expression. "What do you mean when you told Duffy I'd ordered your father killed?"

Jess had a sudden flush of anger. Emboldened probably by the Scotch, she said, "My father's death was no accident. He was run off the road. There is evidence of another vehicle involved and his house was searched. Are you telling me you knew nothing about it?"

"I was in Japan buying a horse when he died and I didn't order it. Ryan phoned me and told me about the accident the next day."

"If it wasn't you, then it had to be Ryan, although I can't imagine him doing anything without your approval," she said wondering what other options there might be.

His voice was quiet and deadly. "Ryan told me that Joe had photos he wanted to talk to us about; photos that showed we'd switched horses. Do you know anything about them? Do you have them?"

She looked at him and saw the cold calculating eyes of the business man.

"So, you didn't arrange his death, but you knew about the photos? I discovered them last fall when I was unpacking the boxes from his house. They show quite clearly that the horses were switched," she said, feeling her anger grow.

Neil bowed his head for a few moments, not even pretending he didn't know what she meant. Then he looked at her. "Could you tell them apart?"

"Arctic Cat had a marking that Wing Commander doesn't have. It's subtle, but I saw it. My father certainly would have noticed it," she replied. She paused for a moment unsure she should tell him what it was.

"What have I missed?" Neil said.

She looked at him again. He's admitting it. That simple question proved she was right.

"How much do you want for the photos?" he said, as calmly as if he was buying a used car.

"Neil, my father was an honest man. He'd have wanted to stop your deception. Extortion was never my intention. But we're talking murder here and I want justice for him and then I want to be left alone. Those photos are my insurance policy. They're in a safe place, but if anything happens to me, there are instructions for them to be sent immediately to the British and American jockey clubs," she said looking at him directly. "I don't know how you managed to switch the microchips, ruin the tattoo, or change the DNA samples."

There was a long silence as he poured himself another drink. "That's my secret" he said turning away.

"And if Duffy wasn't out to kill me, why has he been following me all week?" she asked. "I've seen him several times, at the bank and outside the apartment."

Neil raised his eyebrows and looked across the room at Duffy who was sitting on the arm of the chair, keenly following the conversation. "You're losing your touch, my friend."

"Well, you've got to admit, he stands out in a Latin crowd," Jess said. "So does the Sorento."

"I've been in business negotiations all week and he had nothing to do. He asked if he could keep an eye on you in his spare time. Apparently, he was concerned about your safety. This is a very dangerous city for a naive single American who doesn't speak Spanish. Damned good thing he was following you tonight."

The thought of Duffy being concerned about her was mind-boggling. Why?

"It seems I now have a vested interest in keeping you alive," Neil said with a tight smile. "I'm flying home in the morning. Duffy, take her back to the apartment. Jess, take care of yourself. Don't get yourself killed by someone else, or I'm up shit creek. If you ever decide you want to sell or give them to me, let me know. In the meantime, I need to have a chat with my little brother," he said.

"You should check into his finances too since you're his partner. Antique cars have been disappearing at a rapid rate, and you're lucky no female employee has filed sexual harassment charges against him. None of us were safe with him. That's one of the reasons I left," she said getting up from the chair and looked at him one more time as Duffy led her out the door.

It was a quiet ride home. Duffy pulled the car right up to the entrance of the apartment building. He quickly exited the car and opened her door. He held both her shoulders and looked her in the face. "Please be careful, Jess. Just remember, I'm a security specialist, not an assassin. My job is to protect Neil. I care what happens to you, and have for a long time. I don't go around killing anyone."

She looked at him one last time. He waited until she unlocked the inside door before leaving. He'd never acknowledged her at all until tonight. Right at that moment, she didn't want anything to do with either man. She felt a deep sense of relief as she reached her room and closed the door. She was safe, at least for now. Or was she?

Chapter 21

JESS SLEPT IN UNTIL NINE. NOTHING WAS PLANNED FOR THE day which was a good thing as her energy level was zero. She thought about last night and the fear she'd felt. It seemed to have sucked the confidence right out of her. She'd been so lucky Duffy had been there. It seemed far-fetched that the silent, muscular warrior had been her savior and admitted to an interest in her. Without his intervention, she would probably have been raped or worse. Neil said Duffy was concerned about her. What did that mean? He'd never paid attention to her before. Why now?

She thought about Neil too. At least her suspicions had been confirmed. She also realized there was a world of difference between the rich and the average person. The degree of ruthlessness in him surprised her. There were no ethics, no morals, no empathy, just pure, unadulterated greed for money and power, apparently with little consideration of the human cost.

Her dress lay crumpled on the floor. Examining it, she found it badly stained with dirt in several places, but amazingly not torn. Today would be a good day to get some laundry done and just sit around the pool. The whole episode with Duffy, Neil, and the muggers seemed surreal, like a really bad movie script.

Jess looked at herself in the mirror. There were some abrasions on her left knee and faint bruising on her thigh. Leonardo and Emilia were still sleeping, so she had a quick shower then ate the cereal and fruit Emilia had left out for her even though she wasn't that hungry. She took her soiled clothes down to the basement laundry room and managed to find the right coins to get it working.

She was running events through her mind again as she folded her laundry. The stains had come out of the dress; it looked as good as new. She was nervous when an older male tenant got on the elevator when she was heading back upstairs; she was hyper-vigilant as if expecting trouble. She silently swore at herself for being foolish and wondered how long this reaction was going to last. She'd just gotten her confidence back and now it had evaporated. It had been a bad scare but it was over. She'd survived it thanks to Duffy. She decided to put a smile on her face and deal with it. Squaring her shoulders, she got off the elevator and went back to the apartment. She hadn't decided if she'd tell anyone about the incident.

Emilia and Leonard were up by then and were in the middle of breakfast.

"Good morning, Jess. How was your evening?" Leonardo asked.

"I enjoyed the dancing. I spent most of the evening on the dance floor. It was a lot of fun, but—" words failed her.

"But what?"

"I ran into some trouble when I was leaving."

"What happened?" said Emilia, putting down the coffee pot.

"Well, the Brits took off and didn't tell me they were leaving. I tried to find a cab but there wasn't one. Some guys grabbed me and dragged me in an alley. A stranger saw I was in trouble and helped me."

"Are you alright?" Emilia asked looking most concerned.

"I've got a few bruises, but I'm okay. It frightened me a lot."

"Did you report it to the police?" Leonard asked, his brows furrowed.

"No. It was dark and I couldn't identify them," Jess said truthfully. "I'm alright. Really, I am. I'm just going to be more careful when I'm out. Can you give me the phone number for a taxi company? I didn't even think about phoning for one last night; I was going to walk over to the hotel to get one. Stupid of me."

She saw a look pass between the couple. Emilia poured her a coffee.

Leonardo broke the silence. "Tonight, we are meeting friends and going to a *milonga* club for tango. Would you like to come with us? It's a decent place. You said you were taking lessons."

"I'd love to, if I'm not imposing," she said. "I've been having a really good time in Buenos Aires. I don't want last night to spoil this holiday and make me afraid to do things. It's not usual for the Airbnb owners to babysit their tenants, is it?"

"No, but there are things to see and do here that are unique to my country and it will surely be safer for you to be with us," said Leonardo.

"Thank you," Jess said and gave Emilia a hug. "Now tell me what's a milonga?"

"It's a form of tango, not ballroom but one for the common people. The club we go to isn't fancy like the one you were at last night and it's in a safer part of the city. The music combines African influences as well as Italian and Spanish. Slaves were brought here hundreds of years ago, so there are some different rhythms. The club caters to people of all ages. Sometimes there are professional dancers there but generally it's the average crowd. The band's very good. We already have reservations but I'll call and add one more," Leonardo said, picking up the phone.

Jess went back to her room and looked at her dresses. She selected the aqua-toned one as she hadn't worn it yet. She spent the morning by the pool swimming laps and relaxing on her lounge chair. Her tan was looking good and even. There was no sign of Ann or Sandee. Good thing.

After her swim, she got changed and went to The Gaucho for lunch. "I just love these croissants," she said to the waiter. "They're so flaky. What do you call them?"

"*Medialuna, Señorita.* They have a rum glaze," he replied with a smile.

Now that her left ring finger was as tanned and unrutted as a single woman's would be, no wonder he had called her that. She ordered fruit and a coffee as well. The crowd were indulging in the national past time of people watching, while sipping their coffees and talking on their cellphones. She sent an email to her mother and Marty. No further messages from Mr. Ames.

Hi, folks:

Have been doing all the usual tourist things. Buenos Aires is a fascinating place and I'm seeing a lot. Other than my daily dance lesson, I am also spending time every day in the pool or sunbathing. Having a good time. Sunday, I'll be at the family BBQ, then a city tour on Monday, plus a polo game with Carla and Mateo on Tuesday, and horseback riding on Wednesday. Thursday is a local soccer game. No problem finding things to do. Can't believe my holiday is half over. Jess

She walked to the deli, alert to everything around her and nearly jumped out of her skin when someone bumped into her as she was going into the store. It was an older lady. Jess apologized and held the door open for her, "So sorry; *lo siento, Señora.*" The woman smiled and said something, but Jess didn't catch it.

She placed an order for ribs and a salad and took it back to the apartment for her evening meal, catching sight of Ann and Sandee down in the pool, when she looked over the balcony railing. No point going down there; confrontation wasn't going to change anything. She sat on the bed and decided a siesta was just what she needed.

By the time she resurfaced it was nearly six o'clock. She sat out on the balcony to eat her ribs and salad, watching the activity on the streets below. She then freshened up, taking time with her makeup. The aqua dress looked good on her. She played games on the computer, a mindless way to kill time, until they were ready to leave. Perhaps it was the realization that her holiday was half over that made her feel time was moving at the speed of light. It would be business as usual, back to work, to the humdrum rhythm of her "normal life." Maybe she should just relax a bit and simply enjoy.

They took a taxi to the club which was just how Leonardo had described it—open to the street, full of people and a stage at the back where musicians were setting up. It was noisy with everyone talking at once. Not only were there couples but whole families too.

Their friends had got there ahead of them. Leonardo made the introductions to the thirty-something-year old pair who seemed friendly, moving over to make room for Jess. Emilia explained that both Joaquim and Manuela worked as pharmacists for large company in the city.

"I'll get this round," Leonardo said, ordering red wine.

That seemed to be the drink of choice as Jess casually observed other tables. Soon, the lights dimmed, the band tuned up and the music began. She closed her eyes for a moment and listened as the chatter in the room died and the violins, guitar, drums, bandoneon, and bass swung into melodies distinctly Latin. The center of the dance floor was now packed. She wasn't familiar with the tune but the music was delicious. She found herself tapping her foot and feeling it throughout her body.

Leonardo and Emilia were immediately on the dance floor. She watched their style and recognized the steps and moves they were doing: the rock step, salida, front ocho, ocho cortada—many of the steps Antonio had taught her. Joaquim and Manuela were out there somewhere too. Couples of all ages were on the floor. Some of the older ones, probably well into their seventies and eighties were doing a slightly different style, a closer, more personal one. Their years of familiarity made it look so soft and easy.

By the second dance one particular couple in their early twenties, took to the floor and immediately Jess could see the difference in style, sleek, professional, totally sensual, and incredibly athletic. *You'd need to be a professional gymnast to do some of those moves*, she thought. At the end of one dance the woman's final pose was in the flexed position, her back beautifully arched, her right leg fully extended and her body between her partner's legs, her left knee beside his. Their faces were an inch apart, eyes locked. Absolutely erotic. She watched in complete fascination until her view was blocked by a young man who gave her the look. His skin was ebony, his physique lithe, his suit just as white as his brilliant smile. He looked friendly. She nodded and he escorted her to the dance floor.

As the next dance began, he held her in the open embrace. He moved, she followed and so it went. She wasn't confident enough to challenge. By the following dance she was comfortable with his style and relaxed a bit more. The next embrace was closed with her face against the curve of his neck, her eyes averted. The whole dance flowed. When the music ended, he walked her back to her table where Leonardo and Emilia were now sitting. She was pleased with what she'd been able to do. Being able to follow a total stranger was really an accomplishment. It was one thing to dance with Antonio but a completely different story with someone else. To some extent, she could anticipate Antonio's moves.

It was a delightful evening. The band took a break every forty-five minutes or so, giving everyone time to refuel. Jess bought the next round of wine. She was asked to dance by several other men, giving her the opportunity to dance again. By one o'clock the band wound down, some of the crowd dispersed and a disc jockey took over. The music changed to sexy sambas, cha-chas and salsa, and popular songs by Argentinian groups. A different crowd of younger people filtered in. At that point. Leonardo called a taxi and the three of them went home.

"Thank you so much," she said when they got into the apartment. "I really enjoyed that. I love watching people dance and the music is fabulous." She bid them good night and went to bed, falling asleep immediately.

*   *   *

SUNDAY MORNING AFTER BREAKFAST, JESS WALKED TO THE tourist office. She was surprised it so busy with a lineup of buses ready to take folks on city tours. When it was her turn at the kiosk, she asked the attendant about the guitar concert at the Colon Theater for the upcoming Saturday performance.

"I'm sorry Señorita, the performance is sold out," the girl said.

Jess was disappointed and looked at other venues, but nothing caught her interest. Never mind. She couldn't see everything. It would have been the perfect opportunity to wear her crimson dress but so be it. Maybe she would wear it to her last asado. She went back to the apartment and went for a swim. There was no sign of Ann or Sandee.

Hopefully they had moved on. She decided to talk to Diego that afternoon to see if he would accompany her to see the Campanopolis houses on Monday, after dance class. However, when she looked it up on line, it was only open on Saturdays. The other option was the nature reserve. If they could go by the subway (*subte*) that would be a bonus. He also mentioned something about ice cream.

At one o'clock she changed into her aqua dress again and walked to the Ramirez's apartment. No one followed her. She brought two bottles of wine with her. She really appreciated their kindness in inviting her there in the first place. It seemed the least she could do.

Olivia buzzed her in and gave her a hug. She accepted the wine graciously. Carla and Mateo were already there. Mateo gave her a kiss on the cheek. Jess saw Felipe's mother Maria and brother across the room, but there was no sign of him. Jess decided she wasn't going to say anything about the alley incident to Carla.

Carla placed a glass of wine in her hand and pulled her to one side. "I've got some news you might find interesting."

"Okay," said Jess intrigued.

"Maria just told Mum that Felipe went to church this morning. That's the first time in five years he's done that. What magic spell have you cast on him?"

"I don't think you can credit me with that. I haven't done anything. Maybe he was just ready to make a change. That's a start. Maybe that anger episode with Diego jolted him out of whatever state he was in," she said.

"Or maybe he's trying to impress one beautiful American, who stood up to him," said Carla.

"I'm not sure that makes much sense, Carla. Ten days from now I'll be back in Lexington. Changing the subject, are you ready for the polo match on Tuesday?"

"Okay, I get it. You don't want to talk about it. We'll be ready, meet us at the side gate to the Polo grounds in Palermo at six o'clock. You can go in with us and we'll take care of the horses while Mateo plays. A real game is a lot more exciting than the practice games, especially when the crowd gets going."

Jess sipped on her wine, then wandered over to talk to Diego and Julia.

"Diego, I wanted to tour the Campanopolis, but they are only open on Saturdays. Could we go for a walk in the Ecological reserve at Puerto Madero tomorrow? Are you available?"

"Si, Señora." His smile was so infectious that she burst out laughing.

"Good. I'll talk to your parents then," she said moving across the room. Enzo and Angelica agreed when she asked.

"Get him to take you to Freddo," Angelica said. "They make the best gelato."

"Well, I love ice cream, so that should work out well. I'll get to ride on a subway too, which I've never done before," Jess said. She gave Diego a thumbs up. Sebastian was just going over to set the children up for their demonstration dance. She saw Antonio walk in with his girlfriend; they looked cozy.

She wandered back to Carla and sat down, telling her about tomorrow's trip. As soon as the music started, all talking stopped. This time it was a paso doble. The rhythm was different from the tango. The song was a familiar old piece that Jess thought of as the "bullfighter song." A blare of trumpets had Julia strutting and flaring her skirt, conjuring up images of the bullfighter's cape. Diego on his toes, in his black pants and vest, somehow morphed into the bullfighter. She could see where he'd drawn inspiration from this dance, for parts of the secret dance they were concocting. He spun and turned, guiding his sister. It was sublime and executed to perfection. When the music ended, Julia was in a full left leg extension with a fully bent right knee, gazing up at Diego. Jess was cheering along with everyone else. They were so good!

After their demonstration, everyone else got up to dance. Jess went over to say hello to Antonio. She told him about the milongo the night before.

"Did you try caresses?"

"No," she admitted. "I wasn't ready yet."

He laughed. "We'll work on it this week."

Meanwhile, the chef was busy spreading steaks on the grill with sizzling smoke and pungent aromas rising from the parilla. Soon, everyone was sitting down eating and sipping their wine, the conversation level still high. Jess looked over the scene and felt incredibly lucky that she was part of this amazing family who were so willing to include her in their festivities.

Chapter 22

ROUTINE MONDAY MORNING—ONE HOUR TANGO LESSON with Antonio and one hour secret dance class with Diego and Julia. Her footwork was improving under the continued scrutiny of both instructors. Some of Diego's choreography was a bit advanced for her, but with Julia's help she managed to get the spins and figure eights right, where they interchanged positions in front of him and continued to spin. She was thankful for her old tap dance classes. The foot movement paved the way for the flamenco part of their routine.

Afterwards, she changed from her leotard to a casual top, capris, and runners. Diego took her first by bus then by train to the park. It was fascinating to walk down stairs below street level and climb on board the small train that hurtled through tunnels.

"Come on, Jess," he yelled cramming himself onto the packed train, making room for her just as the whistle blew to close the doors. Folks were hanging onto the straps to keep their balance as it rocketed from station to station. The doors opened at each stop long enough to disgorge dozens, then swallowed more, like a mechanical monster.

"This a cheap, quick way to move a lot of people, compared to gridlock on the streets," she said. He agreed.

They arrived at their destination and managed to get off the train together, laughing. It felt like an amusement park ride to Jess. Diego led the way up to street level and they walked towards the water. The main harbor lay at Puerto Madero with a roadway across the canal, the Ecological Reserve occupying land on the ocean side.

Diego pointed out the yacht club where many beautiful ships were berthed. "People who own those boats are very rich,"

"They're much bigger than I thought they'd be. They're obviously seaworthy for the Atlantic. Imagine the size of the crew you'd need to sail one," she mused. They passed an elaborate marble fountain filled with sculpted naked human figures and rearing horses.

The next few hours were spent just walking the footpath between the lagoons, watching the birds.

"Look, Jess. It's a Great Egret," Diego said, pointing to the snow-white sentinel, poised motionless, knee deep in water, its long S-shaped neck in strike position, yellow eyes fixated on the surface.

Jess watched. Moments later the dagger-like yellow bill punctured the water in a spray, retrieving a small, thrashing silver fish which the bird manipulated to slide down its gullet head first.

There were ducks, a few swans, and the flash of a kingfisher like a blue jewel in the dappled light. A symphony of bird song rose from the swamp. "There are snakes, turtles, and a rodent called a nutria here. I'd love to see a viper up close," Diego said.

"Maybe you want to see one up close but I don't," she said, laughing. Only the turtles made an appearance. It was a quiet refuge from the bustling megacity just one canal away. The pathways were busy with cyclists and walkers, artists, and musicians. The dense shade of the trees made it an oasis of cool.

When they'd had enough, they walked back across the canal. "I don't suppose you'd be interested in going to Freddo for gelato?" she asked, although it was a foregone conclusion. Diego looked immensely pleased and nodded.

A bus ride got them to Callao Avenue. Freddo was on a street corner with tables and chairs both inside and out. By now both of them were hot, hungry, and ready for a treat. Diego gave her the names of some of the flavors, but there were just too many. She picked one that looked like vanilla with some dark berries while he had no difficulty selecting pure chocolate. Apparently, he wasn't allowed to have it very often.

"Tio Sebastian does not approve of ice cream. He doesn't want me to get fat," he said.

"After two hours of formal dance and three hours of walking, I don't think it's going to be a problem, Diego," Jess said digging her spoon into the bowl where the ice cream was melting rapidly. "Oh, this is so, so good."

"I like the way you think," he said with a dollop of chocolate dribbling down his chin. The adult way he spoke sometimes had Jess laughing uncontrollably. She handed him a napkin and the pair of them giggled. After that, they got on a bus and Jess took him home. She then called a cab using the number Emilia had given her, arriving back at the apartment just after six.

She walked over to The Gaucho, having her usual steak with a glass of red wine. Mindful of her surroundings, she walked back to the apartment. No one was following her. Unconsciously, she still looked for Duffy: it had become a habit. It was foolish really as both he and Neil would be in Ireland by now. She was completely exhausted but in a delightful way. After a quick shower, she stretched out on the bed and fell asleep.

She awoke while it was still dark. The clock said two a.m. The apartment was silent. She peeked out her window and saw the moving white and red strings of car lights of a city that never slept. The street lights hung like pearls on darkened residential areas but the entertainment area was still bright with neon. She wondered if it could be seen by the men on the international space station. She sent an email to her mother and Marty.

> Hi, folks:
>
> Had a lovely day yesterday taking a walk along the waterfront and into the Eco Park. Saw some spectacular boats at the yacht club. They looked more like multi-million-dollar ships to me. Just a lovely day looking at birds. Had a chance to go on a subway ride. Great way to get around the city.
>
> I'm going to a polo match tomorrow and on Wednesday, Carla has arranged for me to ride an Andalusian on a ranch in the country. Thursday I will be watching a soccer match. This holiday has gone so quickly it's hard to realize I'll be back home next Wednesday.
>
> Jess.

She marked her map with colored tacks to show the park and Freddo. It was now bristling with pins. Sleep was elusive, so she lay there quietly thinking about what life was going to be like when she got back home. She had more questions now than ever.

Was the Wainright job the right one? If not, what other options were there? Was there any point in taking more dance lessons? What possible outcome was there with the tangled web of intrigue regarding the photos and the O'Connells? Who was Duffy? Eventually, she drifted off to sleep again only to wake up again when Emilia and Leonardo were getting ready for work.

Antonio worked her hard that morning, allowing her to sink almost to the floor with an extension like Julia had done the day before. However, she didn't have the flexibility to do it properly and didn't have the strength to rise once she got that low. He modified it but she still found it awkward. He had her do the caresses until she finally got it right.

Julia came to the door whispering that their classroom was being used for another group, so they'd have to skip their practice session for two days.

She stopped in at the deli and picked up a sandwich for lunch then decided to spend the afternoon by the pool. She hadn't exactly been "relaxing" on her holiday, so today was a good day to do it. She had a nice even tan now. Folks at home in the winter jackets and snow boots would be jealous.

Around four o'clock she went back upstairs and show-ered, changing into a T-shirt, jeans, and her runners. She called a taxi to take her to the Campo Argentino. Hundreds of people were lining up for the match. Eventually, she could see the horse trailer in the queue for the side entrance.

Mateo was taken over driving, so Carla opened the cab door and Jess slid inside beside her. Once through the gates, they joined the other players and unloaded the horses.

Mateo was soon in the saddle. Jess noticed that now there was a referee in his black and white-striped shirt, riding his horse into the melee. The noise from the crowd was deafening sometimes, but the horses seemed used to it. She couldn't talk to Carla even though she was standing right beside her. The stadium held thirty thousand and few seats were empty today.

The riders were extremely competitive, driving their horses often in a flat out gallop but pivoting and changing direction in seconds. How they didn't hit each other with the mallets, she didn't know. It was exhilarating and soon she was cheering for Mateo's team. She was getting quite proficient at getting the horses ready for the next chukka, changing the saddle quickly to the fresh mount, reminiscent of the Pony Express.

In the second chukka, Mateo scored a goal. Jess and Carla jumped up and down screaming. At the end of the seventh chukka, his team had beaten their opponents by two goals. She was hoarse from yelling. The enthusiastic players leaped from their horses, going into a huddle, helmets flying in the air, hoisting the goal scorers onto their shoulders, parading around, and thumping each other on the back, broad smiles on everyone's faces. The people in the stadium were going nuts. Seeing thirty thousand people celebrate blew her mind. The noise was incredible. She felt sorry for the losers; these people were so intense.

Mateo was ecstatic with the little mare's performance. "I'm really pleased with her. She's only four, but I think she's probably going to be the best horse I've ever had. She didn't back off at all out there. She's quick and responsive. She's the kind of horse that will get me to the nationals," he said patting the mare's neck. Jess could see Carla was thrilled, giving her husband a robust kiss that was passionately returned. She enjoyed seeing her friend happy.

They dropped her off at the apartment. "I'll pick you up at the studio about ten-thirty, Jess and we'll head out to the estancia. Listen, Felipe wants to take you to a restaurant afterwards. Would you be willing to go?" Carla said.

"Is he in a better mood than the last time I saw him? Am I safe to go with him?"

"No doubt in my mind, Jess." Carla replied.

Jess got out of the truck and waved good bye as it quickly pulled away, towing the trailer.

*   *   *

WEDNESDAY MORNING WAS A DAY OF HUGE ANTICIPATION. First was her dance lesson with Antonio, then a trip to the estancia to ride the Andalusian. She wondered how she was going to react to Felipe. She hadn't seen him for over a week since his incident with Diego. She packed her jeans, leather ankle boots, camera, and a T-shirt into her carry bag. She wanted Carla to get some shots of her on the horse.

Antonio broke the usual routine with slow ballroom numbers that had them doing the waltz, quickstep, and foxtrot which seemed so different with the Latin flavor of guitars and mandolins. By the end of the session, she was convinced she could do just about any dance if she had a partner who could lead her through it.

At the end of the lesson, she changed into her riding gear. Carla was waiting and they immediately set out for the estancia. For the first half hour of the drive, they did nothing but discuss the game. Carla was so happy. The game was a notch up the ladder for Mateo. Carla told her to read the sports section of the newspaper that was lying on the seat beside her—big headlines. There was a glorious shot of Mateo, his mouth wide open in a victory shout, triumphantly raising his mallet, looking incredibly handsome, the reins in his left hand and part of the mare's head in the shot.

"I hope you're going to get a print of that," Jess said.

"I've already called the sports editor and asked for it," she said with a broad smile on her face.

They left the city behind and drove for just over an hour. The land was slightly rolling grassland with a few trees and more space between the homes. Barns and open-sided arenas began to appear along with the classic ranch-style houses.

"Here we are," said Carla, slowing the truck and pulling into a well-tended driveway. There were a dozen sleek, shiny horses in the paddock. Jess could see that Felipe was already there, talking to their host. He'd borrowed the same car as before.

"Carla, would you mind taking some pics for me?" she said, handing the camera to her.

"Sure."

The man introduced himself as George Hungerford. He was dressed in jodhpurs, full-height leather boots and a polo shirt. Jess picked up on his Texan accent immediately.

Felipe stayed in the background watching, acknowledging her with a nod.

"I'm pleased to meet you Mr. Hungerford," she said, shaking his hand. "What part of Texas are you from?"

"Near San Antonio, and you?"

"Lexington, Kentucky."

"Right then. Come and see my horses." There were two horses in the barn. One was a seventeen hand Hanoverian, then George moved over one stall. "This is Alfonso," he said opening the stall door.

Jess had seen pictures of Andalusians, but had never seen a real one. Nothing had prepared her for the animal she saw. George untied the stallion and walked him out of his stall. Jess walked around Alfonso, looking at his conformation. The white horse was not tall, barely fifteen hands. He was short bodied with a powerful neck, short clean legs, a very wide chest, and muscular hind quarters. His wavy grey mane hung in a two-foot cascade, his tail nearly reaching the ground. His head was refined with intelligent dark eyes that calmly watched her. He had the confident stance of royalty. She stood for a few moments in total awe, her hands up to her mouth.

"Oh, George. he's breathtaking," she said. "He's so different from the Thoroughbreds I'm used to."

George laughed. "He certainly is. I'm very proud of him. Carla tells me you've been riding all your life. He's had dressage training. Do you have any experience in that?"

"Yes, I've have had some. Mostly I've been an exercise rider on several Thoroughbred farms. I would be absolutely honored to ride this horse, George, but if you're not comfortable with allowing a total stranger to ride him, just say the word. I'd understand," she said.

George fitted the black bridle and the saddle on the horse, then held the stirrup while she mounted. "Let's see how you do," he said handing her a helmet.

"Do you have music?" she asked.

"You mean like the Spanish Riding School?"

"Yes. I know he's not a Lipizzaner but I like the Franz Schubert piece."

"I'll find it."

She gathered the reins and walked the horse forward. She spent the first few minutes getting the feeling of his mouth and the degree of contact he was comfortable with. The very familiar military march started to play so she eased him into a slow trot. She put him through every move she knew—shoulder-in, shoulder-out, transitions and changing leads on the diagonal.

The horse was obviously dressage schooled. He responded to her cues, his ears back listening; his movement smooth and fluid. Together, they settled into a rhythm where she felt at one with him. There was no bounce to the sitting trot; she was glued to the saddle. Together they progressed to a controlled canter working from a large circle to smaller ones. He started to resist at one point tossing his head, snorting, and prancing, but she adjusted her tension on the reins and made him work until she got some wonderful extended trots from him.

Finally, she asked him for a hand gallop so he surged forward, the walls of the arena a blur. It was like flying. Slowly, she brought him back to a walk then to a perfectly balanced halt, his neck arched, standing square on all four feet. She bowed her head for a moment then slackened the reins, allowing him to stretch his neck out long and low to relax. On a loose rein, she walked him back to where George, Carla, and Felipe were standing. Sliding out of the saddle, she dismounted, running the stirrups up. Much to her amazement, the arena clock showed she'd ridden for nearly an hour.

"George, I don't have words to describe that. I wish I had more dressage training," she said handing the reins to him.

"Well done. Dressage may not be your forte, but what you do know, you know well. Control was never an issue. He responded remarkably well to you. Even with me, he has his moments when it comes to obedience. You've got good hands." He took Alfonso back to his stall and removed the tack, rolling the door shut. The horse hadn't even raised a sweat.

"Thank you so much. That was an opportunity of a life time," she said shaking his hand and returning the helmet. The three of them walked out to the parking lot, leaving George with his charges.

"Earth to Jessica," said Carla with a huge smile on her face, giving her a hug. "You looked great out there. I don't have to ask you if it was good; you're glowing." She handed Jess her camera.

Felipe was standing with his camera over his shoulder and that cryptic smile on his face.

"Were you able to get some shots?" Jess asked.

"I've taken about a hundred pictures, from every angle I could get," he said, his smile broadening into a grin.

"What's next then?" Jess asked.

"Well, Felipe has a suggestion that you might be interested in," said Carla.

"Jess, if you'd like to come with me, I want to take you to a small traditional restaurant not far from here, where they prepare maté tea, the national drink of Argentina."

Jess looked at Carla. Carla nodded and gave her thumbs up.

"Sure, that's alright with me," Jess said, grabbing her belongings from the truck and changing from her boots to her runners. "In that case Carla, I'll see you on Sunday at your parents' place, my last asado." She had a few misgivings about Felipe, but he seemed normal at the moment.

She slipped into the passenger seat of Felipe's car, fastening her seat belt. He drove through several small towns before slowing down near ancient stucco buildings, shaded by large trees, where he parked the car. The town was merely a huddle of older single-story houses and a well. The sign over the door of the restaurant was so old that the words had completely faded. Wizened, nut-brown old men were sitting on benches, leaning against the wall, looking as old as the buildings. A couple of equally ancient and rather thin dogs lay sprawled a few feet away, sound asleep in the dust. There was an old-fashioned clay bake oven under the tree. It reminded Jess of paintings she'd seen in the museum.

Felipe walked ahead of her, greeting the seniors who nodded with toothless smiles. She followed him inside. The room was small with half a dozen tables and chairs as well as benches. The trees filtered the sunshine, creating a pleasant soft light. He pulled the chair out for her then sat down himself.

The middle-aged aproned man who appeared from behind a curtained doorway was obviously the proprietor. He immediately came over to the table. Jess caught a glimpse of an elderly woman in the kitchen. She listened to the conversation between the two men only recognizing a couple of words: *yerba mate* and *Americana.* Then there was a cascade of words she didn't understand: *bombilla, fugazetta con queso, Moscato.* Eduardo smiled and put a kettle of water on the small stove to heat.

Felipe told her, "I'll give you a quick history lesson. Maté's an herbal tea grown by Indigenous people for hundreds if not thousands of years. They drank it out of a hollowed gourd with a filtered straw. It's had a varied history since the Spanish and Jesuits discovered it. At times it was banned, but now it is commercially grown in some of the provinces west of here, where there's more rainfall. We export tons of it all over the world, the US included."

"What's he doing now?" Jess asked, peering at the man.

"The person who prepares the tea is called a *cebador.* Basically, you fill the gourd with maté leaves and add hot water, put the straw in to filter out the bits and pass it around. There's a whole protocol to doing it. The straw's called a *bombilla.* Back in Buenos Aires you might have seen people carrying a thermos; that's hot water for their maté ."

Eduardo brought the pot over and handed it to Felipe, who put the bombilla in the pot and took a long drink. When he was done, he refilled the pot and handed it to her. She took it from his hands and looked in the pot to see a dense mash of green leaves. She took a sip, finding it a little bitter but not too different from some of the herbal teas she had tried at home.

"This seems a very pleasant way to while away the afternoon on a hot day," she said.

"I thought you might like to try it," he said refilling the pot.

Jess caught glimpses of food being prepared in the kitchen. Another couple came in and sat behind them. They ordered tea as well.

"I have a question for you, Felipe. You don't have to answer if you're not comfortable," she said.

The frown replaced the smile on his face. He waited.

"I spent some time in the art museum last week and I saw your painting of the street vendors. It's wonderful, so different from what I saw at your studio. Why did you stop painting?"

There was dead silence for a minute.

"I apologize. I shouldn't have asked," she said. Talking about it might help him work things through like it did for her at Mrs. H.'s.

"The day my wife died, we had an argument. You've seen what I'm like when I lose my temper. Well, Francesca's temper was the same as mine. It was a very bad argument but then she walked out, got in our car, and two hours later she was dead. It was my fault. The following morning when I woke up, it was like I was in a foggy room. I could see color but it was dull. It hasn't changed since then. All I can think of is gray and black like the pictures you saw."

She looked at him while sipping her mate. How depressing. "Have you ever been to a doctor about all of this? Could there be a physical problem?"

He shook his head.

"Perhaps it would be a good idea, Felipe; you have so much talent. I can't even draw a straight line. I recognized the black hole in those paintings. I've been there too. When my husband Andy and I separated, it scared me to be down there in the dark all alone. The only things that saved me were horses and dancing. I literally kept myself so busy I didn't have time to think or get depressed."

There was a long silent pause. Eduardo brought over two large glasses and a bottle of Moscato.

"Try this wine, Jess," Felipe said raising his glass to her. "Why did you and your husband split?"

She took a sip; it was sweet and strong. "I discovered he was bisexual and had had an affair with a young woman and a young man," she said.

Felipe's eyebrows went up and he nodded.

"Maybe you could try painting over some of those canvases with Diego's yellow paint; fill in the hole, like liquid sunshine. Then you could add a ladder or a rope—anything to get you out of that hole. I don't like seeing you so sad," she said.

The shutters came down behind his eyes, subject closed.

"Go on. I dare you. Find a way out," she said, very softly.

He took a large mouthful of wine, looked long and hard at her, but said nothing.

They continued to sit quietly in a somewhat uncomfortable silence sipping their wine, as yeasty aromas and the smell of wood smoke began wafting in from outside. Eventually Eduardo came in carrying a large, heaped pizza on a metal tray that he placed on the table. Jess couldn't believe her eyes. Of course, it was cooked in the old oven outside.

The older lady brought out cutlery and napkins. Felipe sliced the thick golden crust into wedges. There was a tomato sauce base, but the toppings were dense with mounds of melted cheese and onions. Jess inhaled the smells and thought she'd died and gone to heaven. Between the mmms, ahhs and dripping melted cheese, the mood lightened.

"Argentinians are more Italian than Spanish, you know. Pizza is almost our national dish, after beef of course," Felipe said, returning to safer topics of conversation.

Between the two of them, they finished off the pizza and sat back, sated on carbs and wine.

"Oh, I almost forgot," he said pulling two tickets out of his pocket. "I have tickets for Juan Navaro Carrizo at the Teatro Colon on Saturday. I heard you were interested."

"How did you manage to get tickets? They were sold out!"

"I called in a favor from an old friend," he said waving them under her nose.

"I'd love to go. I hear the building is incredible. I also hear it's pretty formal. What do I wear?"

"Sometimes it's tuxedos and gowns, but for this my black suit is good for me and for you a classic sort of dress. Do you have one?"

"I bought one when I was out shopping with Carla last week and I haven't had a chance to wear it yet. Perfect! What's the best way to get there?" she said leaning across the table to talk to him, seeing his lighter side.

There was a tiny smile on his face now. "Why don't you get a cab to my place and we'll continue together from there, say at seven? That will give us lots of time. We'll have supper after the show. There's a local restaurant I'd like to take you to."

"Sounds good to me," said Jess mellowed by the wine.

Later, Felipe drove her back to the apartment. What a day—a beautiful ride and an unexpectedly pleasant afternoon. There was so much shut away behind those dark eyes.

Chapter 23

THURSDAY'S DANCE LESSON WAS A WORKOUT. ANTONIO drove her hard, knowing his time constraints. With the other studio available again, Diego and Julia were just as driven, determined to get their dance number perfect. They tweaked the routine, sorting out the difficult places and working her until she got it.

"You haven't said anything about what to wear for this dance, Julia. When I was at your home, I remember seeing a red dress in your closet. The only good dress I have is red too. Could we both wear red?" Jess asked.

Julia looked at her and smiled. "Yes! That would work, especially with this music. Let's do that," she said, looking at her brother for confirmation.

Diego stood there thinking. "Good idea. I don't have a red shirt, but I have that white one with the ruffles down the front. That would be effective."

Finally, it was coming together. Tomorrow would be their last chance before Sunday's reveal.

*   *   *

THERE WAS NO NEED FOR HER TO HURRY. THE ONLY THING on her agenda for the rest of the day was the soccer game that evening with Leonardo and Emilia. She spent the day by the pool going through her tourist guidebooks again, knowing that it would be very unlikely to ever be in Buenos Aires again; she simply couldn't afford it. She only had Friday, Monday and Tuesday left for sightseeing. Wednesday she would be home. *Home!* That sounded weird. Lexington. The map on the wall showed her travels. She'd covered a lot of territory in a short period of time.

That evening, Jess ate supper with the Ortizes, as they all sat watching TV. The contents of Jess's two bottles of wine disappeared quickly. She was getting fond of the Argentinian red.

"River Plate's playing San Lorenzo tonight. River Plate are in shirts with the white shield and red diagonal stripe. San Lorenzo has the blue and red vertical stripes. We're supporters of River Plate," he proudly explained.

It was a bigger stadium than the polo grounds and from what Jess could see, there was not a single empty seat. If she had thought the polo fans were the craziest ever, she would have been wrong. Football fans were totally insane. The perfectly normal Leonardo, now transformed from gentle civilized human being into yelling, screaming, fist-pumping, on-his-feet maniac. The arena looked like a scene from a riot. She couldn't even imagine being a fan in the stands. There was enough noise in decibels to render a person permanently deaf.

Jess glanced at Emilia who seemed to be taking it in stride and merely shrugged in amusement. Even Andy with his Sunday football games hadn't been quite that bad.

The door to the balcony was wide open, and she could tell from the noise that there were many others in the building rooting for their team.

The players were just as quick as polo ponies, running, kicking the ball, and avoiding their opponents. Heated arguments broke out over the referee's decisions. She prayed for his safety. She admired the athleticism of the players. They were so fit and tough. The goaltenders were amazing, making spectacular leaps and dives to block the ball. Every play brought a strong reaction from the fans. River Plate finally won the match and a totally exhausted but happy Leonardo staggered off to bed.

FRIDAY MORNING AFTER HER DANCE CLASSES, JESS TOOK A breather. She was amazed they'd managed to have dance time without Sebastian or Antonio discovering their scheme but they did appear to have been occupied with their own classes. The kids had been good at keeping them under surveillance for schedule changes. They too were enjoying the intrigue and keeping the adults out of the loop.

She walked to the tourist office and found a tour specializing in street graffiti. The rest of her day was spent walking the streets with a dozen other tourists and a guide, seeing paintings of every description on the walls of apartments, houses, and stores. Subject matter was wide open: dogs, farmers and chickens, beautiful women, caricatures of politicians, rebels, needy children, hallucinating musicians, outer space, flowers. It seemed endless. Each mural was individual, showing the skill of each artist. Some were very good. There was even one of a hairy man's face, composed of eclectic pieces of metal. She took a taxi back to The Gaucho for lunch and ended her day as usual by the pool.

Saturday, she lay in bed with no need whatsoever to get up. Later she sent an email to her mother, telling her about Alfredo the Andalusian, soccer games, maté, and graffiti. She decided to buy flowers for Olivia in appreciation of the hospitality she had received. The Ramirez family had been very generous to her. Emilia deserved a bouquet too. The nearby florist shop was closed on Sundays, so she'd have to get them that day. She checked her crimson dress. She loved the simple elegance of it with the soft folds of material and the body-hugging form. Having seen pictures of the opulent Colon Theater, that dress was going to be perfect. It also was right for the dance performance at the asado. She thought their performance might give Sebastian a taste of things to come with these two kids.

Later that morning, after stopping at the deli to pick up lunch, she walked to the florists and after much thought opted for two bouquets of white chrysanthemums and roses. Her budget took a hit but it seemed right. Back at the apartment, she found Emilia in the kitchen and gave her the flowers. The woman was flustered with the gesture.

"Emilia, you and Leonardo have opened your home to me and helped me a lot. I'm grateful. Do you have another vase? I'm going to give these to Señora Ramirez tomorrow."

She spent the rest of the afternoon by the pool. She did a few laps in body temperature water then soaked up the sun. She now had a glowing tan. The girls back home would be jealous. Felipe was on her mind too. She had a definite soft spot for him. At times she felt really drawn to him. It was powerful, but he was a troubled man and she didn't intend to be a one-night stand.

She wasn't sure how she'd react if Felipe made a romantic move. She'd try to avoid going inside his shop and the apartment above it. She was looking forward to getting all the divorce matters settled and seeing Andy one more time. She hadn't seen him since November. She had no idea how she would react to him either and whether her broken heart had healed enough for her to forgive him. New relationships were not feasible until that happened and a distance one was basically impossible.

Five o'clock rolled around. She had Emilia order the cab for six-fifteen, allowing for traffic, the pickup at Felipe's by seven, and final destination—Teatro Colon. She applied her makeup and dressed with care. The short hair cut was so easy; just comb, and go. The dress seemed a little looser but that figured; she'd been getting a two-hour workout every day. She looked in the mirror feeling somewhat daring with the spaghetti straps, padded bra top. and bare shoulders. Emilia looked at her, made her turn around and show off the dress. Leonardo glanced over his sports pages and made appreciative noises. As soon as the intercom buzzed, she was on her way.

Felipe must have been waiting inside right by the door, as he came out of the shop immediately the black-and-yellow taxi drew up and honked its horn. He looked good in his black suit and crisp white shirt; it fit his tight, compact body well. He had his black wavy hair pulled back in a pony tail and had thinned out the stubble on his chin. He slipped into the back seat beside her with a greeting but his eyes examined every inch of her in the dress. "Good choice," he said.

Jess couldn't believe the size of the theater. It took up a whole city block, multiple stories high with columns, porticos, and domes. Opulence was again the operative word. The interior lounge areas had high ceilings, more ornate columns, marble statues, massive chandeliers, and brocade-clad furniture with gold-painted woodwork. Some rooms had domed ceilings. In other areas, the rooms went up into open space two floors high with exquisite stained glass at the top. There were throngs of people, all in suits and nice dresses, with a few of the more affluent types in tuxedos and gowns.

Jess clung to Felipe's arm, feeling overwhelmed. He led her along the corridor into the main theater. She gaped at the expanse of seating. Apart from the floor level, there were five floors of stacked narrow balconies. The really important people were sitting up there. The main stage was massive, with huge, draped curtains. On stage, there were a set of drums and an assortment of hand drums, microphones, amplifiers, and several tall stools.

"It seats twenty-five-hundred," he said highly amused by her sense of wonder. "The acoustics in here are among the best in the world," he said. "Many international orchestras and ballet companies come here." Rechecking the ticket stubs, he guided her to the correct row, his hand on her waist.

Jess was spell bound watching the people get seated, noting what they were wearing. The crowd represented people from twenty to ninety years of age who were substantially well-to-do. It made Laura O'Connell's galas look like yard-sale material.

The lights dimmed and the master of ceremonies introduced the three men on stage and the full orchestra with the conductor. All the musicians were in tuxedos with black bow ties. Carrizo was Argentinian and well-known to the audience. He was sitting on a stool, the guitar on his lap; a round of applause went up. The bass player took a bow, the upright bass beside him. The drummer sat on a stool with some drums that Jess recognized, but there was a collection of things that looked like earthenware pots, a bandoneon at his feet.

The trio started off with a melody the audience knew, a melancholy love song. The notes were crystal clear capturing the Spanish touch. It always amazed Jess how a guitar could emote feelings. Felipe handed her a pair of binoculars. She watched Carrizo move his fingers over the frets; his right hand with the long thumb nail picked individual strings or strummed precisely. The next piece was the *Concerto in D* by Vivaldi and the orchestra played throughout, providing a beauty of their own. She handed the binoculars back to him.

The program gave the name of the next number as *Libertango* by Piazzolla. Jess closed her eyes and listened. It sounded like two guitars; one playing the melody, the other the background. Somehow, Carrizo worked the magic with his thumb and forefinger separate from his other fingers. His skill was unbelievable.

For the next few hours, she was spellbound. Most of the pieces were classical. After intermission, the music changed to fast paced modern numbers. The drummer provided the background rhythms, his hands a blur, creating hollow tapping noises, similar to bongos on the urns. Several times he switched to the bandoneon to introduce tangos. She wanted to get up and dance. The versatility of the musicians was incredible.

At the end, the audience gave them a hearty round of applause, demanding more which they got. Finally, the curtain came down. It took a long time for the large group of people to disperse but neither Jess nor Felipe was in a hurry. There was a large green park across the road from the theater.

"If we walk across here, we'll find the restaurant down the street. Well, what did you think?" he asked, holding her hand as they crossed the road. Traffic was heavy especially with cabs and private cars picking up passengers around the theater.

"I really enjoyed that. They played a bit of everything—some of the old songs and some classics. I imagine you're more familiar with the more modern pieces. There was enough variety there to please everyone. Good musicians too. I didn't realize that you could get tours of just the building. It's so elaborate you could spend hours in there."

"It took about twenty years to build, I think. The original building burned down and it had to be rebuilt."

By the time they found the restaurant it was nearly eleven o'clock, the perfect dining hour in Buenos Aires. There was a massive stuffed specimen of a Hereford bull in the main entrance sporting a halter and big blue and white ribbon for champion bull, proof the restaurant served only the best beef. It amused Jess. They stood in line just talking, passing the time until a table was available.

Finally, they were escorted to a table by their white-jacketed waiter.

"Would you care for a drink?" Felipe asked.

"I quite liked the wine we had on Wednesday at that little pizzeria," she said.

"The Moscato? Could I recommend a Malbec?"

She nodded.

He ordered a bottle which was uncorked with due ceremony by the waiter and a small amount poured for Felipe to sample. He swirled it, examined it in the light, sniffed it, took a sip, then gave a nod of approval. The waiter poured a full glass for each of them. Jess took a sip. It was good. She decided her palate wasn't sophisticated enough to tell what fruits were present in the bouquet and she wondered if Felipe did.

"Can you really tell whether there's a touch of cherry and pear in the bouquet?" she asked.

A tiny smile came over his face. He bowed his head and shook a very brief negative, then raised his glass to hers.

She burst out laughing. The meal was delightful. The beef lived up to their expectations and he suggested a dessert called *dulce de leche,* a caramel parfait with a port wine meringue. She couldn't pass it up. The meal ended with a cup of coffee. She felt stuffed.

"Jess, would you consider coming back to my place and staying with me tonight?"

She came close to dropping her cup. He was looking particularly attractive at that moment with stray locks of hair framing his face and his dark eyes swallowing her.

"I'm not a one-night stand, Felipe," she said very gently.

"I know you're not," he softly replied, taking her hand, edging closer to her, so their faces were only inches apart. "I really want you in my bed."

She paused for a moment wondering how to say no without hurting his feelings.

"Felipe, part of me is very attracted to you. I'm not denying that. But, part of my broken heart hasn't recovered and my divorce isn't finalized. I don't know if I've managed to forgive him yet and I need to heal. I don't think I could survive having my heart broken a second time. Besides, by Wednesday, I'll be back in the States." She looked into those eyes; the urge to comply was huge. He was reeling her in.

She pulled back. "I can't."

He sat there looking at her for a few moments. "In that case, Señora, I'd better call a cab and get you home." After paying the bill, he flagged down a taxi and opened the door for her, giving the driver her address. She climbed in and he shut the door, leaving her alone. As the taxi pulled away, she turned to see him standing on the sidewalk.

Chapter 24

SHE DIDN'T SLEEP WELL, REPLAYING THE SCENE AT THE RES-
taurant over and over in her mind. Although she knew she'd
done the right thing, there was a real sense she was going to
regret that decision forever. How would it have felt to have
a man like him want her and make love to her? Would she
have been woman enough to satisfy him? She doubted very
much that he would be at the asado.

Jess looked at her red dress. She'd be wearing it again
for Diego and Julia's big reveal as choreographers. She
couldn't let them down. After breakfast, she went for her
morning swim, letting the water wash over her as she did
laps. It soothed. She slept on the lounge chair for a while.
She couldn't be bothered with lunch, just eating an orange.

At one she booked a taxi for two o'clock and got changed.
She gathered up the flowers for Olivia and went down to the
lobby. The cab was surprisingly prompt and deposited her
in front of the apartment building. She could see Mateo's
truck parked on the street, so Carla was already there. That
was good. It was Emilio who buzzed her in. She walked
into the apartment; it was as beautiful as ever. She was now
looking at things, seeing them for the last time, imprinting
them on her brain. The holiday was winding down.

Olivia came into the kitchen carrying an empty platter. Seeing Jess, she greeted her with a hug and a lovely smile.

Jess passed the flowers to her. "For you, Señora. You and your husband have been very kind."

"Thank you. These are beautiful," Olivia said rummaging in the cupboard for a vase. She arranged them and placed them on the coffee table. "You go out and see Carla," she said shooing her onto the patio.

Carla saw her coming, raising her eyebrows at the dress. "You've finally got a chance to wear it. Looks great."

"I wore it last night. Felipe took me to the Colon Theater, then out for supper."

"Ah, ha. And where did you go?"

"To the restaurant with the stuffed bull out front."

"That's high end. And—" Carla said expectantly.

"And nothing," said Jess shrugging.

"That does not sound like my cousin," said Carla with her hands on her hips and a frown on her face.

"Well, he did try."

"You turned him down? Jess!"

"Carla, I'm not ready and you know it," Jess said.

"I know it but it would have been so nice. Then maybe you could have stayed here permanently and I could see you all the time."

"Carla Santos, you're a schemer," Jess said laughing at her blatantly romantic friend, who was obviously still in the newlywed glow.

Other family members were arriving. Antonio and his girlfriend came in, followed by Felipe's mother, brother, and his children. Felipe was not with them. Enzo and Angelica were the next ones to arrive with Diego and Julia. Julia was in her red dress. Jess casually walked over to them.

"I do like your dress, Julia. That color really suits you," she said, as if it was normal conversation.

Julia was quite ready to play the game. "Thank you. The one you're wearing is very pretty too," Julia replied comparing the color and fabrics side by side. Diego was sorting through the CDs trying to keep his face neutral, but Jess could see the energy bottled up inside both of them, like a ticking time bomb. He couldn't even look at her.

"Are we ready to go?" Jess whispered.

"Yes," said Julia.

Jess walked back to Carla's table and sat down. Sebastian came in with Sofia. Jess asked him if he knew any good dance instructors in the US.

"Do you intend to continue your lessons?" he asked.

"I haven't decided. Now that I know the quality of instruction I need, it depends on distance, the cost of lessons, driving, and time. I work full-time and have an hour's drive each way to get to work. I don't think I'm good enough for competitive dancing. I'm starting too late, but I enjoy it very much."

He disappeared into the apartment returning five minutes later with a list for her.

"Thank you, I appreciate that," she said looking down the list. Georgia, New York, Chicago, San Francisco, and Miami. Chicago was the closest possibility but even that was six hours from home. Not really feasible. "I want to thank you, so much. Antonio's been an excellent teacher for me."

"You're more than welcome," he replied.

She had just sat down when Felipe came onto the patio. It had all the drama of an old B-grade black-and-white 1950s gangster movie. He was wearing black: black shirt, black pants, and a black fedora tilted at a rakish angle. He looked positively feral. He'd left his hair untied, hanging down to his shoulders. He didn't even look in her direction as he sat with his family.

Sebastian got up and prepared the music for Diego and Julia's performance.

Jess could feel the excitement and nervousness building. As usual, the youngsters were totally professional, probably putting performance anxiety behind them at some ridiculously young age. This evening's dance was a tango and Jess concentrated on Julia's footwork. Suddenly it was over. Jess took a deep breathSebastian had just sat down when Diego picked up the microphone. "May I have your attention please. Tonight, my sister and I have devised a special performance for all of you. Tio Sebastian has always supervised our dances. We have arranged something special for him. This is our first attempt at choreographing our own dance routine. We have asked our guest Jessica to assist us," he said with a perfectly even voice, no sign of nervousness. He beckoned Jess to join them.

Sebastian looked perplexed. Carla had the look on her face which clearly implied, "I knew you were up to something" and Antonio looked dumbfounded. She couldn't see Felipe's face. A buzz went round the crowd.

She walked across the floor to join them, standing on Diego's right with Julia on his left. Someone put the CD on. The solo guitar cued them and the dance began. It was a paso doble. Diego raised his left arm, Julia stepped in front facing him, her movement fluid. He lowered his right hand, moving Jess out to the right and slightly behind. And as she curled back in, it was Julia who was turning away. He led perfectly, weaving them together, turning constantly, stamping his feet, posing as the matador.

The music changed to flamenco. Diego turned Jess in a spin to the right then let her go while drawing Julia close to him. Jess went into flamenco mode, arching her back, stamping her feet, tossing her head, and flaring the skirt of her dress with her fingers. She walked toward him, one foot in front of the other in elegant deliberate steps. As she approached, he unfurled Julia to the left, letting her go and reeled Jess in with the right, the bandoneon and guitar providing lush rhythms. Julia did her flamenco routine.

For the finale the guitars, violins, and bandoneon came to a climax, leaving the two girls on the floor at his feet with the skirts of their crimson dresses spread out around them. Diego stood there triumphant with his arms in the air. The music stopped.

There was a pause, then pandemonium erupted with clapping and cheering. Sebastian was hugging Diego and the whole family emptied onto the dance floor. Jess and Julia got to their feet and hugged each other. "That went really well. It was beautiful," Jess said.

"You nailed it," said Julia as they were enveloped in the arms of Enzo and Angelica.

Jess couldn't get near Diego with the frenzied crowd. She suddenly found a strong pair of arms around her. Looking up, it was Felipe. He held her so tightly that he almost crushed the air out of her, one hand across her back, bringing them chest to chest and the other pulling her lower body to him. "The next dance is mine," he said.

Sebastian took the microphone. Gradually, the crowd became quiet. "Today, I realize I have taken these two children for granted. I am used to seeing them every week, for the past seven years. But today I am the proudest dance instructor on the planet. They have taken the initiative to create something completely different and made it work. This routine is unique; it has combinations I would never have dreamed of. Bravo! I can see that their future has expanded exponentially—dancing and choreography. Now, let all of us get on the dance floor and celebrate."

The first music to play was a slow one. All the couples were holding each other close. Jess could feel Felipe rather than see him. She was tucked tight to his chest, her face buried in the side of his neck, under the brim of his hat. She had no idea what dance he was doing but she followed his lead.

His voice was quiet, deep, and husky. "I think the next number is a tango. You have given me challenges; now it's my turn. For a woman to be truly invested in her partner, she must be sensual and give herself to him—the essence of tango. So, I challenge you to give yourself to me on the dance floor." The dark eyes dared her and hypnotically drew her in. She took a deep breath, paused, and went with it.

The intro had them in basic stance. She knew she was the better dancer but could she move outside her comfort zone and evoke the sensuality of this dance? The melody began. He stepped, she countered; he stepped again, she paused in time to the music and did a caress to his left leg, raising her eyes to meet his, quite deliberately challenging him to do more. She exaggerated her foot and hand movements in the elegant way Julia did, making her foot placement exact.

Several moves later, she could feel her body responding to his, feeling pulsations run through her, feeling herself go into a throbbing primal place. Finally, Jess knew what it felt like to be as one with a partner. As the music was coming to its conclusion, he bent low over her forcing her into a full left leg extension, low to the floor, with her right knee tightly bent. She gazed up at him. Their lips were a breath apart. The music ended. He gently raised her to her feet.

"Hold me," Jess said urgently as she felt that gut-wrenching orgasmic spasm run through her and a low moan escaped her lips. Looking up at him, she whispered "You won."

He clutched her to his chest only releasing her when her breathing settled. There was a twisted smile on his face. "I wasn't expecting that," he said giving her a deep kiss on the mouth, then suddenly became serious. "I may have won but now I know exactly what I'm losing." He walked her back to where Carla and Mateo were sitting. Then he was gone, through the patio doors and into the apartment and did not return. Jess sat beside Carla, who promptly poured a large glass of red wine and placed it in front of her. They didn't speak for a few minutes. Carla knew something had happened. Jess pulled herself together.

The teens were swaying and rocking to *La Vida Loca*. Even Diego and Julia were dancing. She grabbed Carla and dragged her onto the dance floor.

"Come on, Carla," Jess said seeing her friend was reluctant with Sebastian present. "I've already broken all the rules tonight. You can blame me."

Carla grinned and the two of them let loose with free form samba shimmies and shakes. At the end of the dance, Carla whispered to her "Let's do another one."

Both of them gave Mateo the eye and beckoned him to join them. He burst out laughing and shook his head "no," so the girls went back to their routine. After that, they sat back down.

"Sorry, Señoras. I'd be safer playing polo than dancing with you two," he said. Carla gave his hand a squeeze.

The chef had been busy and the smell of cooked beef signaled the end of the dance. As usual, the beef was superb. When it was time to leave Jess thanked everyone again. Carla and Mateo drove her back to the apartment.

"Jess do you want me to come with you to the airport Wednesday morning?" Carla asked.

"My flight is early. It won't work for you and Mateo. It's just as easy for me to take a taxi. Besides it's a work day for you. It's okay, I can manage. I've had a wonderful holiday here."

There were hugs and tears. "I promise to keep in touch. Send me emails when you can. Now I know your family, I want to know what happens to them. I start my new job next week, so I'll have news for you. Keep an eye on *el primo* Felipe," Jess said.

With a wave, the truck merged into traffic and was gone. Jess went up to the apartment and into her room. As she sat on the bed, she thought about all the things that had happened that day. Diego's dance routine had been superb and she was pleased with Sebastian's reaction. Maybe now he would give those two kids a bit more leeway. She would never have believed she was capable of having that reaction with Felipe. But to have an orgasm on the dance floor; never had she been so aroused. It was a good thing it had been crowded. She didn't think too many people noticed.

She gently hand washed her dress in cool soapy water and rinsed it out, placing it on a hanger in the closet to dry, then went to bed.

Chapter 25

ROUTINE MONDAY—DANCE LESSON WITH ANTONIO. WHEN she got there, he was smiling. "Well done, Jess. You did a good job getting those kids organized. Was that your idea or Diego's? Your dancing has improved immensely. You've worked hard and it shows. Now, for these last two days, I think perhaps instead of lessons, we could just dance."

"I merely hinted he should try something else and have a little fun with it," she said. For the next hour they danced everything from waltz to tango. When the tango began, Jess went into tango mode but this time it was sensual not sexual. She teased and gave him the look but it did not generate the same response as it had with Felipe. As a matter of fact, Antonio seemed amused. She simply enjoyed herself. It flitted through her mind that the tango had originated with Italian migrant men who danced with each other because they'd left their families behind and there were no women to dance with.

"See you tomorrow," she said when her hour was up. She peeked in the room next door. Diego and Julia were leaning over a table listening intently to Sebastian as he was explaining something. She didn't interrupt them and went outside. Another beautiful day. She felt lazy and walked down to the deli to get her lunch. She had planned on find a tour of some kind for the afternoon but really couldn't be bothered, so she spent the time by the pool.

Jess ate her supper at The Gaucho again. She almost felt like a regular there and the waiter brought her standard well-done steak with red wine without even bothering with the menu. Afterwards, she went back to the apartment and started packing. She took down her map of Buenos Aires and folded it, tucking into the side pocket of her suitcase. Most of the literature she discarded. She sorted through her clothes, decided what to wear on Wednesday's flight and packed the rest.

Tuesday morning was her last day. She got teary-eyed saying goodbye to everyone. Big hugs from Diego and Julia. "I may be a long way away, but I'm going to keep track of you two. One day I'll be able to say I danced with world champions Diego and Julia," she said. She cleaned out her locker, making sure she'd got everything and went back to the apartment.

Last afternoon by the pool. She was so brown now that no one was going to recognize her. When Emilia got home from work, Jess had her book a taxi for five-thirty Wednesday morning. She had a quiet evening with the Ortizes and thanked them again for their hospitality. She packed her camera and laptop in her carry-on bag.

Wednesday morning, she was up at four-thirty. She double checked the closet, ensuring she had her passport and ticket. Emilia had left fruit, cereal, and sweet rolls for her. She took one last look around and left the apartment key on the kitchen counter. The taxi showed up on time and half an hour later she was at the airport, as traffic was quite moderate. Jess had some difficulty getting her boarding pass on the self-serve, but an attendant assisted her and she found herself in the departure lounge with her carry-on bag. She found another mystery novel to occupy her time.

This time Jess felt like an old pro, knowing what to expect. As the plane took off, she watched Buenos Aires and the Rio de la Plata shrink to tiny dots. It had been an experience of a life time. She spent some time thinking of the people she'd met, all the places she'd seen and realized how she'd grown with the experience. She was completely different from the naive untraveled woman who'd left Lexington three weeks earlier.

Jess had just enough time in Houston go through customs and change planes. It was dark when it finally landed in Lexington. The first thing she noticed was the cold. Slipping her jacket on, Jess's immediate impression was that everyone had pale skin. She quickly found a cab and was home in no time. It felt weird not having to calculate the exchange.

Her car was still in the driveway. She patted it and thought of Diego. Although it was late, Mrs. H.'s lights were still on, so she knocked on the door.

"Oh Jess, come in," Mrs. H. said, giving her a huge hug. "My goodness, the tan, and you've cut your hair. Let's have a look at you," she said, turning Jess around. The next thing Jess knew, she was sitting down having a cup of coffee with a plate of home-baked cookies in front of her. They talked for over an hour, then Mrs. H. gave her the keys and she went home.

The apartment looked tiny. She'd spent three weeks seeing grand, elaborate places and now she was back. She looked at her father's pictures on the wall and the Kentucky rifle. Small it might be but it was home. She pulled out the sofa bed and made it up. The plants looked healthy. There was a stack of mail on the table. It was then that she saw the flashing light on her phone indicating saved messages.

There were three: one from Mr. Ames, reminding her to call when she got back, one from Karen asking her to go for coffee, and one from Duffy. That one caught her attention.

"Jess, this is Duffy. Neil and I are still in Lexington. There's a lot going on and none of it is good. PLEASE, do not under ANY circumstances come to the stables. It's not safe. This place is a powder keg that could blow any time. Repeat: NOT SAFE. Call me on my cell as soon as you get back, regardless of the time and I'll fill you in."

She wrote down the call back number and somewhat reluctantly dialed it. The phone rang a couple of times then he answered sounding like it had woken him up.

"Duffy, this is Jess. I just got home."

"Thank God you got my message. I need to see you in person. Some of this can't be said over the phone. When are you available?" He sounded very concerned.

"I'm don't have to work until Monday but I do have some things to do tomorrow."

"Can you meet me at the drive-through on Man O' War drive at five-thirty? The O'Connells won't be awake that early so it'll be safe for me to leave."

He sounded so serious that she agreed.

"I'll see you in the morning then," he said, hanging up.

Jess stared at the phone. She'd only been home a couple of hours and the intrigue was starting all over again.

The alarm clock rang like a rooster, startling her out of a sound sleep. It took a few moments to orient herself, then she showered and dressed in jeans and a T-shirt. Ah, back to normal. She looked at the thermometer: thirty-eight degrees. She slipped on her winter jacket, making sure she had her gloves. The car started well so she sat for a few minutes, letting it warm up. What a blessing to have her own car. No more taxis. She drove over to the drive-through and parked the car. She couldn't see Duffy, so she waited.

A few minutes later, a cab pulled in and Duffy got out. She noticed his tight athletic body in his gray jogging suit and the wooly hat. He saw her and indicated for her to stay put, entering the coffee shop. He exited shortly after with two coffees and walked over to the car. Getting out of her car, she grasped the coffee from his outstretched hand. His eyes were constantly scanning the other cars and customers. They stood there for a moment or two, keeping their hands warm on their cups.

"So, what's happening?" Jess asked.

He put his cup on the roof of the car. "When Neil and I left Argentina, he decided to come here before going back to Ireland. He's gone over the finances and, basically, Ryan's bankrupt and is in debt for millions. He questioned Ryan extensively about the night your father died. Ryan was in Atlanta at the casino, not at the house and was not responsible for your father's death. Joe did tell him that he had photos proving the horses had been switched but Ryan was going to deal with it when he got home."

Jess stood there frowning. "If not Ryan, then who?"

There was a moment where Duffy looked at her and put his hands on her shoulders. "It was Laura."

Jess dropped her coffee and stood there with her mouth open. Impossible. "Laura? But she's been so good to me. Why?" she said, totally confused. She found herself buried in his arms, her head on his chest as he gently pulled her close.

"After your father called Ryan about the photos, Ryan phoned her first from Atlanta and later called Neil. The cops have the phone records. I think Laura took it upon herself to remove the threat in order to protect Ryan. I haven't heard yet if they've traced her call to the guy who drove the truck. That's why I don't want you going there. She's capable of anything. Ryan sent the kids to her parents in Miami."

"What's next?" Jess asked, looking bewildered.

"Neil's pulled the plug on the partnership. The stable is finished. He's already moved some of his mares out. Arctic Cat has a few mares to breed this week, then he'll be shipped home. We'll be around 'til then. Paul Wagner's selling off some of the other horses. The antique cars are being sold to pay wages. Staff have been given notice. The house may have to be sold. I don't know if Laura's parents can help her out. They're wealthy in their own right. It's a mess and all of them are constantly arguing. The kind of people Ryan's in debt to are bound to make trouble."

She looked up at him, still in a quandary.

Casually, he kissed her on the forehead. "Sorry, Jess, but I've got to get back. Can I have your cell number just in case there's another emergency?"

"I'll drop you off somewhere close," she said, giving him her number. It was a completely silent ride back to the stable. A block away from the mansion, out of camera range, she dropped him off, then he was gone, jogging down the road. She went back home, feeling totally deflated.

Chapter 26

TWO COFFEES LATER, JESS WAS STILL SITTING IN HER FATHER'S chair trying to digest the information. Her dad would have gone back to the stables if Laura had asked him. That made total sense. Jess could understand that if the photos went public, there would be loss of status in the community and business, exactly what was happening now with Neil shutting it down. Laura's father was one of the biggest bourbon distillers in the state. Laura was wealthy before she married Ryan. She had a university degree, was a high-society woman, and had a lot to lose.

Jess thought about the times Laura had done nice things for her, like having her attend the galas and granting days off. Had Laura done that out of guilt or convenience? She'd always thought she been hired because she knew the locals. Maybe it was to keep an eye on her. Finally, she gave up and began to tackle her to-do list. She phoned Mr. Ames' office.

"Hi, Mrs. Johnson, it's Jess Coxwell. I'm back from vacation. He wanted to see me. Is there any chance he can fit me in for an appointment today or tomorrow? I'm starting a new job in Louisville next week and I don't get back to Lexington until after six. Tomorrow at four-thirty— that's great, thank you."

She hadn't expected Duffy to be so considerate. He'd been an absolute rock, once again saving her from disaster. Her position on him was mellowing. He'd been a threat at the beginning. His concern seemed genuine. She sure appreciated the warning. She could have blindly gone in there about a feed problem, not knowing the risks. That reminded her she needed to call Mitch.

In the meantime, she needed groceries. Later Jess sent an email to Karen requesting a date and time for a coffee at the mall. She phoned the dance studio and booked an hour on Saturday for a tango lesson, wanting to strut her stuff even if she wasn't sure she'd continue. For the time being, she wasn't going to ride at Stattler's until she knew the demands of the new job and any time restrictions. She didn't need to be so busy.

The trip through the familiar streets to the grocery store had her smiling; yes, there were skyscrapers and traffic jams but not miles of them. Lots of people were on the streets, even a few business types but just about everyone wore jeans.

Back home, after unpacking the groceries, she checked her email. Karen was free Friday night around seven. She was good with that and sent a reply. She called Wainright's, and tracked Mitch down.

"Hi, Mitch I'm back. Just wanted to touch base," she said.

"Did you have a good time?"

"Absolutely fabulous, so much to see and do, so different. I'll be there Monday morning to get started. I've got information you need to know. Are you aware the O'Connells are bankrupt and the stable is closed? Please don't let any Wainright staff go near the place, including Todd. Horses are being sold off. Tensions are very high. Do we have an outstanding feed bill?" she asked.

"We do. Damn it, Jess, I'm surprised. I'll hold deliveries until I've got a clearer picture of the situation. I'll let Len and Todd know. You sure chose a good time to change jobs. I'll see you at head office on Monday," he said.

She could picture him sitting frowning, weighing the options, and putting the ball in motion. Her loyalties now lay with Wainright. Those farmers deserved to be paid. A large debt would hit the company hard. Mitch was right; by pure luck she'd chosen the right time to leave.

The meeting with Mr. Ames was brief. The assessments had been made and she'd been allocated more than she expected. Andy probably wasn't going to be happy about that, but she was going to get half the proceeds from the house sale. The date for signing was March 29th. Jess was pleased and felt the solution was fair, considering Andy's income in comparison to her own. She'd have to tell Mitch she needed to leave early that day.

Jess walked into the mall and went to the coffee shop, finding Karen and all the girls there. "Hello everyone," she said. There were instant comments about her haircut. One of the other girls had been to Florida, so they compared tans.

"Well, did you meet any sexy Latinos?" Karen said jokingly.

"As a matter of fact, I did, and I danced with some fabulous guys," she said. Jess managed to satisfy their curiosity without actually giving them much information. Felipe was vaguely referred to as "an artist" in her story.

Saturday, she turned up at the dance studio in her high heels and leotard. Jim and Jean were waiting for her.

"Well, we're curious to see how you made out," Jean said. "Did you get much instruction down there?"

"I did. First thing every weekday morning, I had an hour with Antonio Ramirez, Sebastian's son, and then sometimes I got an extra hour with Diego Ramirez and his sister Julia. They're junior champions in Argentina. It was great. So be warned, Jim. I'm going to put you through your paces this morning," said Jess, giving him the eye.

He laughed.

Let's see if he's still laughing when we're done. She was going to have fun with it. Jean put on the music. The Latin guitar rhythms immediately brought Jess back to Argentina. She followed the first step he took, but on the second, she challenged. He had to ad lib. She did extensions and gave him the sultry look that she had achieved with Felipe, so now she had Jim working. She did the caresses. It became a duel. When the music ended, Jess did her final extension, gazing up at him.

He shook his head.

"Well, aren't you a surprise?" Jean said.

"Jess, you've totally changed. I can't believe the difference in just three weeks. You must have worked your butt off. You've got confidence now and it shows. I had trouble keeping up with you on a couple of sequences."

"The question is, Jim, what do I do with it? My body's not flexible enough to go to competition level, but I still enjoy dancing. The young ones are almost gymnasts. Sebastian gave me a list of Argentinian dance instructors in the US but the nearest one is in Chicago, so that isn't going to work. Is there anyone at all that I can partner with regularly to keep this momentum going?"

"I'll have to look into that further for you. In the meantime, let's do some salsa, or cha-cha," he said.

He didn't get much respite with those dances either. After an hour, he seemed more than happy to see her leave, patches of sweat darkening his cotton shirt. Jess winked at Jean who hid a smile, as Jess booked an appointment for the following Saturday.

Monday morning, she met Mitch at head office in Louisville. He had prepared a large map of the state, showing the locations of the farms and stables she'd have to visit periodically.

"I've also marked the locations of feed stores that stock our products. I tend to visit the ones farthest away in good weather and save the nearest ones for the winter months. Our biggest customers are the poultry producers. The boys in R&D can give you info on each of the feeds we make. We'll visit them after lunch."

"What about fairs and horse shows?" Jess asked.

"It's early yet but by March they should all have their schedules and you'll need to make arrangements for a booth for the big ones. You'll work those weekends and take days off during the week in lieu," he said. He went on to discuss dairy ration, horse ration, seed corn, and the access Wainright had to oats, barley, and hay, not only in Kentucky but the four-state area.

After lunch, he took her around the building introducing her to the staff, including the CEO. Len Wainright rose to meet her when she entered his office and they shook hands. He was in his early sixties, but Jess could see the family resemblance between Todd and his father. The man was about the same height but had the look of the farmer who had spent his life outside, the reddish hair fading to gray, a ruddy complexion, and strong body that spoke of hard physical labor. His rolled-up sleeves revealed tanned hands and forearms. She'd bet a dollar his upper arms were snow white. He struck her as a methodical, practical man and could picture him driving one of those huge tractors around his fields.

"Welcome aboard, Jessica. Is Mitch treating you right?" he asked.

"Sure is," she said smiling, feeling the assessment of those hazel eyes. "We're just going over the map."

"We appreciate your heads up on the O'Connell situation. Todd is looking into that. They owe us nearly a hundred-thousand dollars," Len said.

"Don't let Todd go there in person," said Jess. "Seriously, Laura's a loose cannon."

"Yes, Mitch told us. What are your plans for tomorrow, Mitch?"

"We've got a road trip. Forecast sounds okay, possible snow on Friday. Anything in particular you want me to discuss with the Owensboro folks?" Mitch asked.

"Nothing right now. What's on your agenda for this afternoon?" Len asked.

"I'm taking her to R&D to show her some of the science we're dealing with." They left Len and walked down to the far end of the hall. R&D occupied the entire end of the building with an open expanse well-lit by large plate glass windows on three sides. The fourth wall was covered in maps. Jess scanned them quickly, seeing they were soil and weather maps. Four expectant male faces looked up from their desks and Mitch made introductions.

Jeff McKelvey was the resident science guy and the other three were his assistants. Jeff explained that he created the formulations for each of the feeds, then hired out the production end of it.

"Right now, poultry feed is our current project, which is really important, given the popularity of fried chicken. We do our feed trials on several poultry farms, one here in Kentucky, the other in Illinois. The four of us set up the trials and then we all go over the results. Sometimes, we have a new variety of grain, and it may or may not be better than what we've been using. I get feedback from other crop scientists across the country, who have different weather patterns and soil conditions to work with."

"Are you doing the trials on our co-op members' farms?" Jess asked.

"Wherever possible. We'll provide the seed and they'll do a test plot. We try to source locally or within the four-state area. I understand Thoroughbreds are your main expertise. Next time you're in the office for a day or two, we'll set up some time together and go over that," he said.

Jess thanked him for his time and took a good look at the maps on her way out. There was a list on the wall, showing which crops grew in specific areas. By the time she got back to Mitch's office, she realized she had totally forgotten the names of most people she had met that day. She scribbled herself a quick note, a list of department heads and any names she could remember. There was no sign of Todd though.

On the drive home, she looked at the thickly forested limestone hills and fields still tipped with snow. It was like she was seeing Kentucky for the first time. It had taken a trip to Buenos Aires to make her realize the beauty in her own state.

Chapter 27

TUESDAY AND WEDNESDAY WERE ROAD TRIP DAYS, VISITING farmers, stable owners, and feed stores. Jess made lists of everyone she met. She now had her own personal shirts with the Wainright logo and her name on the pocket. She asked questions about the operations, how long it took the chickens to grow from hatchlings to market size, the amount of milk produced by a dairy cow and she marveled at the automated milking systems. It all became a blur by the end of the day. As Mitch drove, she made notes and asked questions.

"You've had years to learn the names, the farms. How am I going to learn all that and the business end of it in a month?" she said.

"If you get stuck, I'm only a phone call away. I'll let you handle things starting next week. We'll increase it each week."

"I'm going to have you on speed dial. Oh, talking about the end of the month, on March 29th I'm going to need about an hour off that afternoon. I've got divorce papers to sign at my lawyer's, at four-thirty. Could I work my lunch hour?" she asked.

"Sure, that'll work," he said.

Wednesday evening was the bereavement group meeting. Jess had prepared a fruit and cheese tray the night before, as she only got home from work just in time for the meeting to start. She was curious to see if her take on things had changed.

It was good to see the women again; it had been so long since she'd attended. There were hugs all round. They oohed and aahed over her haircut and tan. Jess was seriously thinking the haircut was here to stay. She'd have to find a salon to keep it that way. She listened to the stories. Elly was looking good. That evening there were no critical situations. After everyone left, they chatted for a while.

"Jess, you've changed. Did something happen there?" Mrs. H. asked, perceptive as usual.

"It did. I had the opportunity to help someone who was deeply trapped in grief. I told him some of the things I'd learned from you and made a few suggestions. I've no idea if it helped or not. Latino men are not well known for taking suggestions from women."

"Are they really like that? I thought it was only in movies," Mrs. H. said.

"Oh, no. We are just poor weak creatures and they are always superior and in charge. However, I tried. I did spend a lot of time dancing and really improved. My new job is interesting and I like it. I'm having a hard time remembering all the names, where the farms are and what they raise," Jess said.

They hugged each other and Jess went home.

Thursday was another day on the road. This time, Jess visited a pig farm that raised sows and their litters. The barn was enormous. She found the piglets so cute, but oh-so noisy with their high pitched squeals. She checked out the feed being used and talked to the farmer. She had to established her credibility with these men. Later, when she was homeward bound on the I-64, it was slow. She was about twenty minutes out from Lexington when a news flash interrupted the music.

The commentator sounded excited. "We have a breaking story! Gunshots have been fired at the O'Connell Stables in Lexington. Police and paramedics are on the scene. There is no information available at the present time. Stay tuned for further developments." He went into more background story on the O'Connells but she tuned him out.

Jess almost ran her car in the ditch, but corrected and pulled off at the next exit, her heart pounding. She found a place to pull over and tried to calm down. Had someone been shot? Who? Was Duffy alright? She knew he'd put his life on the line for Neil. She'd call him as soon as she got home.

On the rest of the drive home, her mind kept racing and she was thoroughly glad when she finally pulled in the driveway. She turned on the TV and watched the late version of the news showing the helicopter view over the estate. Police cars were still parked around the circle and news vans were on the street with a gathering crowd.

The commentator was saying, "One person has been taken to hospital in life-threatening condition. At this time, police have not released the identity and are still on the estate."

Duffy didn't pick up so she sent him a text.

Duffy, heard the news on the way home. Are you alright? Please call me back whenever you can, regardless of time. Jess

Her phone rang about ten o'clock.

"Jess, it's me," Duffy said, sounding tired.

"Are you okay? I was worried you'd been shot."

"No, Laura shot Ryan."

"What!!"

"They argued last evening. She was furious—he bankrupted both of them. I think the final straw was a phone call from the cops wanting her to go to headquarters and bring her lawyer. Neil and I were having lunch in the dining room while they were in the front foyer arguing again. Both of us heard her scream "You ruined us. I killed for you," then 'bang.' Both of us ran out. She was standing with the gun in her hand. He was lying on the floor clutching his chest. She dropped the gun and knelt beside him, crying. Neil called the police and paramedics. Ryan was bleeding like a stuck pig, even when I put pressure on his chest. I doubt he'll make it."

"So, you've been tied up all day giving statements to the police?" Jess.

"Yeah. The phone's been ringing off the wall, with reporters."

"What happens now?"

"Neil's beside himself. Despite the crap that's happened, they're still brothers. Neil's not leaving the hospital until he sees the doctor. He's got me running errands. The police have Laura in custody. Arctic Cat's being shipped back to

Ireland tomorrow. I'll keep you posted if there are any new developments but I've got to go now," he said.

"Thanks, keep in touch," she said to the man who had rescued her not once but twice.

*   *   *

JESS SPENT MOST OF FRIDAY MORNING IN R&D AND HAD JEFF explain the difference between pig, horse, cattle, and chicken feed. That kept her mind occupied. At lunch time, she left the building with her head crammed with facts about percentage protein and supplements for each species. Quickly, she slipped over to the coffee shop to grab a bite to eat. The first person she saw was Todd Wainright, sitting on a stool at the counter. He was frowning, deep in thought, a half-eaten burger on his plate and a cup of coffee in his hands.

"Good morning," she said sliding onto the stool next to him. She caught the eye of the waitress and indicated she'd have the same as Todd.

"Hi, Jess," he said, the serious look receding to a smile. "You look great with that haircut. So, how was your first week?"

"Thank you. Crazy busy. So much to learn. I'll eventually make sense of it. Mitch is great to work with. I just hope I can become as knowledgeable as he is," she said.

"With regard to our problem, I talked to Neil O'Connell this morning. Ryan had emergency surgery last night but is still critical. Neil said he'd look into the feed bill when he had time. Right now, it's not his priority. I understand that.

If they declare bankruptcy there's not a lot I can do and that will really hurt our bottom line."

Her coffee cup was filled and shortly a fully loaded plate with a burger and fries was placed in front of her. They chit-chatted about the spring fairs and kept the subject light. She quickly had her coffee and ate her burger. There were too many fries. Todd looked at his watch.

"I've got to go. See you later, Jess," he said.

"See you," she said and watched him walk back to the office.

The trip down the I-64 went relatively quickly. She thought about Todd. Her first instincts had been correct. He was a very nice man but there was no chemistry, no spark for her. Felipe came to mind and while he had awoken that spark, she seriously hoped it hadn't spoiled things for her as far as dating other men.

She thought about the pictures of Arctic Cat and Wing Commander. How weird that she had an element of control over both Neil and Andy with photographs. Once again, she thought about the sex scenes but this time it wasn't hor-rifying, just kind of gross. Both sets of photos had served their purpose and she would be glad to get rid of them when the right opportunity presented itself. She wanted to protect her interests without harming anyone. She spent the rest of the afternoon with Mitch going over the lists of fairs they would be attending and submitting applications for booths.

On the way home her phone rang. She put it on speaker. It was Duffy.

"Jess, I want to see you tonight. Can I meet you at the coffee shop? It's hard to get out of here. There's still a crowd outside the gates and van loads of TV crews. I'll see if I can use Ryan's car. I'll be there around six if that works for you," he said, sounding very business-like. She agreed.

It was quarter to six when she got there. Duffy was already there, leaning against the car, a coffee in his hand. Hers was sitting on the roof. He wasn't handsome; he just looked so ordinary. That had been such effective camouflage for him. As he handed her the coffee, she could feel the tension.

"Jess, Ryan died an hour ago. I'm leaving for Germany in the morning. I'm weeks behind in my security work at Neil's other companies. He'll be here for a few more days."

"Well, he's paid a high price for being a crook. It cost him his brother. I don't think Laura's going to be able to get out of that charge, even with her father's money behind her."

"Enough about them. I've been coming here for the past five years and each time I wanted to get to know you. You were married so I didn't pursue it. Now you're divorcing your husband, please give me a chance. It's not the right time for me to talk to Neil about changing jobs but I will when things settle. I could be based here as his securities manager. I want us to get together."

Jess looked up at him stunned. "So that's why you were stalking me in Buenos Aires!"

"Guilty," he said, smiling. "I loved watching you. Didn't appreciate the men you danced with much. Put down your coffee and me a hug," he said. The smile completely changed his appearance. He was tentative as he pulled her closer, looking down at her. He very gently kissed her on the cheek.

She looked up at him, surprised. "Oh," she said, but didn't move away, conscious of his arms around her, the smell of him and the look on his face.

"I think I'd better leave now or we could end up in the back seat like a couple of randy teenagers," he said with another grin, and released her, getting into the car. He waved goodbye and pulled out of the parking lot.

The thought of fogged up windows and heavy petting made Jess burst out laughing. She watched him drive off and she went back home, wishing she'd kissed him back. The spark was there. Would he get in touch again?

It had been a long time since she'd emailed Carla, so she sent off a long missive all about her new job and a tamed version of the O'Connell saga.

Saturday at dance class, she spent most of her time talking to Jim. "I know I've improved but I don't have the flexibility to get to competition level. It's unlikely I'll ever go back to Argentina."

Jim looked at her. "I haven't been able to find anyone locally to partner with you," he said.

"So, my question is what now?" she said.

"Well, why don't you simply join one of the teen classes and use it as an exercise class?"

She thought about it. It would be a lot cheaper and it would keep her in shape. "I'll give that a try then. What time do you want me here next Saturday?"

"We've got a ten-thirty class that's a lot of fun. I'll book you in," he said and that was that.

On the drive home, she was a bit sad but it seemed the best option for the time being. When she got home, the light was blinking on the phone. The message was from Duffy, wherever he was.

"Jess, Neil just informed me there was an accident when Mick was loading Arctic Cat into the horse trailer. There was a fender bender between two TV trucks and as if that wasn't enough noise, one of the TV choppers flew overhead and he spooked. He reared in the trailer, smashing his head, and damaging his front leg. It wasn't operable so the vet put him down. Neil has asked about the photos. Let me know what you intend to do with them. If you decide to send them to Neil, I'll give you the address and you can send them registered mail. I'm in Germany right now. Will be in touch later. Duffy."

Poor old Wing Commander. What a ghastly accident. By rights he should have been on a plane heading for Dublin and green pastures after his exhausting breeding season. Was it really an accident? The timing was incredibly convenient. Now, the big question was what to do with the photos. The deception terminated with the horse's death. He'd be dog food by morning. She didn't need the photos now and could give them back to Neil. He was a ruthless business man but he wasn't a killer.

The photos would support the inmate's claim that Laura hired him. On the other hand, the inmate would probably be charged and found guilty on the forensic evidence of the glass pieces. It would be his word against Laura's that he'd been hired for the job. No matter what happened, Laura would be charged with Ryan's death. Neil and Duffy had virtually been witnesses. All Jess could think about was getting rid of the photos.

She brooded about her decision all evening and Sunday and finally decided to give them back to Neil. Part of her was really glad that it was Duffy she had to deal with and not Neil in person. She sent a text message to Duffy.

> Have decided it is in my best interest to return the photos to Neil. Will send them by registered mail as you suggested. Please give me the address. Jess

She had it within the hour. Jess phoned Mitch and apologized to him explaining she would be late getting to work in the morning and would work through her lunch hours to make up the extra time. He suggested they meet at a farm about an hour's drive southeast of Louisville. That was a good compromise.

Monday morning, she was at the bank as soon as it opened and took both sets of photos from her safety deposit box. She also removed and destroyed the letter of instruction. Jess mailed the horse pictures to the Dublin address by express post. It's done. Andy could have his photos back too at the first fair she saw him at. By ten o'clock she was heading to the farm to meet Mitch. The day went really well, and she had a chance to see Charolais cattle on that farm.

The rest of the week promised to be normal. Every place she accompanied Mitch to was a learning experience and she found she was enjoying meeting the down-to-earth hard-working families who had formed Wainright's co-op.

On Thursday evening, the phone rang. It was Detective Peterson. "Hi Jess, I need to talk to you. I'm in the neighborhood," he said.

"Sure, come over." She gave him the address.

Ten minutes later, there was a knock at her door. He looked business-like but not threatening.

"Come in, have a seat. Do you want a coffee? I've only got instant."

"That'll do," he said, parking himself on the sofa.

She boiled the kettle and filled the mug. "Milk? Sugar?"

"Both," he said, calmly appraising her and the apartment.

She handed him the cup then pulled up one of the kitchen chairs and sat facing him. "So, what up?"

"This winter, you came to me with questions about your father's death. You told me you thought it wasn't an accident. The glass found at the scene came from two vehicles and we've been able to find the Chevy truck involved. The red pieces were from a Dodge, likely your dad's car but the white pieces came from the Chevy. The inmate did own a Chevy truck at the time, according to DMV records. The guy is in jail for break and enter and a theft unrelated to this case. We found the Chevy in the garage on his property. There was damage to the passenger side head light assembly that matched the broken pieces we had. He made the mistake of blabbing to another inmate that he'd run a guy off the road in the ravine."

"Did he admit to breaking into Dad's house?" she asked.

"Not yet. Did Joe leave any photos of Arctic Cat?" he said, subtly scrutinizing her reaction.

"Dad's photos were in boxes when I got them. I spent the winter sorting them and putting them in albums," she said, pulling one album from the shelf, and placing it on the table. "This album has the last pics he took, on his trip to Ireland at Neil's stable. He'd only been back from holidays about two weeks before he died."

Peterson turned the pages, looking at the individual pictures, his lips pursed and forehead creased in concentration. There were at least six pictures of Arctic Cat.

Jess knew full well that none of those showed the scar on the horse. She sat quietly, sipping her coffee, watching him.

"Do you have any other photos?" he asked.

"No. Are you looking for something specific?" she asked.

"I'm just following up a lead. Jess, I want to take one of these with me," he said.

"Sure. Will the inmate be charged with my father's death, now you've got evidence?"

"He's been formally charged."

"Take whatever you like." Jess didn't want to talk about "the photos." She no longer had them. Nothing could be proven. After Peterson left, she sat there for a long time, flipping pages in the albums, lost in earlier years and simpler, happier times. Timing had been perfect. Jess hadn't lied to him. She'd quite honestly shown him all the photos of Arctic Cat she had.

Chapter 28

THE NEXT TWO WEEKS AT WORK WERE BUSY. MITCH WAS letting her take the lead with the customers. Jess was getting used to having discussions with some of the younger ones who'd look things up on line and fire questions at her later. She spent time phoning R&D to get answers, learning as she went. She made a point of meeting the farm wives, to set the tone, not wanting any "situations."

"You know, Mitch, it might be a really good idea if you had a question-and-answer column on your website. Then we could deal with these questions directly without necessarily driving all over the country, maybe even have Jeff do a monthly blurb that would interest them."

"Talk to him and see what he thinks. Did you send in our application for table space at the fair in April?" he asked.

"Yes, I sent that off last week and I've got a list of the other fairs on my wall. I'll mark them off as I go." She had always enjoyed the local fairs and had shown horses as a kid, but had never been on the vendor side of the business.

Emails from Carla arrived periodically, updating her on the family goings on.

Hi Jess:

Mateo has been doing very well this season. His goal average has gone up. That new mare is perfect for him. It is a huge amount of work to keep the horses ready and get them to the stadium on time each week plus work at the other stable.

Diego and Julia just won the Buenos Aires junior class championship. Sebastian is allowing more of their input into their routines. Diego's in a growth spurt. He's taller than Julia.

Felipe has been coming to church periodically, and I noticed some paint on his clothing, so I hope that means he's painting again. Still quiet and moody.

Was surprised to hear all about the O'Connells. Our asados seem very quiet without you. Keep in touch. Adios. Carla.

Jess kept in touch with her mother and Marty; nothing much was happening on the west coast. She still went for her dance class on Saturdays. The teen class was fun. She just got home in time on Wednesdays to make the group meetings of the bereavement group. She was quite comfortable in her own skin at that point and tried to be supportive to the other ladies. She realized she had indeed worked through some of her issues.

Todd had let her know that Neil had paid his half of the feed bill, so they were going after the estate for the balance. Not a perfect solution but an improvement for the farmers anyway. She wondered if that had anything to do with her giving the photos back. Her relationship with Todd had settled into a co-worker one and that suited her fine. He seemed to know from her lack of response that she wasn't interested in anything beyond that.

When she opened her computer, there was an email from Duffy.

Hi, Jess:

Still in Germany. Had a major security problem which turned out to be internal. Had to revamp the whole system and catch the guy. Will be back in Ireland next week and will speak with Neil first chance I get. I think about you a lot. Please keep in touch. Duffy

The fact that he was actually going to talk to Neil, meant he was serious about moving to the US. That in itself was amazing.

Hi, Duffy:

Good to hear from you. I don't even know where to start. We've known of each for five years but actually know very little about each other. I only ever saw you as Neil's body guard. You were the ghost who kept himself fit and could disappear in the blink of an eye. Staff at the stables told me you were ex-SAS. I had no idea you were interested in me. If you are coming back here, let me know and we can get together. Have never properly thanked you for the rescue in the alley or for warning me about Laura.

The end of the month rolled around and suddenly it was March 29. Leaving work early, she arrived at Mr. Ames' office. She had a brief wait until the earlier client departed, then Mr. Ames called her in. She examined the document and read every word. The legalese bogged her down a bit but finally she put her signature to the last page and initialed all the others.

"The money will be in your bank account shortly. You've managed very well through all this. You'll be getting copies for your records within a week or two. What's next?" he said.

"I don't know. I've got a new job and it seems to be working out. Now I'm legally free, so we'll see what happens."

They shook hands and she walked out feeling like she'd been released from prison. Free!

*   *   *

TWO WEEKS LATER WAS THE FIRST SPRING HORSE SHOW AND fair. She had the company van to carry the portable tent and tables, plus sample bags of all the horse product lines they produced. Mitch helped her load. This was their last weekend to work together. Mitch was moving on to his new position Monday.

"Mitch, how am I going to manage this when you're in Tennessee? I can't erect the tent by myself, and I'm going to have trouble moving the grain bags."

"There will always be two reps staffing the booth. Gary from Illinois will be in to help as well. You'll help him on occasion. There will be two other fellers here shortly, local guys who help us out every year."

Jess found their booth site and with the arrival of help, the four of them had the tent up and the pegs firmly hammered into the ground. She was thankful it wasn't windy. They unloaded the folding table. Jess draped the table cloth over it and strung up the Wainright banner across the open front of the booth. Mitch helped the guys unload the sacks of feed. They also had four folding chairs that she placed around the table. She started unloading pamphlets and brochures about their products to display on the table. She had brought several of her reference binders that listed all the ingredients for each type of feed and put them under the table.

Several ideas she'd had for promoting their products had been approved. She was running a daily draw for a bag of horse feed and was handing out small sample bags of horse feed to anyone interested. A big easel showed a photo of head office and some of stables using their feed. She also had a clipboard and pen on the table for people to ask questions.

She was wearing her green shirt with her name and company logo, as well as dark green slacks. She felt as ready as she could be to do her spiel to the public. Mitch brought her a coffee. She checked out neighboring booths and found several vendors she knew. The blacksmith who'd done the horses at O'Connells, also did hand forging of medieval swords and daggers, which was a surprise. At the far end she could see the booth for the Agricultural College. She caught glimpses of Andy. The sight of him made her stop and think. There was no rush of adrenaline or negativity. He was just someone she knew. The photos were in the glove compartment of the van if she met up with him.

As soon as the fairgrounds opened at ten o'clock it was pleasantly chaotic. The midway was open with screaming kids as the Ferris wheel and roller coaster gave them their money's worth of thrills to loud canned music. Horse events were going on in three rings including Western, English, and horse pulls. She didn't get time to even have a ringside view of any events. Kids and candy floss were everywhere.

Suddenly, Andy was walking by her booth with a young man. It was the young man from the photo. Momentarily, all three paused and stared at each other. Again, he was the same old Andy—mid-thirties, six-feet tall, and good-looking, but a lot had changed. She didn't feel anger; she didn't feel much of anything, so she approached them.

"Hi Andy, how's it going?" she said.

Very well," he said eyeing her tentatively.

"I'm glad I've run into you. I have something for you," she said. "Will you wait a moment?"

He nodded. She saw a look pass between the two men, but she went to the van and took the envelope.

Walking back to them, Jess could see that Andy was chewing his lip. The younger man stood back a bit. She handed the envelope to Andy. "I hope life's good to both of you," she said and somehow meant it. Whatever she had felt for Andy was completely gone. There was no spark whatsoever. He opened the envelope, scanned the contents, then closed it again. Their eyes met for a brief moment and he gave her a thumbs up. She returned the smile and they went back to their respective booths. Mission accomplished! She'd never seen Angel with them; maybe it was just the two men now. She couldn't forgive Andy for the lies and deception, but the anger had gone. She had Mrs. H. and the bereavement group to thank for that, and now she had something to share with the ladies on Wednesday night.

Those envelopes had been baggage in their own way and that was over. She was not the same person she had been.

By the end of the day, Jess was exhausted. She couldn't even guess how many people she'd spoken to. A teenage cowgirl won the bag of feed for her buckskin Quarter horse and rode him over to the booth to pick it up. That was a good photo op.

As soon as the gates closed, she drew the curtains around the tent and tied them closed. Mitch drove her back to head office.

"Well, Mitch. I think that was a good day. How did I do?"

"Jess, you're a natural at it. No problem talking to people. You answered their questions and were accurate. The draw went over really well. Are you driving back to Lexington?" he asked.

"No, I booked a motel room. Quite frankly, I'm tired and tomorrow's going to be another busy day."

Sunday was a carbon copy of Saturday. One of the child riders from the pony class won the bag of feed. Mitch took a photo of that. It would go on the website too. She'd even met Brenda in the crowd and was pleased to hear she'd landed a position at another stable, and the fate of other attendants from O'Connells. It was dark by the time she got home. She was so tired she just pulled out her bed, changed into her old T-shirt, and fell asleep.

Chapter 29

IT WAS WONDERFUL TO SLEEP IN MONDAY MORNING. THE weekend had been so busy, fun but hectic. She was quite content to just lay there for a while, before getting up to shower. She made a toasted bacon and tomato sandwich then checked her emails. There was one from Carla.

Buenos dias:

I sent you a package from Felipe. I think you'll be pleased. Nothing else happening around here. My parents have relatives from Spain visiting, so Sundays are as crazy as ever. Weather is much cooler now. I'm still busy with the horses.

Carla.

She'd answer that one later. There was also one from Duffy.

Hi, Jess:

I have a brief stopover in Lexington on Friday, enroute to Chicago. My plane lands at five. Is there any chance we can get together? Neil and I discussed my interest in you and he has agreed to allow me to become part of his security detail at his Chicago office. Don't know all the details yet but at least I'll be able to see you more often. Duffy

P.S. I'm not ex-SAS; never was. No wonder you were scared of me. I bloody well would be too. Those guys are deadly, about the same of your Navy Seals. Knew a few of them in my army days. I'm a pussy cat compared to them. Luv Duffy

Jess sat there totally enthralled. He was serious about her. She felt her interest in him escalating. He was a man dedicated to his job. He had principles and had kept her safe. How far could she trust him? Enough to start living again?

Hi, Duffy:

Purrfect! I'm so pleased for you. I'm sure that move will open up work opportunities and you won't be a million miles away. Am looking forward to seeing you at the airport around five, depending upon traffic delays. Jess

She spent the week visiting some of the local beef farms, learning about their operations. In two weeks, she would be driving to Illinois to help Gary with a big local fair.

Friday rolled around very quickly and she felt the excitement build as she was heading home. How was she going to react to Duffy? The last time she'd seen him they had been tied up with the O'Connell business. That seemed like ancient history. There was no denying he tweaked her interest. The spark was there and now that she was divorced, she was free to do as she pleased.

There were a few spots where construction slowed traffic otherwise it moved along at the usual Friday pace and she got into the airport at five-ten. She parked quickly and ran into the building. There was no sign of Duffy yet, although she could see the big jet on the runway along with several others. He'd have to clear baggage and customs so she took a seat and waited. Twenty minutes later, passengers started straggling out of the customs exit. When he came through the doors, her heart started to pound. He was in a pale-blue business suit that fit his athletic body like a glove. He only carried his briefcase and a carry-on bag. His eyes sought her. Once again, his appearance completely changed as a big smile blossomed over his face. He opened his arms and she calmly accepted the hug. He planted a kiss directly on her mouth, that she returned, then he released her and they looked at each other.

"How much time do we have?" she asked.

"I have a private plane coming in at six-thirty."

"Private plane? What's the occasion?" she asked.

"Let's grab a quick coffee and a burger in the cafeteria, and I'll tell you," he said as they walked over to the lounge area. Sipping on his coffee and finishing his fries, he explained, "After Neil and I got back to Ireland and I got caught up on our business backlog, I had time to think about what had happened. I wasn't happy with the situation with your father, his death, and the whole issue around the horse. My job involves being a security manager for Neil's companies, everything from security systems, computers, cameras, hiring practices—anything security-related. I wanted to be closer to you so I asked Neil if I could move solely into that role instead of body guard detail that I sometimes did when Neil needed it."

"So, he knows about our interest in each other and he's okay with it?"

"I've worked for him for more than ten years. He's a good man to work for. I'm loyal to him. I will be operating out of Chicago, covering the half dozen companies he's involved with here, although I may still be servicing his German and Italian assets for a while yet. The money's good and I get to travel, which in the past was an advantage but not so much anymore. I'm only here for the weekend to meet some execs, then I'm off again. I'm waiting for my work permit."

"Maybe we can see each other more often," Jess said.

"That's my plan," he said with a grin on his face. "Hopefully I'll have more time on my next run." They sat in the departure lounge and talked.

A small plane landed and taxied in. A few minutes later an announcement came over the public address system "Would Mr. McDuff please report to the desk."

Duffy gave her a hug and a deep sensual kiss this time, which she didn't find offensive in the least. Then he was gone. She watched him walk back to the plane with the pilot. It was airborne within minutes, to disappear into the dusk. She watched until the lights were out of sight then drove home feeling quite content. That spark of interest was now glowing.

Several days later, a package arrived, covered with Argentinian stamps. Eagerly, she opened it. There were two pictures inside. The first was one of the gray eight by ten paintings that had been on the floor during the incident at the studio with Diego. The huge difference was that the cave was empty; the desolate man was gone. Felipe had painted over it in broad brush strokes so the yellow sunlight flooded the hole and a black ladder leaned against the wall. She smiled, recognizing his flamboyant signature. *I challenged him to find a way out and he has.* His success made her feel warm inside. She still had a soft spot for him but knew deep down that she had made the right decision. He wouldn't have been a reliable mate, although he'd aroused a passion in her she hadn't thought she was capable of.

The second picture was a poster for his gallery opening. He'd called it *Girl on a Horse.* It blew her away. He must have been inspired by some of his photos from the day she'd ridden the Andalusian. The picture was basically oranges and yellows. It was a frontal view that showed the horse's face and arched neck with the long wavy, flowing mane sweeping over the naked woman rider, her long hair covering her breasts. Rich teals and blues outlined their bodies. It was beautiful in a sensual way. There was a note inside from Carla.

> Hi, Jess:
>
> He did very well at the gallery and sold five paintings. They were all done the same way but from different angles. Somehow you kicked him into painting mode. Any time I see him, he's splattered in paint. You've worked a miracle. His mother is the happiest woman on the planet. Carla.

After supper, she fitted the pictures into frames. She had very little wall space but managed to squeezed them in beside the TV and her father's photos. They brought a bright splash of color to an otherwise neutral-toned room.

*   *   *

THINGS WERE GOING WELL AT WORK. HER IDEA OF A QUEStion-and-answer section on Wainright's website was being very well-received. She either forwarded the questions to the experts or researched them herself. She tried to respond to every correspondent. It was definitely appreciated by the younger farmers and a steady dialogue was developing as her knowledge base expanded. She was slowly making friends with women in the offices, even if only on her lunch hours at the moment.

Life at home revolved around dance class on Saturdays, occasional rides at Stattler's and Wednesday's bereavement group. Occasionally, she met the girls for a coffee at the mall, but she was losing touch with them due to the length of her commute and little time. Updates from Duffy appeared every few days. He was signing his emails "Luv Duffy." A few weeks later, there was an email from him:

> Hi, Jess:
>
> I'll in Lexington on Friday. Will be arriving around four p.m. and have three hours available. Can you meet me? Please. Luv Duffy

Excitement filled her. Three hours was better than nothing. She could feel her heart thumping in her chest, like a school girl on a first date, as she quickly sent a reply.

Hi, Duffy:

Will be there as soon as I can. Will work my lunch
hour and try to beat the traffic. Maybe we can go to
my place instead of the coffee shop. Jess

She needed to know more about him before anything
physical happened. Her body was craving him but common
sense was putting up red flags. She knew very little about
him other than his connection with Neil. There was nothing
on Facebook or Twitter. Fortunately, she had a busy day
ahead of her and no time to think about it. She was scheduled to visit one of the huge poultry farms near Louisville.
She worked through her lunch hour, discussing the feed
protocols with the farmers. It was a multi-generational farm
run by cousins, grandchildren, and brothers as well as the
very elderly founding parents.

She was on the road by three o'clock, reaching the airport
around four-twenty. Duffy was in the waiting room. He was
on his feet the moment she came through the door. This
time his hug lifted her right off the ground.

"We'll go to my place, rather than the doughnut shop.
It's not far from here," she said. She took shortcuts through
the back roads. It took twenty minutes to get to the apartment. Unlocking the door, she flung it open and welcomed
him in. The apartment suddenly felt very small.

"Make yourself at home. I'll put the coffee on."

He looked around taking in everything, running
his hand along the rifle's wooden stock and looking
at the titles of her books. He didn't miss the signature
on Felipe's paintings either but his face gave nothing
away. Jess handed him his coffee and he looked at her.

"I've missed you," he said, gently removing the cup from her hands. He put his arms around her and kissed her. "I looking forward to getting settled in Chicago. I expect to be there permanently in about two weeks. I've sublet a furnished condo for a year, so that will simplify things for us."

Us? She kissed him again with more passion this time. She loved the fact that he was letting his hair grow and she could actually run her fingers through it. He looked far more like an executive than a body guard. He responded to her kiss by pulling her body tight to his and ran his hands down her back.

"Duffy, there is so much I don't know about you," she said looking up at him and trying hard to stay rational. She gently pushed away from him, picked up her coffee cup and sat in her dad's recliner. With a sigh, Duffy took the hint and made himself comfortable on the couch.

"I've always known you as Duffy. Is that your first name or your surname?"

"Actually, it's a nickname. My name is Jonathan McDuff. Dad's a Scot, Mum's half Irish, half English. They live in Dublin where I was born. My sister lives there too. You can keep calling me Duffy if you want," he said.

"Are you married?"

"No, I'm divorced. I married very young. It didn't work out. Debbie couldn't deal with me being deployed for up to six months at a time with the army."

"Did you ever have kids?"

"No, we didn't."

"So, you never were in the SAS? It was common gossip at the stables. I guess it added to your aura as Neil's body guard. What happened in Buenos Aires? What was that all about?" she asked.

"After seeing you at the stables, I looked on your Facebook page and your friends posted you were divorcing your husband. I decided it was my opportunity to hook up with you. In Buenos Aires you were so damned naïve, it was scary. You left yourself wide open on many occasions, especially at those dances. I asked Neil if I could cover you in my spare time. So, I did. It blew me out of the water when you thought I was out to kill you. It never crossed my mind that you'd be afraid of me."

"Duffy, there was no way for you to know that I suspected Neil of being behind everything that happened to Dad. Initially, I was so scared in that alley and you rescued me, but later when you pulled the gun, I automatically thought he'd sent you after me," she said. I'm so grateful for what you did." There was a long pause.

"When Neil and I came to visit Ryan over the past five years, I watched you. I've seen you working with the horses and the staff, managing Laura's galas, and I've seen you dodge Ryan. He really pissed me off sometimes. I was impressed with how you conducted yourself' You've got integrity and principles. That's what attracted me to you in the first place," Duffy admitted.

"Well, you're pursuing it now, aren't you?" she said.

"You're right, I am. Come here, another hug would go over really well," he said with a twinkle in his eye. Together they rose and gazed at each other. The face that looked at her was not handsome, but the man knew how to kiss and it took her breath away. His hands roamed her body and pulled her in closer.

She could feel herself letting go. "Duffy?"

"Uh-huh?" he said nuzzling her neck

'"We'll have to leave soon to get back to the airport on time," she said checking her watch.

"Damn. Look, I'm excited about moving to Chicago. I've never had my own place. At Neil's, I had the apartment over the garage or I've been at hotels on business. It's going to be fun to invite you to my home. We'll have more time then," he said, holding her tightly. "I have to confess, being settled in one place will be a whole new experience for me, and I'm out of my element. I might even bring my parents over at Christmas."

They chatted casually on the drive back to the airport, asking questions about their families, where they grew up, school, and first jobs. After a last-minute kiss. She watched him meet his pilot and disappear into the night. When she got home, she sat there thinking about the enigmatic man she was falling in love with. To love him, she had to not only learn to love but to trust again. She might have gotten over Andy, but the fear of betrayal still lingered. Thank God for the bereavement group. *I don't want to mess this up*, she thought. *I really like him.*

Chapter 30

TWO WEEKS HAD FLOWN BY. JESS HAD HELPED GARY AT THE Illinois fair and it had gone well. Thursday night, she had a call from Duffy.

"Hi, Jess, I'm in Chicago. Instead of you driving here tomorrow, I've booked a flight for you with a pilot named Eddy. He'll pick you up at the small plane departure lounge in Louisville at five-thirty' You'll be in Chicago by six-thirty."

She could hear the excitement in his voice. "That beats a six-hour drive. What do I bring in the way of clothes for this special occasion?" Jess asked.

"Well, we'll be staying at the condo. It has three bedrooms, so you can take your pick. But, I've booked us for a fancy dinner at one of the hotels, so bring your best dress. I've got to spend tomorrow at the office getting organized. I'm in the process of unpacking here, not that I've got much to unpack. It's going to take me a while to sort out what I need now I'm here permanently. I need groceries."

"I could help you with that on Saturday," she said.

"Good idea. See you tomorrow," he said, and hung up.

Jess dug out her suitcase from the back of the closet and looked at her clothes. The little black dress looked dated so she threw it out. Her two cotton dance dresses looked good but didn't impress her much. The crimson silk dress was at the back. It instantly reminded her of Argentina, tango, and sexy Latino men. She loved the feel of the sleek material, as she folded it into the suitcase. She took a pair of slacks and a cotton top, along with sandals and dance shoes. She always slept in a T-shirt. She didn't own lacy, frilly things. She'd be wearing jeans for work so there was no point in changing for the plane ride.

FRIDAY WAS A NORMAL WORK DAY. SHE SPENT IT PHONING customers, getting orders, and slipping up to R&D to ask questions on the new chicken pellets. The rest of the afternoon was busy enough that five o'clock came before she knew it. As she left the building, she felt her own excitement spiking. She had looked up the location of the small plane airport earlier in the week and found it without any difficulty. After parking the car, she extricated her suitcase from the trunk. There were several small planes on the tarmac.'

"I'm Jess Coxwell, and I'm looking for a pilot named Eddy from Chicago," she said to the woman in reception.'"He's here already," the woman said, placing a call to the pilot's lounge. A pleasant-looking man in his early forties came through the door and walked towards her, a pair of aviator sunglasses stuffed in his shirt pocket.

"Jessica? I'm Eddy Anderson," he said, shaking her hand. "If you'll follow me, we'll get going. Duffy's a fanatic for punctuality."

She followed him out the exit door, towing her suitcase. The plane was a small four-seater Cessna 182. Her eyes got big when she saw how small it was. Apprehension started to build.

Eddy noticed her concern. "First time in a small plane? No problem. You just have to sit still and let me do the flying. I've been a pilot for more than twenty years. It really is quite safe." He stowed the suitcase in the small luggage compartment behind the cockpit and helped her into the passenger seat. "This normally would be the co-pilot's seat," he said.

As she buckled her seat belt, Jess looked at the instrument panel; it was a mass of dials. There were dual controls. The barf bag was in the side pocket if she needed it. Eddy completed his checks, climbed into the pilot's seat, and put on his head set, offering her one. She could hear the pilots communicating with the tower.

At the turn of a key, the single engine roared to life and the propeller started spinning at a tremendous rate, becoming a blur. Eddy got his instructions from the tower and the plane started moving forward away from the buildings. He waited at the threshold point until the other two planes cleared the runway.

Now it was their turn. The revving engine pulled them forward, and with a mighty roar and thrust, they were airborne. Jess let her breath out. Once her heartbeat returned to normal, she watched Eddy monitoring the dash. One dial showed the plane relative to the horizon. She could see the air speed and altitude. This was so different from being on an airliner where cockpit and crew were hidden behind a closed door.

She enjoyed being high enough to see the countryside without the wing blocking her view. Below she could see the traffic on Hwy 64 and was glad she wasn't driving. It looked busy and there was construction. Within twenty-five minutes, they skirted Indianapolis heading north. Half-an-hour later Eddy was calling the tower near Chicago, not O'Hare but a private landing strip. The plane landed with a solid bump and rolled to a halt outside the terminal. He shut off the engine; the propeller blur slowed to three separate blades, then stopped altogether. He got out of the plane, opened her door, and grabbed her suitcase.

Jess could see Duffy in the waiting area. He greeted her with a quick kiss and shook Eddy's hand. "Thanks, buddy. I really appreciate this. What time on Sunday do you want me to have her back here?"

"One o'clock would be good. This must be one special lady," Eddy said, with a wink.

"She is," replied Duffy with a grin as he picked up Jess's suitcase and led her out to the parking lot. He took her over to his rental SUV, stowing the suitcase in the back seat.

Chicago traffic was worse than Louisville's and it took them a while to reach the suburbs. Jess was busy watching as the office towers gave way to malls, car dealerships and high-rises. He pulled into the parking lot of a twenty-story building. "Here we are," he said, escorting her inside. The elevator took them to the ninth floor. Unlocking the door of the apartment, he ushered her in. "Welcome to my new home."

It was classy—high ceilings, neutral colored walls, and functional modern furniture. But it was totally devoid of personality. The only sign of occupation was his computer sitting on the glass coffee table.

"We don't have a lot of time to spare. Dinner is at eight-thirty," he said showing her the bedrooms. She chose the middle one which had a queen-sized bed. She took a brief warm shower, feeling the water wash away some of her nervousness. She combed her hair, applied her makeup, and slipped into the silky red dress. It looked gorgeous. The illusion of sophistication came over her again. Duffy was sitting in the recliner waiting for her, dressed in a formal dark gray suit, white silk shirt, and dark red tie, looking and smelling like a slick ad for men's cologne. He took her by the shoulders, scrutinizing her from head to toe. "I bet you bought that in Argentina," his voice soft and husky.

She laughed. "Well, you did say I should wear my best dress. It's one of my tango dresses, but of course I'm not expecting you to dance."

"It wouldn't be pretty; I've never danced," he said.

He escorted her to the parking lot and they drove downtown. The restaurant was on the main floor of one of the high-rise hotels. Light from the gold wall sconces was dim, decor exquisite and the tables set formally with an array of silverware and fine china, on pristine white linens. There were red velvet draperies and semi-circular booths with velvet cushions. Although the room was full of diners, the conversations were hushed. Their waiter, dressed in black trousers and a formal white shirt and vest, greeted them formally, "Mr. McDuff, if you'll follow me please," and took them to their table. He then presented the menus and wine list.

Jess chose an Argentinian red wine and Duffy opted for an Irish whiskey.

"Jess, has your divorce been finalized?"

"Thankfully, yes. It's been interesting. I saw Andy and his male partner at the fairs when I was working the Wainright booth. I don't know what I was expecting but I was okay with it. It was a relief to get it settled. I knew at that point I could start dating again."

"Have you dated?" he asked with a serious blank expression on his face.

"No, I've been waiting for you," she said. "You've been a surprise. I wasn't expecting to have these feelings. You said you'd watched me for years. Well, I was aware of you too. I'd watch you doing push-ups and jogging early in the morning when I was doing rounds with the horses. You have an amazing ability to disappear in a crowd, so I rarely saw you at the galas. That attack in the alley shocked me. You saw the worst side of me that night. I really thought Neil had ordered you to kill me. I still don't trust him. In your mind, he's a good boss but to me he just plain ruthless."

"Jess, I am serious about you. I intend to make Chicago my permanent home. Just think—I'm thirty-eight and it's the first time ever to have my own place. I can't offer you a normal nine to five sort of relationship yet. I'm still going to be traveling. Neil's got interests across the country. A lot of the business I can do on the computer, but sometimes I have to go in person. You'll have to decide if you can deal with that. I haven't the faintest idea, what you're looking for in a relationship, whether you want a family or anything like that. I've had relationships in the past, but they never lasted because I've was on the road so much."

Jess sat there thinking. Neil was smart. By letting Duffy move here, he was keeping a valuable employee and she would never be in a position to jeopardize him, because she loved Duffy. He'd got them exactly where he wanted them. As for wanting a family, she had no clue. A woman had to trust her partner, so it would very much depend on their relationship; if there was one.

The waiter brought their drinks and took their orders. Jess was silent for a long time as she sipped her wine. "Duffy, I think a lot of those questions will be answered once we know each other better." He gently squeezed her hand and held it, his eyes firmly fixed on hers.

Gazing back at him almost made her melt. It wasn't a spark now, but an out-of-control brush fire. She was glad when the waiter placed their meals on the table.

The meal was delicious. She thoroughly enjoyed the linguine and the shrimps were huge. Duffy worked through his steak. Jess sat back and thought about her past relationship with Andy. What had bothered her the most about the breakup? Number one: the lies, the deception. If he hadn't been happy, he should have said something. Number two: Angel was eighteen. The threat of a younger, more attractive woman? Not to mention the young male lover! Her self-esteem had taken a big hit.

Jess declined the dessert menu and just ordered a coffee. The bereavement group had taught her that hurt ran deep and colored everything that came after; it had to be dealt with, not shelved to taint the future. Although she had been attracted to Felipe, she knew he'd never be faithful. Perhaps the fact she hadn't been divorced at the time was only an excuse. She simply hadn't been ready.

Looking at Duffy sitting across from her, she had a decision to make. Either she would give herself to him totally as her body was craving or bail out. He seemed a good man. He had lived a life on the move, working for Neil. But, now he had changed his job and moved to the States to bring them closer together. He was right—their life together would not be conventional. He'd still be on the road for the foreseeable future.

No point projecting too far ahead. Chicago had many possibilities, including horse-related jobs. She could even continue dancing, with the man Sebastian had suggested. The only friend that mattered and would be left behind was Mrs. H. In time, her Wainright acquaintances would fill the friendship void.

"What are you thinking?" he asked.

She took her time answering him. "I feel very strongly about you. To be honest, it's scary. It means uprooting myself from everything and trusting you."

"Whoa. Let's take it one day at a time. The attraction is there between us. Let's enjoy it."

He paid the bill, then took her back to the car. It was dark except for the neon lights down the streets, much like the evenings in Buenos Aires. She caught glimpses of the lake and wondered if there was a good view from the condo balcony. He'd been so quiet she was uneasy, but then she felt his urgency as he ushered her into the apartment.

"Can you see the lake from here?" she asked. He opened the patio doors and they walked outside. Buildings blocked most of the view, except for one small area where lights of a large tanker could be seen on the lake. She felt his arms around her, his lips on her neck, nuzzling into her hair and his fingers sliding up to fondle her breasts. Oh, she wanted him, yet she hesitated.

"What?" he whispered.

"Duffy, I've only ever slept with Andy. You're a man of the world. You've been around."

"You mean you didn't sleep with Felipe?' he said skeptically. "He was coming onto you at the ranch."

"I only met him that morning. I just wanted to see the horses. He did ask later but I turned him down. I'm not a one-night-stand. My divorce hadn't gone through, and I wasn't ready to get involved. I just couldn't do it. If you're thinking about that poster, I've got photos of me riding that stallion; I was fully dressed. That's wishful thinking or artistic license on his part." She paused.

"I know you're not a one-night-stand. You can come to me or you can go to your room and we can just be friends, if that's what you want," he said, pausing outside his bedroom door. "I know what I want, but you need to decide."

Jess paused, looking up at him. She was strong enough to take whatever came, whether it lasted or not, and prayed it would last. She put her arms around his neck and kissed him, her eyes watching his. Pupils dilated. Breath raspy.

"One more thing, do we need protection?" she whispered. "I'm on the pill, but . . . "

He moved over to his dresser and pulled out a slip of paper, giving it to her. It was an Irish medical lab report—negative for all the sexually transmitted diseases listed on the sheet. There was a box of condoms too. He'd thought of everything.

"I tested negative last fall after I found out about Andy," she said. Slowly he slid the zipper of her dress down, then pulled the shoe-string-straps over her shoulders. She undid his shirt buttons, baring his chest as the dress slid over her hips and gathered in a scarlet heap around her feet. As she moved her fingers over his chest, his rib cage, and the curls of his chest hair, she could feel his heart pounding as hard as her own. Heat was pulsing in her groin and there was the pressure of his hardening. He picked her up in his arms and lowered her gently onto the bed.

IT WAS LATE THE NEXT MORNING WHEN JESS AWOKE, AWARE of Duffy's warm body beside her. He was still asleep, his back to her. Sunlight was bright on the blinds. A quick glimpse at the clock registered ten o'clock. She gently kissed his back and ran her fingers down his spine. At first, he twitched as if startled, then rolled over.

"Good morning," he said, sleep-tousled, touching her lips, his weight pinning her down.

"I think it's time we got up," she said. "Do you go for a run in the mornings or did you have enough exercise last night?"

He chuckled and kissed her. "I think I'll skip the run for now. Ran a marathon last night," he said, with that quirky grin. He rolled out of bed heading for the bathroom. She went to the spare bedroom and showered. She looked at her slacks then opted to wear her jeans. She could smell bacon. He was making breakfast. She thought of them in bed. He had been gentle but profoundly virile. He could teach her a lot.

He was at the stove, stirring scrambled eggs and strips of bacon. She slipped her arms around him, then rescued the toast which was close to setting off the fire alarm. "Duffy, there are a thousand things I want to say, but they all seem inadequate. I hope I was enough."

He paused momentarily munching on a strip of bacon. "No complaints in that department. You and I are a good fit. I need to know what pleases you. We'll learn from each other," he said.

"I'm looking forward to that." He was smiling again. "Does Wainright have a Chicago office?"

"I have no idea. I'll have to find out. There are race tracks and lots of stables around here. For the time being, I'm going to stick with Wainright. You can't keep hiring Eddy to fly me back and forth all the time though," she said. "It'll cost you a fortune."

"Don't worry about the cost. I've lived cheap for a long time. It didn't cost me anything to live over Neil's garage. I can afford Eddy. Even if you moved to Louisville once your probation's finished, it would still work," he said.

"I know there's a dance studio around here with a good Spanish instructor. Sebastian gave me a list of names, if I can find it. I'm sure there must be stables around where I can ride."

"Does that mean I'm going to have to learn to dance?" he said getting up from the table with an exaggerated look of mock panic.

She laughed, got up and put her arms around him, holding him in dance position. "Are you going to get jealous if I dance with another man?" she asked.

There was a pause. "Point taken. That's blackmail, isn't it?" he asked trying to look serious but failing.

"Well, maybe, but the only other option is that you learn to ride," she said looking up at him and they both burst out laughing.

"Not likely. Given my options, the dancing sounds safer. We'd better go grocery shopping now or we'll never leave the condo," he said moving towards the door.

Jess paused for a moment and looked at him standing there in his jeans and T-shirt, plainly enjoying himself. She'd overcome obstacles, dealt with her some of her fears and had grown in ways she never thought possible. All she needed was the courage to follow her heart and trust in herself to allow it. With that, Jess squeezed Duffy's hand and joined him.